To Pam,

all the very

Chris!

Christopher James Rhodes

University Shambles

Published by

MELROSE BOOKS

An Imprint of Melrose Press Limited
St Thomas Place, Ely
Cambridgeshire
CB7 4GG, UK
www.melrosebooks.com

FIRST EDITION

Cover designed by Catherine McIntyre

ISBN 978 1 906561 39 0

Printed and bound in Great Britain by:
Short Run Press Limited,
25 Bittern Road, Sowton Industrial Estate
EXETER, Devon, EX2 7LW

AUTHOR'S NOTE

The city of Evergreen is a fiction and accordingly its municipal technical college, polytechnic, and finally Evergreen Epstein University (EEU) are merely virtual figments of it. Nor is nor was Charles Rae, to the best of my knowledge at least, a mortal man, although his ambition undoubtedly rampages disembodied down numerous corporate corridors. Did he go mad? That is a good question. Where the norm is insane, the sane might appear abnormal, and hence mad, at least to insane minds. I seem to recognise Charles, and his ambitions, perhaps as some long-lost glimpse of someone I once knew, or just a distant shadow that flickers now and then, peripherally, when my eyelids begin to drop their guard. Could any civilized country, one without a social and economic death wish that is, possibly allow its university system to descend into the chasm of an EEU at the behest of the market forces? I contend most assuredly not. In some alien environ it might be almost conceivable, but in the present illumination, the system would become a shambles. Accordingly, all events, characters, acts and scenes are entirely the fruit of some febrile imagination and have no basis whatsoever in reality. What remains, of course, must be true.

1

It had rained a lot on Charles Rae, and the outlook was not fair. As he stared at the bubbled glass of a sodden city office, suddenly glimpsing the image of himself spattered against the afternoon of a January storm, he was overwhelmed by the metaphor of it all. Trapped against the rain. Such was his lot. Stuck as a lecturer in a lower, mid-ranking university with no recognition of his achievements. The words echoed back to him.

"Promotion?! Ha ha! Well, young man, when I was at about your stage in career... Ha ha...!"

Jasper Totter had been forty-five when he got his readership, then he'd had to wait until fifty-five before they made him a professor. At thirty-two, Charles realised that these year-stones would be the effective riders on his own progress.

"...When I was at about your stage in career... Ha ha...!" Charles wondered if Jasper had *ever* been "at about (his) stage in career". As he looked out, the horizon appeared grey – uniformly lacklustre and unlifting, like lead. It was time for a change, or for a crisis, mid-life or otherwise. The clouds had to be lifted, or swept away.

At once, the phone heralded, "Dr Rae? We need your services."

"Indeed?" thought Charles.

He was being headhunted. Here was that change. At thirty-two he was being offered a professorship. It would mean moving to the far-flung city of Evergreen, and all that might entail, but he was blind. The title smoothed over him like a caress. Blind ambition is a dangerous faith, and as with all passions, it lacks foresight or an awareness of consequence. He knew it was blind ambition: the Holy Grail.

"Professor" but that was too embarrassing to admit, even to himself. Especially to himself. So he tried to justify it inwardly by telling his colleagues.

Life would be better: more money – quite a lot more money. That title "Professor", like a laurel wreath. It would really piss off his peers. It did. He could read it in their faces. Cheaper housing, no commuting, more time with his wife.

"Oh yes. Quality of life. That's what really counts." He glowed inside. "Lucky man," he thought.

Having basked in the warm radiance of success, and grown accustomed to it, Charles picked up the phone purposefully.

"Jasper. Yes. I'm leaving. I've been offered a professorship at Evergreen Epstein University."

Silence. Yes, here was a pissed-off man.

"Will you come up to my office?"

"Sure." He climbed the steps jubilantly, and faced the door – "Professor Jasper Totter: Head of Department". He knocked.

"Come!

"Yes, sit down, Charles." Jasper appeared to have recovered his vantage point. "Well, I know it *sounds* good, but it is at one of the *new* universities."

It struck – wounded pride. He had somehow expected something of the sort, but it knocked the breath out of him. He dodged back. His hands were fists in his pockets. That smarmy politician's grin, which invited oblivion. The material strained against his knuckles.

Yes, he was definitely leaving. He was almost pleased. It reminded him of all the other times. It justified his will. He felt cleansed and absolved of all doubt. But this sense betrayed the germ of anxiety, which he had felt all along. He was probably making a very bad move, but pride doesn't turn back; especially hurt pride.

Letter to Personnel: Dear Joan…

★   ★   ★

Three months later the train pulled into Evergreen City Station, with its warming sign, "Welcome to Evergreen!" The message should have started with the word "You're".

What a mess!

★   ★   ★

When Charles arrived at the EEU Faculty of Technology building, it *was* quite a mess that met him. Perhaps there had been an earthquake in Evergreen? Certainly the foundations were exposed.

"Professor!" Hamish Humble, the head of department, waved. "Mind your step now." Friendly advice from a friendly man. Soft Scots call; extended hand.

Stepped over the broken bricks; twisted ankle. "Ouch!"

"Are you all right? Aye, Charles, sit down for a wee minute."

Not a good start. "Ouch!"

"Would you like a cup of tea?"

Too hot; burnt his fingers. "Ouch!" The pride flinched once more.

"I'm afraid we've got the builders in. Sorry about the mess."

Weakly, "That's all right."

"You'll have to prove your qualifications, I'm afraid. I hope you did bring your O-level and A-level certificates with you. You can give them in to Personnel at your induction course."

"What? But I'm a professor!"

"Aye, well, but we can't be too careful. We've had some queer folk come here in the past."

"What else will they want to see?" Charles felt insulted. It was a *Chair*, after all.

Hamish could sense his annoyance. "Och, I'm sure they'll fill you in, if you ask them. It's just one of our funny wee ways."

And then, more thoughtfully, as though the possibility had only now occurred to him, "I dare say you'll find things a bit different at the poly – sorry, *university*. I've been here thirty-two years and I cannae break the habit."

But he was right. It was "The Poly". The old sign lay outside under the rubble, and in its place a proud new banner proclaimed: Evergreen Epstein University (EEU). Just the same, Charles didn't feel very proud. That ankle still hurt and he should have put his fist under the tap, before he'd signed the "Professorial Contract".

"When you've settled in, I'll take you to meet the vice-chancellor."

Well, that was something. The last time he'd met a vice-chancellor was at his old university, imploring Charles to remain there. "Well, my boy, you must do as you see fit, but I can't help thinking you're too good for them!" But he was here now, not there.

★ ★ ★

Knock on oak. "Professor Stirling George, vice-chancellor." Shake of hands."How are you settling in? Do you like living in the Evergreen River-lawns Development?" Stirling George shone the corporate beam.

Charles had got a flat there – for now – while he decided what to do. Charles did, at least, like the flat. Sheer concrete, but with potential, or it could just be left as *Bauhaus* minimalism. It was its setting, however, that lent appeal. Set above a marina, with glass on each side, it conveyed a water reflection at once of river and bay, sail and block, dock and town. The light welcomed the morning in bright spangles, drifting among the bobbing boats, which pulled in the breeze like small dogs on leads, eager to be on their way.

On a weekend afternoon, and other afternoons when Charles was in the shadow of his office in EEU, the flat became a greenhouse, where one might move a chair around the brace of windows, following the light, like a warm cat keeping its back in the sun. The nights were never dark, since the lights from the outline forms of buildings and the masts of boats all shone their own reflections. A peaceful place of solitude, away from home.

"Good! I like Evergreen. I like the people. They have great pride. It is the Evergreen people we are here to serve." The sales pitch snapped Charles back from his wharfside reverie.

"We don't have students; we have customers!" Stirling George's fist smacked the table, and the oak murmured back affirmatively. "We are faithful to our roots as the Evergreen Mechanics Institute of 1823. I have no interest in research, which is not our function. Our role is teaching: customer supply, I prefer to call it! Anyone who joins the staff here intending on a research career had better look for a job somewhere else. Like up there, for instance!"

Charles' gaze followed the movement of his hand, as Stirling gestured dismissively toward the older University of Evergreen.

Hamish nodded weakly, and glanced pleadingly at Charles to keep mum.

"Don't tell the vice-chancellor any bad news; he doesnae like to hear it...! And whatever you do ... *agree* with him!" he had pleaded beforehand.

Charles listened to the V-C in incredulity. An astute man, he could scent the hairs prickling on Charles' neck.

"Don't get me wrong," he sidestepped. "I assure you that if you do something *good*, I'll be the first one to shout about it. We *need* good publicity! But you should never forget that is not your real job here!"

The oak table agreed resoundingly. Charles stumbled away. Yes, he'd made a terrible mistake.

"Och, it's no so bad," Hamish tried to console him. "Maybe he'll turn a blind eye to your research work; that way we can just pretend for now that we just got you here to teach – sorry, supply – our customers, and he'll be none the wiser!"

"But you told me this was a research appointment?"

"Och, it is. Don't take it so hard, Charles. It's just that we have to play that down at the moment. Things are a wee bit up in the air for the department just now, and I don't want to rock the boat. So if anyone asks, just tell them what you're going to be *teaching* – sorry – *supplying our customers with*. If they get wind you've got any *research* credentials, they'll alienate you. You just won't fit in, you see?!"

Charles didn't see… It was the first step of a long march into the twilight zone.

"But I was a successful researcher before. I've published more than a hundred papers on my research; you knew that when you appointed me. Isn't that *why* you appointed me? You told me you wanted to build up research in physics here!"

"Aye, all true, but why do you think we kept the vice-chancellor away from your interview?"

"Doesn't he know who I am?"

"Well, he *does* … I mean … he did agree to the appointment, after all. But his views … how can I say? …can be a wee bit *capricious* at times. He seems to have changed his mind about the whole idea, since then."

As he walked on through the building, feet scuffing against the shagpile, past the garish portraits of Stirling George shaking hands with the chairman of Evergreen Football Club; smiling at the Queen; and accepting a large cheque from Randolph Epstein – the university's benefactor; Charles began to feel very sick, very sick indeed.

★ ★ ★

The early courtship between Charles Rae and Jasper Totter had not shuddered tinglingly into a honeymoon consummation. At the time of their first acquaintance Charles was working in the polytechnic, whose high-rise vista obstructed the skyline of Jasper's department. The twin history of the two institutions was marked by askance gestures of mutual contempt and rivalry. From the viewpoint of "The University", "The Poly" was an icon of contempt, the university all but spitting on the floor at any mention of them; while the poly, being only too thoroughly and constantly reminded of the perceived pecking order, railed at the university in an anthem of bitter resentment: "It's all right for those bastards! We do the same job as them. I'd like to see how well they'd do if they were working under our conditions – not in their ivory bloody tower!"

It was sour grapes, of course. The two sides didn't do the same job, nor had the two brands of institution been forged for a single purpose. The polys were conglomerates of technical, teacher training and other colleges, whose units were retained by the local authority for the inculcation of the indigenous workforce; while the universities were autonomous, elite icons. A few of whom, like Jasper's, had long since been elevated from former technical college to the academic peerage, whose haughty role was the "pursuit of knowledge" – an activity now known as "research"; and the fuel of "research assessment exercises" (RAEs). In accordance with this mantra, the nature of staff in the polys and universities also differed. A vacancy had arisen at the university in the aftermath of the divorce from Jasper of a talented young academic, Simon Soames.

When the advertisement appeared, Charles read it in a spirit of soaring elation, sensing a potential lifeboat into which his research career might be hauled. The post was advertised as "Lecturer in Materials Physics", which seemed a little remote from Charles' own field; then again, there is often an element of flexibility in such matters, especially when the mainstream candidates' credentials are unexpectedly weak.

Charles was not happy at the poly. In line with accepted prejudice, the idea of joining such an institution held little appeal, but as the dole queue beckoned at the close of his post-doctoral contract, no university lectureships having been advertised at all that year, he had applied for a post there, and now found himself in a condition whose bleak prognosis did not disappoint his prior qualms.

His own credentials were good: following the post-doc, which had proved highly productive, Charles had worked his arse off at the poly, he told himself, to get out of the bloody place. It would be a stepping stone or a tombstone, and he was determined not to die with his boots on there. All in all, he could claim nearly fifty publications (including some marked "in preparation") on his CV, which almost certainly, he surmised, would see off any of its rivals. Although the inference did indeed prove correct, the matter of it would not act immediately to his advantage.

★　★　★

"Professor Totter. Yes. I have all the applications in now, for the lectureship in Materials Physics. Shall I bring them over? I must say though, apart from one of them, they are hardly the best I've ever seen."

The rider jolted a sense of dampened expectation over Jasper, and fifteen minutes later, the cloud cloaked fully around his shoulders. They were, on the whole, far worse than Jasper had expected. He placed Charles Rae's application separate from the rest, for later consideration.

"Sam. Could you pop up to my office? Personnel have just brought over the Materials Physics lectureship applications. There are some issues we need to discuss."

The tone was clipped and fretful, quite unlike Jasper, and Professor Sam Burrell rose contemplatively from his desk, wondering what could be wrong.

"How do they look?" Sam asked him.

"Oh. Better sit down." Jasper pushed the small pile of applications over to him, using only his fingertips, in an unconscious gesture that he didn't really want to touch them again.

Sam's voice hovered on the edge of incredulity. "Is that it?!"

"Not entirely." The two small words posted a message, which was finally delivered. "There's this one too."

With a cautious air, Sam reached out his hand, as though to exchange an either precious or capricious cargo. It could be either gold or nitroglycerine, and they were unsure which kind of material Charles Rae might prove to be.

"His publication record is remarkable," Sam volunteered. The two shared an uneasy glance.

"Yes. Almost fifty papers. Fifty!" agreed Jasper.

"And he's been working in that place over there..." The lights of the poly twinkled back inscrutably at them through the window, as they surveyed it. "For the past year. How come?"

"Yes. If he's so good, what the hell's he doing at the poly?"

"But, Jasper, we can't afford to dismiss him out of hand." Sam shuffled the papers, studying them in detail. "Rae seems to have a somewhat chequered background – used to be a technician, according to this – unlike the others, who are rather more, well ... Establishment. But they're awful! Some of them don't seem to have published anything since their PhD. It's almost insulting that they've applied to us. What do they think we are, here?!"

Jasper nodded. "Yes. I think it must just be a bad time. There have been more lectureships advertised in Physics overall this year than I can ever remember. Even more than there were during the university expansion in the '60s, and a lot of the good candidates must just have been snapped up elsewhere. We should have been quicker off the mark probably, but it's taken until now to get the funding for the post approved by the university."

Sam's eyes panned quizzically upward from the sheets in front of him. "What do you propose we do, then?"

Jasper met his gaze steadily. "We wait a while. If we leave it six months, then the system should have settled down again. Then we readvertise. There are bound to be other good ones coming through by then...finishing post-docs in the States – the other places will be full – and they're the sort of candidate we want to net. We have to remember that we are trying to replace Simon Soames – and whatever I might think of him personally, he was good enough for Effington University to snap him up with their offer of a senior lectureship. That is the calibre we should be looking for, and taking this Rae fellow on – *from the polytechnic* – just doesn't sit comfortably with the image we are trying to uphold."

Sam looked thoughtfully wise. "I agree, Jasper, but just supposing there *are* no other decent candidates the next time around. And Rae has meanwhile found himself another position – and he might well do, given his research output, if someone else decides to take a chance on him."

Jasper adopted a contemplative posture. "OK. As an insurance policy, I'll write to him explaining ... well, that although we are impressed by his CV, there were no strong candidates ... *exactly in the field we are seeking to develop*. I'll put it like that, and tell him that I'll send him over a copy of the readvertisement when we've drawn that up, and ask him to make a new application then if he wishes to do so. That shouldn't cause any offence to him. It also covers us, since he is unlikely to find anything else within the next six months, as the nationally available positions will mostly be filled by now, for this year anyway, given likely budgetary constraints. We have the advantage that the funding for *our* Materials Physics lectureship is in hand, so we can still make an appointment, say, in early summer."

So it was agreed, and so it was done.

★ ★ ★

When the letter arrived, Charles tore the envelope open excitedly, and then felt a pop of deflation. He was not, however, too miffed to dismiss *them* out of hand either. It was liability cover for both of them, as although another job had appeared on the horizon, there was no guarantee he would get it. So, to affirm the agreement, but also in the hope of forcing Jasper's hand to appoint him now, Charles read between the lines of the policy again, before endorsing it:

> *Dear Professor Totter,*
>
> *Thank you for your letter, which arrived this morning. I am, of course, rather disappointed not to be able to join your department at the present time. I have no wish to remain at the polytechnic for longer than is absolutely necessary, given the current circumstances here, and an all too clear future which is entirely inconsistent with my reasons for embarking on an academic career in the first place. I am encouraged by your positive comment regarding my CV, and your invitation that I apply at the next stage of the appointment process.*
>
> *I feel it only fair to mention, however, that I have meanwhile been invited to apply for a post at another university, so there is the distinct prospect that this delay will mean that I have already signed another contract by the time the new advertisement appears for the Materials Physics lectureship in your department.*
>
> *Yours sincerely,*
>
> *Dr Charles Rae*

Jasper could read between these lines too. He knew full well that Charles Rae was trying to force his hand. If Rae went somewhere else, that might be for the best, such were his reservations at taking on someone from "the poly". Jasper's eyes defocused from the text, to assimilate the tower-blocked concrete eyesore whose presence had irked him since his first sight of it on the day when he had himself been interviewed for a lectureship at the university, in the dim furrows of his youth. His own interview had, as was common then, been a perfunctory formality: a paper show to substantiate a nepotistic arrangement of matters made during a single phone call between Jasper's post-doctoral mentor and the then head of department, whose post Jasper now held in succession.

"He's a good chap – Totter. I'm glad you phoned to ask for my help in finding an appropriate man for the job. I recommend Totter. I know he only attended a, well … rather minor provincial university. His A-level grades weren't really the ticket. Then he only got a 2:2, so he stayed on there for his PhD. Not a boy-genius exactly. I had my reservations about taking him on as a post-doc, but his PhD supervisor wrote a most complimentary reference for him, and, I have to say, he shaped up well, here. Quite a tricky experimental project, as it turned out … then he seemed to grow green fingers in the second year, so I expect to write up certainly three decent papers from it all!"

Archibald Hammond had issued a proclamation which, all things being relative, and spoken by him, resounded as an honour roll of unabated praise. Three papers "in preparation" were enough to get a lectureship in the '60s, if you knew the right man! And that man was Archibald Hammond.

★ ★ ★

"Totter? It's Hammond." There was only one (Archibald) Hammond. "It's been a while, but I wanted a quick word." The voice jarred an ominous chord, as it had even in Jasper's days as a post-doc with him. Periodically, there had lurked the threat of repayment of debt, or so it seemed, since Jasper knew that without Hammond's strong recommendation and thinly-veiled threat, the head of that department in the early '60s might well have given his job there to someone else.

"Yes … Archie …" After thirty-odd years, Jasper remained uncomfortably removed from an intimate footing with him. He was still his post-doc.

"I see you've taken on this chap, Rae."

"Charles Rae. Yes, he's quite a worker."

"Productive, you mean? Lots of *papers published*?" Archie stretched out the words from praise to fault.

"Yes. We're quite pleased with him." Jasper sounded awkward.

"It's too much. He's publishing far too much. This is intended as a friendly warning. You can still nip it in the bud. It's been noticed, you know. I was talking to Conrad Connery and Alistair Blakeley only the other day. They both mentioned it. You've been around long enough to know how things work. If Rae carries on like this, he is likely to offend the great and the good. And you know what that can mean, don't you? Especially in these days of RAEs. Have a word with him, quietly. For both your sakes. If the Establishment takes against him, their wrath may extend to the whole department. I hope you will consider my advice, *wisely*."

"Thank you … Archie." As he replaced the receiver, Jasper felt rather disconcerted, unsure of his next move. Others were highly flattering of Charles Rae. What had rattled Hammond's cage so?

In contrast, Archie was quite sure what he would do next. On his desk was an application to the Physical Sciences Research Council, sent to him for review. He read, with smug satisfaction, "Principal Investigator: Dr Charles Rae". It was a gift from God. He had sown the seeds of doubt with his head of department.

"That should hold his promotion prospects back for a few years," he muttered, and smiled an anonymous smile, knowing the research council would protect his name from any feedback to the applicant. Now, if he could cast doubt on the man's *work*, that would ensure he was not funded now (or perhaps ever). He could extinguish Rae's ambitions summarily in a few swift strokes of the pen, swatting him like a fly:

> *Dear Secretary,*
>
> *I have read the application for funding by the Physical Sciences Research Council, entitled* Cosmic Ray Spectroscopy of Ionic Systems, *submitted by Dr Charles Rae as Principal Investigator. I would have some sympathy with the aims of the applicant, since he is a newly appointed lecturer, but for his excessive publication rate. I see he has already published fifty papers, which is entirely inconsistent with someone of his age. This rather casts doubt on the quality of his science.*
>
> *Furthermore, the project is of no real significance and reflects Rae's inexperience. I would be more concerned if a more senior scientist had submitted it. In conclusion, I find myself unable to recommend support for it.*
> *Yours faithfully,*
> *Professor Archibald Hammond (FRS)*

From a Fellow of the Royal Society (FRS), written about a newly appointed lecturer, this was, as Archie knew well it would be, the kiss of death, but he was not finished with him yet. The next time Charles submitted a paper for publication in *The Journal of Physical Sciences*, Archie would be waiting in the wings to throttle that too.

2

In 1992 the university underwent major reconstructive surgery. A change of face on a grand scale. In the first phase, the constructors, contractors and handymen up and down the nation were doing well in their spontaneous erections.

"Down a bit. Wait. Don't lose it! Bugger!" Then it crashed to the ground. "You OK, mate? Right, give it here. Shit! Heavy, innit?" It was definitely a two-man job.

And so the proud insignia of "Evergreen Epstein University(EEU)", its logo designed at the cost of hundreds of thousands, had superceded the name of the polytechnic, giving birth to "the uni", as it would colloquially be called; in a similarity with "unisex", where one cloth covers all.

"What do we do with the old one?"

"Ah. Just leave it there. Someone else'll pick it up. If they want us to take it away, we'll charge 'em extra. Easy money, eh!"

A wind of political change had swept across the land, bearing in its breath the seeds of a new, more equal society. This was to become a mainly post-industrial age, with amended expectations and adjusted roles for its citizens. There was indeed, all were assured, "no such thing as society": a self-fulfilling prophecy if ever there was one, and which ushered in the fragmentation of a robust nation.

In a struggle for power, the trade unions "had to be broken", a mandate turned into limp flesh by crushing the industrial bones that supported them. With the manufacturing industries abated, thus arose a service economy fuelled by banking. Permanent jobs were long gone, and even temporary jobs of any quality fell in short supply. The unemployment statistics began to rise, and their projection, particularly in the 18–25 age group, predicted a huge embarrassment for the Government in a very short time.

Fast action was required. Voters were still having kids, and some worthy purpose must be found for them in order to avoid an election defeat. The opposition were already burying their landmines, whose destructive imperative would become profound at "Prime Minister's Question Time" and in far more militarily effective leaks to the press. They had to be ready with their secret weapon, to counter instantly such an all-out assault on their governance. The style of headline was not hard to imagine: "Government Policies Fail the Young", "PM Policy Blunder Leaves 18–25s on Scrapheap", "Dole Queue Beckons for Our Brightest Kids". Permutations of these sentiments could continue *ad nauseum*; and more seriously, *ad destructum*. The prediction was that in three years' time, according to current trends, almost one million of the nation's youth would be on the dole, coinciding with the year of the next election. Unthinkable! But what could be done about it?

Creating so many jobs, and so quickly, was not a practical proposition. Not even with short-term, rolling contracts. What other options were there, that could handle the scale demanded? There was, of course, education and training. At present, around a hundred thousand of the young attended university or polytechnic, but if that number could be *quadrupled*, sustainably year on year, the million excess would be comfortably absorbed in advance of the ballot boxes. Failure would become success, and provide a glowing record from which the next government would bray its election manifesto: "Education, Education, Education!" A true *coup de maitre*. They would be indeed perceived as "the caring party", into whose hands could be entrusted the cradle of the nation.

Through their massively expanded programme of higher education, aimed to correct the disadvantage of *our* youth "as compared with the rest of Europe", a re-election result was inevitable. Amid the air of wild enthusiasm, a niggling question still lingered: Why would the universities and polytechnics *want* to take on four times their present intake?

Quite obviously, they wouldn't *want* to, so some means of gentle *encouragement* was required to persuade them it was in their own interests to accede to Government will. Firstly, the ingrained institutional defences had to be breached. The polytechnics were split off from the local authorities as free-standing institutions, leaving them entirely vulnerable to planned or incidental vagaries in government funding, directly through the allocated *per capita* fee of their student numbers. By the Government setting this low, a bums-on-seats funding regime took hold, and in a nutshell, if the polys *refused* to absorb the numbers the Government demanded, their income would not meet the staff salary bill. So, nothing short of the massive expansion target was an option for them.

That was round one, but the policy had to be applied across the entire higher education sector, otherwise what remained from the million unabsorbed young would still jeopardise the election. Therefore, the universities had to be brought to the same master's heel, although tradition made this a little more awkward. Unlike the polytechnics, the universities had what was proudly hailed as their *autonomy*. This meant they were beyond direct government interference and control in their activities, serving as an independently governing, autonomous body of unconstrained free-thinking and self-determining academic community. It was hardly that, but inasmuch as all prior attempts to scale its ramparts had been repelled, "the university" remained unbidden.

> *Dear Minister,*
>
> *I am astonished by your letter. We cannot possibly teach the numbers you suggest. The figures are simply preposterous. If, hypothetically speaking, we were to attempt this feat, where would that leave time for staff to pursue their principal activity, which is surely research?*
>
> *We are not a polytechnic!*
> *Yours faithfully,*
> *Professor Sir Malcolm McKenzie,*
> *Vice-Chancellor, University of Effington*

This was a fair representation of the responses the minister had received from the nation's body of vice-chancellors, and there would remain an unbroken *status quo* if he did not exercise considerable strategic leverage on the situation. At the request of the Minister for Education, the Prime Minister summoned his senior ministers to an emergency brainstorming session: What were they going to do to bring these truculent buggers to heel?

The polys never had any rights and did as the local authority told them, so bringing them into line went uncontested, without even the vestige of resistance that might be expected from some of the left-sympathetic city councils toward an apparently right-party Government. Then the next stage became obvious. If the polys could be bent to the Government's will by the lack of autonomy tradition had passed down to them, then surely, by collecting the entire catch of institutions, both polys and universities in a single system, the universities could be similarly controlled.

In effect, the universities would become polys, overnight, with the same desperate and irresistible dependence on the government shilling. Their funding would no longer be ring-fenced by the University Funding Council, and certainly not by its descendent generations.

What should they call the new system though? Maybe they were all polys now, but it would not do at all to say so in so many words.

"No need to rub their noses in it, and indeed one does owe some debt of gratitude to the *alma mater*, after all!"

There was only one course of action, a more clever and subtle strategy than its appearance first suggested: "Call them all universities!"

The polys jumped at the chance to become "universities", not only for snob value, and that the downtrodden bodies of their staff would feel some belated sense of worth, rather than just second rate, but from a genuine belief that the Government, having elevated them to that grander rank, would upgrade all their facilities so they really could become universities, on a fully equal footing with the older guard. That would not come to pass, however, and the only winners were the big, research-intensive universities, with massive research funds, who could still pay their staff from these, while avoiding the considerable inconvenience and corrosion of their working conditions that the majority would endure as they retooled for the mass education melee which was about to ensue.

The ranks would then divide: quite naturally and without culpable government intervention, simply in response to the economic gradient imposed upon them. Knowing which side their bread was buttered, the big universities formed a pressure group, banding together to secure the bulk of the nation's *research* budget for themselves. This would shore up their position, while "the rest" – the smaller (and newer) boys – fought like rats in a sack for their share of the devalued *teaching* currency... fought for the privilege of absorbing vast numbers of the million virtual unemployed young, to accommodate them on mainly cheap degree courses of all kinds. Consequently, subjects like leisurewear soared while physics crumbled.

When the Government's coffers began to wobble under the weight of so many new bottoms, the number of whom grew bigger than planned, the Chancellor flustered. The vastly expanded view had cost a fortune. A mislead calculation in covering up the youth unemployment figures had cost them more in the end than the dole would have done, or indeed, supporting the industries that otherwise might have absorbed them. Then, he experienced a brainwave. "Top-up fees, that's the answer! Get the bums themselves, or their parents, to cover the deficit!"

Since student grants had already been deftly discontinued in favour of student loans; this would ensure that, along with paying off their credit card bills, mobile phone charges and the like, the students would be in debt forever.

To complete the systematic transformation, 1992 was also the year the "research assessment exercise" (RAE) was impressed upon the newly shining one-size-fits-all university system. In a scheme rather like hotel listings, a grade 5 was a suite in The Dorchester or The Hilton, say, whereas the unmentionable, the grade 1, was a bunk bed in a Bosnian Salvation Army hostel, four to a room.

The price differential was similar, with a grade 5 department able to command a comparatively vast income, which fell off exponentially down the ranks 4, 3, 2 and 1, until the 1 would get nothing at all. In that pecking order of things, the Sub-Department of Applied Physics at EEU had found itself firmly in the Balkans, and its funding had followed suit.

★ ★ ★

Hamish Humble, head of the Department of Applied Physics and Astrology, held his head in his hands, and wailed in despair, "Och, Tommy, what are we going to do?!"

Hamish, a gaunt, tall, thin man with almost transparent skin, palmed together his unsupple hands of graveyard fingers, then wrung them over the grey leavings of his hair. Under his shiny scalp, an unsteady fast mind paced and paused in anxious frustration.

"Well, there's only one thing we *can* do," Tommy Wakefield advised him. "Get somebody really *good* in from outside. We're never going to get anywhere with the existing staff!"

Tommy, a solid, well-formed, practical man, with both feet firmly set, and the best researcher in Physics, was under no illusions as to their situation, and looked at Hamish steadily, face on, his hands flat on the table. Hamish looked back at him, now thoughtful and calm.

"But how can we attract someone of the calibre we need? Why would anyone *good* want to come *here*?" he responded. "Especially after this."

"Well, if we pick someone young, under thirty-five, say, and then offer them a Chair, which they'd probably have to wait several years for where they are, they could perhaps be persuaded! Even if we only hang on to them for a few years, they might get our RAE rating up to a grade 2 or even a 3," Tommy replied. This became the plan.

"But the university has never appointed anyone directly to a professorship. All our professors have just come up through the ranks, like me," Hamish chuckled. "It'll need the approval of the vice-chancellor. I'll make an appointment to see him."

★ ★ ★

"Vice-Chancellor, I've come to talk about our admittedly poor performance in the RAE..." Hamish donned sackcloth and ashes for it, yet again.

"Mmm...the grade 1. Yes... the lowest rating in the entire university... in the entire country for that matter. A crushing embarrassment!" Stirling George growled, glowering.

"Well, yes, I know... but I think I can solve the problem. I'll need your approval though."

Stirling George levelled his gaze, permitting an atom of reconciliation. "Go on then, I'm listening. What do you have in mind?" he followed on with a measured but unconvinced curiosity.

Hamish knew his balls were against the blade's edge, and responded squeakily, clearing his throat to regain composure. "The reason for our low rating is the staff we have. They've all been here for years, me included. I'd got my PhD anyway, before I came down and joined the poly as an assistant lecturer. Most of the others hadn't. They did it part-time while they were working on the staff here. We need some new blood. Someone young, with a good research track record, from outside, to give the place a facelift. If we can get someone from one of the older universities, that would be all for the better. So, what I'm suggesting is we advertise for a professor of General Physics. I mean, we make the appointment at the level of professor, otherwise there is no incentive for anyone half decent to come here... especially not with the grade 1. So, if you agree, Vice-Chancellor... it will, of course, require your formal approval."

Stirling George nodded carefully, comprehending the situation. Hamish was right. The physicists were a bunch of old deadbeats. Most of them had done their degrees at the original Evergreen Municipal Technical College, and then been taken onto the staff of the polytechnic when that first re-labelling occurred. While on the staff they did part-time PhDs validated by the Polytechnic Assurance Authority, and in some cases supervised by more senior staff without a PhD themselves, who had also studied at the technical college. All of them had practically no published work, hence no one outside the institution would ever have heard of them. But Hamish had them assessed in the exercise anyway – a big mistake.

The RAE submission was accordingly unimpressive. The Assessment Panel had greeted their document with mirth and derision, EEU living down to exactly the kind of standards prejudice might expect of them.

The only remotely credible entrants were Tommy Wakefield and Hamish Humble, but all their grants were from industry and foreign governments, and hence were regarded as "dirty money". The RAE assessors could congratulate themselves that all their funding was of the clean, research council granted kind, overlooking, in a moment of self-appreciation, their parallel membership of the Physical Sciences Research Council, and that it was they who determined who would receive support and who would not.

In addition, the confidentiality arrangements attendant to their funding were sufficiently stringent that all Hamish's publications were merely reviews in books he had edited himself, and Tommy's were reports internal to the company which sponsored him, with nothing from either of them that had survived the test of peer review, as a journal article would, if it were published. All in all, to a panel suited in their Dorchester grade 5, EEU were in that Balkan bunk bed, at grade 1, and if there had been a grade 0, they would have awarded them that instead.

"If I agree to your plan, what grading do you think you might get, *realistically*?" Stirling asked him, thawing a little to the idea.

Hamish hesitated, but, levelling his voice, ventured optimistically, "We included too many staff last time who are really dead wood, but if we manage to get someone really *good*, with an international name, and focus mainly on them in our RAE submission, perhaps along with myself and Tommy Wakefield, we could be looking at a grade 4 next time."

The V-C was won over, and to seal the bargain, Hamish unfurled his final flourish. "And the money we'd get from a grade 4 would more than cover the cost of the salary for the appointment; and along with whatever grants, overheads and contracts they brought in, we'd be making a fair profit on the deal at that!"

A formal advertisement had to appear, announcing the vacancy for a professor in General Physics, but meanwhile, there was nothing to be lost in approaching any potential candidates informally; if, that was, he could think of anyone who might be interested.

★ ★ ★

"Tommy? It occurs to me that we might be able to prime our appointment procedure by approaching some appropriate candidates. An informal chat, you know, to encourage them to apply."

"OK. That's not a bad idea. Who do you have in mind?"

"I rather hoped *you* might have some ideas on that one," Hamish hinted a self-effacing flicker of a smile.

Tommy pondered the matter, looking fixedly into space. Then it struck him. "Actually, there is one person I can think of who would be *ideal*, but he seems to be doing pretty well where he is. He must be a reader there, so I'm not sure the step down to EEU would be worth his while, even for a Chair. You could ask him though. No harm in that. His name's Charles Rae."

"On the other hand, we know what it's like here – he doesn't," Hamish winked knowingly.

★ ★ ★

When the advert appeared in the issue of the prestigious science magazine, *Nature*, to which Hamish Humble had directed Charles Rae's attention, its requirements of the applicant appeared exactly as one would expect for a professorship, and it read:

> *Evergreen Epstein University (EEU).*
> *Department of Applied Physics and Astrology.*
> *Vacancy: Professor in General Physics.*
> *The post is intended to enhance and strengthen research in applied physics at the university, and is part of a programmed expansion of the Sub-Department of Applied Physics. Applicants should have an international reputation in an appropriate area of applied physics, as attested to by a distinguished publication record in internationally regarded journals, and the potential to attract significant funding for research. For an informal discussion, please contact:*

> *Professor Hamish Humble, Head: Department of Applied Physics and Astrology, Albert Einstein Building, Evergreen Epstein University, Evergreen.*

It was just as Hamish described to Charles over the phone. A wonderful opportunity, and it had his name written all over it! This was his time, and he would seize it.

* * *

The contents of the letter came as no surprise; indeed, Charles would have been astounded had they been otherwise. It was like winning a raffle, having bought the only ticket on sale:

> *Dear Dr Rae,*
> *We are delighted to inform you that your name has been placed among those of the candidates shortlisted for our currently vacant post of Professor in General Physics. The interviews are scheduled for the afternoon of Monday, the 18th of April.*
> *Please confirm that you intend to attend for interview at Evergreen Epstein University, and if you require any further information or overnight accommodation, please contact me directly.*
> *Yours sincerely,*
> *Justin Pollock*
> *(Executive Human Resources Manager)*

Of course Charles intended to attend for interview, absolutely, but he noted a minor detail that needed to be addressed. He was due to be working in Germany on that date, actually as part of a two-week visit to work on the European particle accelerator facility, so if they wanted to interview him then, they would need to fly him back for the event. In the back of his mind the notion glimmered that if EEU were put off by the expense of a "non-Saturday night cheap flight", they were not worth working for, and he would be absolved of the inconvenience of a move up to Evergreen.

In his heart Charles knew he didn't really want to go there, but he had set the plan in motion, the stages of which would run him on to that final conclusion: It is a *Chair* after all, which were precisely his words when Justin Pollock balked at the cost of his return plane ticket to Evergreen – "That's nearly a *grand!*" before conceding the point that it was a drop in the ocean compared to a professor's salary. Moreover, as there were no relocation expenses offered to the successful candidate, it remained a very cheap deal for EEU compared with the overall appointment package met by most universities. Exactly how cheap the deal was to prove itself, as yet lay below the threshold of Charles' imagination.

"I don't like it, but I'm stuck with it," Justin continued in a chiding tone. "You did know from the further particulars when the interview date was, but you ignored it."

It was *Creep in a Suit Syndrome* (CRASS). A modern pandemic. Personnel officers, middle managers, estate agents, independent financial advisors and newly qualified solicitors. Charles found an increasing annoyance at such people, observing wryly, He probably doesn't even have bloody A-levels, but he thinks he's better than me.

"Hang on," Charles responded, "you sent me the wrong 'further particulars' the first time around. They were for a… now what was it? Oh yes, a *research assistant* in *Modern Dance*, as I recall, which is to be interviewed for in May. I've only just got the documentation for the *professorship* in *General Physics*; it arrived yesterday as a matter of fact, after my receiving an empty envelope in response to my first phone call about it, and then having to phone your department again. And while this was all going on, I was suddenly allocated some additional time on the European particle accelerator facility. This is worth around two million quid, so I can hardly turn it down just for a job interview. They might never let me use the facility again… and my research career would be finished for good!"

These last words were to prove prophetic.

3

When Hamish Humble received sight of Charles Rae's application, he was agog. As a fish-wearing God-fearing man, it seemed the Almighty had answered all his prayers in the form of one man. His messiah had been sent to seed the barren earth that was Applied Physics at EEU – at grade 1, the pariah of the university. As he told him later, if Charles had been unable to attend for interview on the 18th, Hamish would willingly have recalled the panel the following week, or for that matter, practically *any* other time at Charles' convenience, just for him; so far above the other candidates was he.

In this reverie of enthusiasm, Hamish had temporarily forgotten that the Department of Applied Physics and Astrology was technically bankrupt, and that he, Hamish, had passed the last six months in sleepless nights, pacing the floor of his bedroom with the worry of it all, while trying to summon a solution to the impending financial crisis. The main problem was the shortfall in student numbers who wanted to study Physics at all, a condition that seemed irredeemable. He had hoped that the department might secure a respectable research rating, to which the grade 1 had been their final body blow. In retaliation, the dean of the Faculty of Technology, Norman Rayle, had merged them with the fledgling subject of astrology, in the hope that both vessels, as the Department of Applied Physics and Astrology, would sink together.

★ ★ ★

Hamish tried to chivvy the long-serving staff into producing some research output, but it was hopeless. He first approached Donald Smallpiece, Paddy Bowens and Neville Farmer, the oldest members, but his pleas were rebuffed with a curiously indignant pride.

"I joined the poly to *teach*! There's nothing in my *contract* that says I have to do research!"

And so it was. The sign outside might well now say "University", but the contracts told an older story.

While from Tarquin Tupper he was met with remonstrations that "Ah *do ree*-search. But it's all industrial and 'ush-'ush like. So how can ah publish anything. No! They're not going to give me any grants *here*! It's all done *there* … at *their* place!"

There was nothing Hamish could do to improve undergraduate recruitment, so research was his final refuge. Tommy Wakefield was right: they did need to get someone in from outside, and on looking through the mostly weak applications, it had to be Charles Rae, and in whose hands would rest the future of Applied Physics, and indeed that of Hamish, himself.

It was a gamble at best, and the circumstances were far from being the best. The vice-chancellor, Stirling George, had been rumbling for some time, beneath a veneer that could breach at the slightest modicum of pique, and sweep the department into ashes. And on a stable day, when his magma was still, he had acceded to Hamish Humble's supplications not to close them down, but to draw in new blood. A messiah was called for, rather than a grim horseman bearing a purpose-hardened scythe. In his accordance with Hamish's volition to "get someone *good* in from outside", Stirling George had engendered in him the false impression that the department was now "safe".

It was, of course, still bankrupt, and only a man driven by the utmost desperation could ignore the fact. But that was Hamish, desperately naïve. He had only become head of department because no one else wanted to be. A miserable, thankless task, which no one would thank him for; least of all Charles Rae. They had, at best, a stay of execution, but this would not be clear for six months. Exactly six months to the day that Charles Rae took up his post, Stirling George would be persuaded to close the department in which Charles Rae had been appointed as its new professor.

It was scandalous, but in the body of EEU, which lurched among different crises of its own making, so much was, where careers and lives of individuals were deemed irrelevancies; superficial on the EEU grand plan, which maintained its status quo in having no grand plan. The whole enterprise was so perfect an example of chaotic order that scholars might wonder at the beauty of it all. When the lack of scholarship among the senior staff at EEU threatened to reduce their staff ratio of professors to the rest smartly and well below the national mean, possibly a few professorships might be randomly scattered, in a fur-coat-and-no-knickers deception, with a chaotic educational bias: "educational chaos", "chaotic education", perhaps; as the term "education" and its derivatives often has little to do with either learning or comprehension.

Whatever else was done, the vice-chancellor would continue to pay himself well above the going standard for V-Cs running the nation's more prestigious universities. He would argue that this was justified because EEU produced vastly more graduates than "these other places put together!" even allowing for its growing number who never made that final furlong. Off the record, and away from the ear of the media, Stirling did express quiet concerns about EEU's dropout rate, and what might be done to stem the weeping wound.

The reply that EEU were prepared, albeit grudgingly, to stump up "the grand" to fly Charles to Evergreen and put him up in a swanky hotel overnight also lent some confidence in him that the deal was true. It was a Chair after all, and they were pushing the boat out (that would have been cheaper) to seat him in it. As he flew back, first class, Arabian Airlines, Charles felt propelled on the winds of destiny. He would be the youngest professor of Physics in the country; a real "elevation to the scientific peerage" as Dai Davis wrote to him later. A final bus ride from the airport to Evergreen City, and then to find the hotel.

Charles walked circumspectly out of the railway station, round the side, and then the back, to find an entire rank of "hotels", mostly DSS dosshouses... No, surely, they can't have booked him into one of these, could they? Then the scene opened out into a bluer sky, and there it was – magnificent! – The New World Hotel.

The building itself retained the overall grandeur imbued to it by the leading architect of its time. It was, for many, to be their last look at an old world while contemplating a new life in fresh lands across the great oceans, dividing common destinies into parallel lives endorsed by Christmas cards and brave faces. Shiny faces held their parents' hands and tousled heads were reassured that the move was a good one: they were leaving for a "better life" while they were still young enough to make it so; and the old stayed behind by familiar firesides of smoky coal that fuelled the vessels of journeys or imaginings, and hope fired its embers in the human soul, whether that of voyager or firesider.

★ ★ ★

Charles Rae was also on a journey. The further particulars had not been too explicit as to where he was supposed to go for his interview, and so he found himself urgently propelled on a grand sightseeing tour of Evergreen City. The passage proved rather tortuous, since it appeared that just about every other large building was an outlet of Evergreen Epstein University, broadcast in an impressive new logo, whose aesthetic design had cost them thousands. Then something struck Charles as oddly familiar.

Yes, Maypole Street… Maypole House – that's what it said on the headed notepaper. Human and Administrative Resources, Central Offices – that must be it. Charles pressed the buzzer.

"Yes, can I help you?"

"I'm here to be interviewed for the professorship in General Physics. I was sent a letter by Justin Pollock about it. I'm Dr Rae."

Mumbles in background. Charles could catch "'Ave you seen Justin today? 'As he been in?" and then "Hello? Dr Rae? Yes, Mr Pollock is interviewing today. He won't be back 'til later."

"Yes, I know. He's supposed to be interviewing *me*! But where exactly do I need to go?"

"Ah, yes. Hold on."

More backstage mumbles… "Where did 'e say 'e was going?" and finally, "Right. Yes. Mr Pollock is over in Marion Street today. Interviewing."

"I know!" Charles responded, agitated.

"Yes, OK. I'll let you in." Wait for the buzzer. "Probably best if I draw you a map. You didn't know you were supposed to be at the Marion Street site?"

Charles sighed, feeling helpless.

"No. I agree. It's not very clear is it? There seem to be some pages missing from your human resources portfolio. Sorry about that, but if you just take a left out of the main entrance… on past the car park and the radio mast, then ask again at the shopping centre. You should find it OK…"

★ ★ ★

Fortunately, Charles had plenty of time, having risen early, awoken by the incipient sun searing into his torpid brain through frays in the curtain.

Though The New World Hotel maintained its external glories, within it lay a general tattiness that struck Charles as a down-at-heel splendour, drawing in the faded lines of more opulent days. It was, thus, a metaphor for the city itself, whose splendid original architecture contrasted and humbled the hodgepodge constructions of the later century.

"Marion Street is just past the flyover," his mapmaker had told him. Then on, over the flyover itself, which, in its time, merited an award to its creator for innovative construction, but was now so riddled with concrete cancer that its rusting reinforcements were unconcealed beyond any doubt. As Charles continued walking, the vista opened on the building itself: "EEU Faculty of Technology, Albert Einstein Building". Originally the Evergreen Municipal Technical College, it too had seen better days.

In the swirl of that day's events, Charles didn't notice the poorly repaired subsidence which urgently threatened to cast down much of its large utilitarian facade into a hail of rubble, as it shattered upon the flagstones below it.

"Dr Rae? Oh, I'm glad you could make it! I'm Hamish Humble, head of Applied Physics and Astrology here. We spoke on the phone. I was afraid we'd have to reconvene the interview panel for next week if you couldn't manage today."

This all sounded very promising to Charles; they were indeed serious about having him, as he'd been led to believe. Hamish continued, "Now, I'd like to introduce you to two other members of staff. In fact, they'll both be at your interview this afternoon. This is Tommy Wakefield. He's our reader in Theoretical and Particle Physics."

They shook hands. Charles had heard of Tommy Wakefield; he was quite good. In fact, Charles recalled their meeting at a conference a few years ago, which Tommy confirmed.

"And this is Tarquin Tupper, our reader in Industrial Physics, and an ace committee man!"

Charles had never heard of him, but then before that fateful telephone call, he'd never heard of Hamish Humble either.

Tommy seemed genuine and straightforward, as Charles remembered him to be. He recalled them both having a lot to drink at a conference banquet a couple of years back, when Tommy had been less than flattering about the abilities of students at EEU to comprehend the merest modicum of anything remotely mathematical. Not that he was too buoyant in his description generally of conditions at EEU:

"Constant mergers and remergers of departments and divisions, rotten management, knife-in-the-back politics, crap academics who are anti-research, incompetent technicians."

The list went on and on – chaos! – but now it had been decided to build up the Sub-Department of Applied Physics, and to appoint a new professor: a *research* professor at that, such was their commitment to take research forward there.

"About time we had some serious research policy here," Tommy muttered grimly, a sentiment to which Tarquin Tupper nodded in assent, with a smile like a firm handshake; but somehow there was something impalpable that made Charles instantly distrust him. They eyed one another like two cats on a wall, before displacing their attention with a quick lick of a paw.

The interview itself ran to a perfect mechanism, following the measured sweep of hands past faces, becoming nods and smiles. The panel itself consisted of Hamish Humble; Tommy Wakefield; Tarquin Tupper; someone from the board of governors; Justin Pollock from Human Resources; and perhaps surprisingly, *not* the vice-chancellor, but the professor of Astrology, Mervyn Omen, who was also the university pro-vice-chancellor for research – a pleasant, youngish man whose main role was to preside over the proceedings.

Ten minutes in, Charles thought, "If I can keep my nerve, I've got this." And he had.

"How can we improve our Physics RAE rating?" This was what it was all about really, and Charles had the answer. They had to make a serious investment in physics at EEU.

"Well, there is this appointment, of course, plus another lectureship to be filled," Hamish declared. But that was nowhere near enough to impress the Physics RAE panel. Charles pointed out that three departments in the "older" universities which had scored a grade 2 in the first round of the exercise all managed to rise to a grade 4 the next time, after the investment of about a million pounds in *research infrastructure,* quite apart from making some good new appointments.

Hamish beamed, "Och, that's it! The university has had the teaching labs repainted, and the main corridor replastered and repainted too. Now, the work has been costed by 'Estates' at about half a million, so aye, I think we can say we've done our bit there."

Well, that was better than nothing, even if it had nothing to do with research.

The previous night, Charles had sat late in the hotel bar, trying to antic-ipate their line of questioning, and he seemed to have sized up the situation pretty well. The hangover, which concerned him earlier, was almost gone; swept from his brain in the flood of adrenaline. He was young, and by EEU standards especially, well-qualified to the point of embarrassment.

"You've published over a hundred papers, but it says on your application you're still a lecturer. Why is that?" Hamish Humble asked him quizzically, and almost in the tone of a demand.

The question had, for a split second, disarmed Charles, but only for that, and he countered it swiftly. "Ah, yes, a good point. As you see, at present, I am working in a rather traditional university, where it is almost impossible to be promoted before the age of about forty, and that is why I am looking elsewhere, now." A fair answer. The panel all nodded knowingly, smiling, and were satisfied that it was the truth.

When it came to Tommy's turn, he asked, "How do you think your interests would fit in with the research already going on here?"

That was an easy one, since Charles and Tommy both had an interest in ion-physics, and also that some of Charles' work could be applied, or at least stretched, to complement some of Hamish Humble's research into the phys-ical properties of lard.

Tarquin's question was one of "What grants do you have?" which Charles answered simply by listing them all, from the top of his head. Charles noticed during their subsequent years together that Tarquin would often ask this question, usually of younger staff members, although in his own long service at the Evergreen Municipal Technical College, the Evergreen Polytechnic and finally EEU, Tarquin had never, ever had a grant himself. It was one of his many diversion tactics to prevent anyone from looking too closely into his own academic achievements.

★　★　★

As Charles walked back across the concrete flyover, he felt ten feet tall – head and shoulders above the corroded dilapidation that chafed him before. He knew he'd got it: "Professor" Charles Rae. It was a sunny spring after-noon in mid-April, the 18th and three days before his thirty-third birthday. He remembered a holiday in Turkey three years previously. He and his wife had gone with friends to Cappadocia, an area with an almost lunar land-scape of soft volcanic rock, carved and eroded by winds and antiquarian floods. Among the sculpted legacy of these twin forces are the so-called "fairy chimneys", which look for all the world like a petrified army of giant phalluses, with stone helmets poised upon shafts of lava stone.

And there is a "lucky wall", too: a sheer cliff of pumice into which hollows have been etched by centuries of wind and water, with shallow shelves, sloping downwards. The locals have a legend that if you take a stone – a good one about the size of your fist – and throw it upwards while making a wish; if it lands on the shelf and stays there, the wish will be granted. In time the successful stones must fall or be knocked out, presumably, but that is only in the nature of wishes – such ephemeral things.

Charles had done it. Taking a stone from the ground, he seized his window, then closing his eyes and forming a Zen-like singularity with it, he sent the stone upwards on a journey of destiny. "I'm going to be a professor by the time I'm thirty-three," and it had landed sure, so now, in the promise of time, the wish was made solid. But it has been said, and there is anecdotal evidence that it is true: "Those whom the gods wish to destroy, they first grant them their wishes".

Poor sods. Poor, poor sods.

"Be careful for what you wish: it might just come true" is another proverb worth recalling.

★   ★   ★

The fountain of elation did not leave Charles for several days. The following morning, he phoned Justin Pollock for confirmation that the panel had selected him, which of course it had. It was now only a matter of waiting for a formal contract to arrive. Charles decided to sit tight and say nothing to anyone. This made sense, ostensibly because something *might* yet go awry, although this was practically impossible; but also that the knowledge he would shortly be moving on, and on to a *Chair* at that, distilled in him a rising sense of smug pleasure. This he found enhanced finally to the level of euphoria by the unabated superciliousness of Jasper Totter.

When the latter culminated, coincidentally on the day the contract arrived from EEU, in Jasper's announcement that the departmental deadbeat was to be placed in charge of Charles' teaching duties, the hours of which "would have to be doubled" as it transpired, he decided the time had arrived to break his silence. The event had been contrived in the form of an ambush. Never particularly fond of staff meetings, finding them generally tedious and futile, Charles had walked into this one with his widely acknowledged enthusiasm on such occasions.

To Charles' surprise, presiding over the meeting was Dudley Dudd, rather than Jasper, who usually assumed responsibility for all meetings "departmental". Indeed, he normally insisted on it, in a paranoid anxiousness that his rank might otherwise be undermined as head of department. Dudley Dudd, being the only research-inactive member of the department, frequently found himself the single butt of Jasper Totter's acerbic contempt. "What the hell does Dudley do with himself all day? He's just dead wood!" and any crap jobs that were going, you could be sure would be going Dudley's way, and if he protested at all, "Well, you've got to do something to earn your keep! Look at some of the younger people, Charles Rae, for example. Why can't you be more like him?" This had caused a resentful and jealous maliciousness to rise in Dudley toward Charles, for whom he would lie in wait, watching the clock for him.

"You've finished your lecture five minutes early," Dudley would announce loudly in front of all the students. "You're not giving them value for money!"

"Fuck off, Dudley! Haven't you got anything better to do than check up on me?" was a typical reply, hissed menacingly into a gnome-like ear, whereupon Dudley would scuttle back into his office, to plan the next raid.

Sadly, Dudley was a dud. His blue touchpaper had flared into skyward promise, with the top double-first in his year, followed by a PhD in the most prestigious university the nation had to offer, then an exemplary post-doc in the US. His record was impeccable and so, when a lectureship became available, Dudley Dudd was headhunted for it. Such was the enthusiasm to get him, any formal interview process was waived, as then was their right, and Dudley was appointed lecturer in General Physics.

But, Dudley was a dud; a damp squib, and having found himself in a permanent, tenured post, his glowing fuse almost instantly fizzled out, never to deliver its charge. In retaliation for this, he had never been promoted above the rank of lecturer in all his thirty years there. But Jasper had found a new role for Dudley, as he explained:

"I've called this meeting of all staff, to explain some new arrangements that I feel are required to ensure the efficient running of the department. As you may all have heard, I have been elected as the new dean. This, naturally, will mean my taking on a whole host of new responsibilities concerning the running of the Faculty of Science. Now, I shall remain as head of this department, but in order for me to do so, it will be necessary to delegate certain of my current tasks and responsibilities. As you know, I have always believed that as head of department, I should be in control of allocating the teaching duties of my staff. However, I realise that with my own duties as dean, I no longer have time to do this effectively, and so I have deputised Dudley as 'director of undergraduate studies'."

This, Charles thought, did not bode well.

"Dudley's role will be to assign their overall teaching and teaching-related duties to individual members of staff, and to keep a progress check on it all, just to... as I said... ensure that everything runs efficiently." Jasper smirked condescendingly, concluding a *fait accompli*.

Jasper had noted too, that "We are moving from an elite system of higher education to a system of mass education... This means we will have to provide formal proof that our procedures are properly validated".

Someone had commented to this: "But what about our professional integrity and judgement?" to which Jasper had replied: "In effect, we are all going to become polytechnics, and they are accountable to official inspectors, and have to provide full documentation of their procedures and practices. We will have to do the same. It's probably quite right that we should, too."

Everyone knew that Jasper's wife, though now retired, had made a highly successful career in the Polytechnic Assessment Authority, lending him an insider view into the true nature of that draconian world, which they could only as yet suspect.

"Now, I'm going to hand the meeting over to Dudley, who has a few words for us all."

This was Dudley's *magnum momentum*. From being a slinking dog, hiding in shadowy corners out of aim from his master's boot, now he had some authority. Jasper had also offered him a juicy bone: that if he made a decent job of this, he might have a good case for promotion to a senior lectureship. Dudley, however, cowed from years of expecting the unannounced steel toe-cap, had honed his cunning. Because he had never been promoted, the university remained bound by the terms of his original contract of "tenure". So, unless he committed fraud or embezzlement, or molested one of the undergraduates – which he didn't feel capable of anyway... not these days... as he glanced down wistfully – they couldn't get rid of him, no matter what.

If he was promoted, that would mean a new contract, containing the phrase "terminable by three months notice in writing from either side". And Dudley, an albeit dejected but still a clever and well-trained animal, had noted some unwelcome changes in his environment recently; like a dog finding molehills appearing in his once pristine green parkland. Recruitment had not gone well, and although numbers were not bad, the entry grades were, so they were now taking students with two E's at A-level. Ten years ago it would have been unthinkable.

If Jasper was right that they were heading for "mass" education, with survival dependent on student numbers, the system would become far more competitive; and they had plenty of competing neighbours, like the polytechnic, who would scrape further down the barrel and frankly leave them with too few students to survive.

"Then, what about me?" Dudley thought. He thought a great deal in his doghouse. "If they start cutting staff. My God! I'll get the push! It'll be the likes of Charles Rae they'll want to keep. Not the likes of me! They'll hang on to the research-active staff, who can do the teaching but also publish the papers and bring in the research income. But, if I don't apply for promotion, I'm here 'til I'm sixty-five, whether they like it or not! Just as my contract says! Ha ha!" Regarding the contract almost as a talisman, Dudley smoothed a hand over the yellowed paper, which matched the faded colour of his lecture notes, and locked it back in his desk.

Dudley was being thoroughly astute, in fact. The whole business of his new role was a subterfuge by Jasper, and part of a grand plan to hack away the remaining dead branches: pension off the "old deadbeats". There was now only Dudley left. He realised that Jasper would resent his intransigence to stay, when the time came, but meanwhile Dudley could relish his days of glory. For once, he had some status, and he could crack the whip of resentment on Charles Rae.

Who did he think he was, anyway? He'd been taken on from a poly, for God's sake! The man could hardly contrast more lowly with Dudley's own unbowed credentials. This view of matters was, however, unique to Dudley's mind. While Rae received praise, he earned contempt. Now was the time to get his own back.

"Thank you, Jasper." Dudley adopted the mildly pompous air of self-defence he usually did when summoned from his safe, hidden world into the public gaze of derision. Today though, there was nothing to hide from; his moment had arrived.

"Jasper and I have been discussing my new role in the department, and *our* requirements regarding teaching. One aspect that is clear is that the staff teaching loads are quite unbalanced. The same unfair distribution applies to teaching-related administration. For example, Charles' hours are dramatically lower than most."

Dudley glanced toward Jasper for reassurance, which he found granted in an authoritative nod, both sets of eyes singling Charles out from the pack.

"But Charles publishes far more than anyone else – about half the department's output, as I recall – so surely his research must be protected? That's why we gave him less teaching than, say, yourself, Dudley, wasn't it?" said Sam Burrell, looking askance.

This was true, which both Sam Burrell and Jasper Totter had agreed on when they first appointed Charles Rae, and voiced by a senior professor, who was also Charles' section head and until now had assigned his teaching duties to him. The argument bore some mass, but Jasper interceded, "That was *then*, Sam. We are now looking forward to the new challenges and opportunities facing us."

Professor Sam Burrell shrugged acquiescently, "OK, if that's how you see our best use of his talents…"

Dudley knew he'd won this skirmish, if not the battle, or yet the war, and produced an overhead slide, depicting before-and-after teaching hours and admin burdens, projected toward next year's target of undergraduate numbers. Even Sam Burrell sucked in his breath at this, and looked sympathetically at Charles, who was down for nearly double his current hours plus a load of administrative duties, against which, curiously, the initials DD had been crossed out, and CR written in their place.

If Charles had been undecided about Evergreen, he was no longer so. The supercilious smirks from Jasper and Dudley – from *Dudley* of all people – were the clincher.

"Jasper? Perhaps I could discuss something with you tomorrow? I have some news. I'll give your secretary a ring in the morning to make an appointment."

And then he was gone.

4

Stirling George was an astute man, an unusual man. But this time he had gambled heavily. As director of the Evergreen Polytechnic, in 1992 he became vice-chancellor of Evergreen Epstein University, named in honour of Randolph Epstein, a local businessman and benefactor who made a sizeable fortune buying and selling scrap iron in the 1930s, which he then invested wisely in government bonds, returning a vast profit in the late 1940s and making him a millionaire, even then. In a handshake with Stirling George, Epstein made a gentleman's agreement to leave Evergreen Polytechnic £50 million in his will, in return for it naming the university after him, but when he finally died, aged 103, and the will was read, it contained no mention of either the polytechnic or Evergreen Epstein University.

In a somewhat premature gesture, the polytechnic commissioned a craven idol, a ten-foot-tall bronze cast of Randolph Epstein, to stand by the main entrance of the Faculty of Technology. Being a rags-to-riches practical man, his strong right hand pointed from an industrial age which brought that city forth, aiming toward future prosperity. As he stood proudly outside the new university, the students would adorn him, usually on Thursdays, when an evening of "happy hours" could be found time-tunnelling through the bars of the city. Traffic cones embellished his head; an umbrella graced his arm; a cigarette projected from his unyielding fingers, toward the new sign of higher education: EEU. That was quite a climb: a good twelve feet. In winter a scarf or a makeshift bin bag jacket would be wrapped around his broad shoulders, with snow on the lapels.

The family lawyers proved it was all down to a simple misunderstanding, but, in a show of goodwill, the Epsteins were willing to cover Stirling George's sponsorship of (1) a local radio station: "Evergreen City, where it's at, 96.7 MHz"; and (2) a train: "Evergreen Epstein University". The latter found particular use in the recruitment of students from beyond the environs of Evergreen, and in transporting them there – mainly international students who had never before been to EEU or indeed Evergreen City at all, and for whom both venues would provide an indelible learning experience.

★ ★ ★

Stirling George was not an academic – more streetwise, he thought. His formal qualification was a third class degree in Human Studies, and he had then risen in the ranks of the Polytechnic Assurance Authority. He felt he was still assuring quality-assured "customer supply". When EEU was formed, he awarded himself first a doctorate, and then a professorship, becoming professor of Customer Supply Assurance. His title married well with Letticia Jolanda, who, having sold off her Knightsbridge fashion warehouse, moved to Evergreen as assistant vice-chancellor of EEU, and professor of Retail Therapeutics.

As Stirling explained, "It's not for me, you understand. But I have to deal with senior academics and vice-chancellors from other – especially the 'older' – universities, and they are all professors and hold doctorates, and well… I just can't see EEU disadvantaged, so I am prepared to accept these titles for the benefit of my colleagues. You *do* understand, don't you?"

"Of course, Vice-Chancellor. Thank you. We all appreciate your sacrifice."

Stirling was a public-spirited man. Indeed, he paid himself more than any other vice-chancellor in the country. A true martyr to the cause of Evergreen; and martyrdom comes with a price in its pocket.

As the polytechnic expanded into the new university (EEU), its student population nearly tripled, and space became at a premium, but its costs were prime too. They needed more lecture rooms – and far larger rooms, since some of the classes had doubled or more in the number of students taking them – and new, up-to-date science labs were demanded. Stirling made some shrewd negotiations and bought some of Evergreen's finest property.

On making the grand tour of Evergreen, prospective students found its signs seemingly everywhere: in a proud new logo, on the facades of buildings, hotels, former city council offices, and even on the front of the main railway station. As his empire put on weight, its foundations became increasingly compressed, and rumours of cracks began to appear.

How was he going to pay for it all? But he was shrewd. He took out loans against EEU's existing collateral – borrowing £20 million in all. The deal was made in the manner of provision of starter homes for newly cohabiting couples, with no repayments due in the first year, but a first repayment in the second year and then more in subsequent years. Even without the anticipated Epstein legacy, Stirling calculated that with increased undergraduate recruitment – particularly of customers from overseas, and paying full fees – EEU's income should cover these initial costs and those of all further payments over the years to come. He had drawn up the business plan with the university's accountants and Tony Naismith, the bursar, by which the bank was sufficiently convinced to release the loans. All appeared sound until the free market kicked in – a market whose vagaries are often unpredictable in both their direction and their impact.

Stirling had been delighted to meet Professor Sharleen La'Coy. Not that she could be described as coy. A tall Texan redhead, and a hardnosed and groundbreaking professor of Business Studies, whose international reputation preceded her, her theories on business education were the talk of seminar rooms at conferences and university business schools around the world.

"Ya see, Stirling – size does matter. You Brits, you're just too small!"

She was at once frightening and exciting, and Stirling's personal holding vacillated between incipient phases of contraction and expansion.

"Your *Business School*, Silly!" she laughed, beginning to massage his upper arm slowly with purposeful, tactile fingers. "You simply *can't* run a successful business school with less than *two thousand* students...! and that's where *I* come in."

He was hooked and mesmerised, both by her presence and her glamour and a chameleon calculation that two thousand bums on seats, reckoning at, say, £10,000 per bum, which you could get away with for a "Business" course...would mean £20 million *additional annual* income for EEU! The sticky tongue connected with its target – slurp! *And business subjects were cheap to teach too. Not like those damned science courses,* he thought, *which cost us a bloody fortune.* Stirling began to enthuse, You could have five hundred students in a lecture room... if it were big enough, naturally... with just *one* lecturer at the front. Anyway, if the room only held two hundred and fifty, he or she could just give the same lecture twice; or if it only held a hundred and twenty five, they could simply give it four times over. Easy! Maybe the size of the lecture rooms wasn't such a problem after all... even the smaller, fifty-seaters... the same lecture, ten times... maybe a bit much in the same day, perhaps... but... well, I'm sure the staff could use their initiative. He was entranced. He *had* to *have* her. EEU *needed* her, or so ran his thoughts.

"Well... OK, Stirling... but I'll need a free hand, y'know."

"*Anything*, Sharleen, *Anything*."

Truly, she had been sent from the divine – the answer to his prayers and to those of the EEU accountants and the bursar, who were beginning to glimpse a hole, rather like the newly discovered ozone hole, in their financial firmament. With a vastly expanded business school, there could be an unrivalled reign of expansion at EEU. It would be the largest provider of business education in the country – far greater than any, even among the more established, older universities. Her current employer, The Midwestern Baptist University, could not even approach matching Stirling's offer, and conceded, sadly, that all hope of retaining Sharleen in-post there was lost.

Stirling George was forced to confess that the logistics of teaching another two thousand business students did pose certain tactical challenges. The EEU insignia graced the former New World Hotel, which had been accommodated into his empire to embody the "EEU Modern Business School", as the sign now read. It *was* a splendid building, as only a building built on the slave trade could be, and still not cheap at five million pounds, but with the student numbers Sharleen La'Coy's image had promised to bear, he would have his money back in a year – and some! What a coup she was!

Stirling couldn't believe his luck in persuading her "across the pond" to EEU. It was just too good to be true. Admittedly, Sharleen hadn't some cheap either, since he was paying her far more than he was the dean of her faculty, and as much as a vice-chancellor might typically earn nationally, present company excepted, whom he paid well above the gold standard. It was his ambition to retire at sixty with a knighthood for... services to Evergreen City. "God bless yer, Sir Stirling!" Tears in their eyes. A feudal lord in his fantasy parade. "Arise, Sir Stirling..."

But what exactly had Sharleen arisen in him? At a £5 million outlay for the premises, then £120K for her, as an *annual* outlay, his balls were heavy, but they would yield a spectacular issue, and he eyed them swollen in his pockets.

"It's gonna take *time*, Stirling! Business *is* a competitive industry.

"We need a complete refit of the building. It's just so *old*-fashioned!"

High ceilings, sweeping marble staircases for fluent ball-gowns – a nightmare to heat the place! Rewiring – a full overhaul. Study-bedrooms – partitioning some of the larger rooms and adding in more *en suite* facilities. Lecture theatres – knocking through some of the ground floor bedrooms, and putting in IT facilities, "Powerpoint" and such things of which he'd never heard. The list went on and on... he could add another £5 million to the initial cost of the building, reduced to a mere shell, and still the bloody woman wasn't satisfied.

"Vice-Chancellor, it's Professor La'Coy again... Oh! She's on her way over... that was her mobile..."

"Stirling...!"

That voice, initially so seducing, became a plane, rasping the nerves on his skin. He shuddered in a cold sweat.

"I'm sorry, Vice-Chancellor..." His secretary had been slow in fielding the door, and the red ball was in.

"*There* you are!"

"Ah. Sharleen. Do come in." Stirling George motioned a hand to calm his ruffled first line of defence against all intruders, who withdrew into her own outer chamber. He would deal with the matter, quite calmly and capably.

"Please take a seat."

She did present a striking figure, he considered: something like Bodicea or Margaret Thatcher, but more formidable.

"Stirling," she breezed, "we need to talk."

Cool green eyes held him steadily, anticipating the game.

"We're just not getting the applications in."

Red fire cascaded across her shoulders, brushing over the freckles and straps of a backless red dress. Lovely long legs, crossed with intriguing rustles... What a woman...

"Sorry, Sharleen...what do you mean?" Stirling spoke tersely, abruptly recentred by the portent of bad news.

"We only have a hundred applications in for our Business course next year."

"A hundred... that means... about a million pounds in fees," Stirling calculated aloud. "We were banking – literally, as I've had to borrow against our projected returns on the course – on a take-up rate of *two thousand* students per annum."

This was not what he hoped to hear, but maybe it was a glitch that could be fixed.

"Can't you get some more over from the States?"

"None of them want to come. Ya see, Stirling, air travel is a sensitive issue since last year. And your strong currency doesn't help..."

"Then what do you propose?" He was genuinely scared. This was his masterstroke. If it went wrong, EEU would owe millions, with no easy means to claw them back.

"There *is* one strategy," Sharleen spoke deliberately. "Suppose we drop the price?"

"Student bursaries, do you mean?" Stirling replied.

"No. Better than that. How about running a two-year Business degree, with a third semester? That way they only pay fees for two years, not three."

Stirling suddenly spurted ahead of her, and took up pen and paper.

"Now, let's see how this might work out... we need to calculate the 'dead time' in a standard three-year degree programme. One semester is fifteen weeks, but with the exams, reading week etc, there is only *ten* weeks of actual *teaching*. Then there is a break of about six weeks over Christmas before the second semester begins; then the Easter break, which takes out April typically, leaving a couple of weeks teaching in May, and then the exams begin again... all done and dusted, degrees awarded by mid-June. Then three months of nothing before the new academic year commences... so we could easily fit in another semester between June and September. Six semesters in two years rather than three!" His face shone triumphant.

"But, Stirling, now you put it that way... if we were to dispense with the exams, and assess the course simply on *coursework*, we could squeeze *four* semesters in. Imagine that – a sesquiennial degree! All over in eighteen months! Start in September, get the certificate in the April following the next fall!" Their partnership was back in the groove.

Since the existing mass of lecturing staff were deemed sufficient to run the "optional sesquiennial Business degree"; other than a little more electricity and water, it would incur no additional costs. Therefore, the standard £10K flat fee for Business courses could still apply, effectively reducing the upfront cost of a degree by half, and by more than that since living costs had to be found for just eighteen months, not nearer thirty-six. Priding himself that EEU was a modern innovative university, Stirling George launched a major publicity campaign, headed by Letticia Jolanda and the university public relations team. Unfortunately, this resulted in contemptuous newspaper headlines, and even the vice-chancellors of some of the other new and more innovative universities drenched the notion in scorn, probably wishing they'd thought of it first.

Determined to trash such potential competition, the valid point was bandied that the "gaps" in a degree were there because "the assimilation of knowledge requires a 'gestation period' to bear the full fruit of comprehension". They also served the purpose that the students, having to find living costs and pay top-up fees, needed to get jobs during the "gap" periods, so they didn't have to work during the examination weeks, when they might otherwise fall asleep on the paper and fail it.

Stirling began to consider a broader question: If the sesquiennial plan seemed workable for Business courses, what about the others?

Imagine, EEU could be the first university in the world to offer sesquiennial degrees in select vocational courses like Business, Media, Astrology, Nursing and Psychology too. When he suggested that the approach might be extended to subjects like forensics and physics, mathematics and law, biology and engineering, he was reminded in a uniformly scalding petition from the deans and heads of departments, that such courses did require exams if they were to be taken seriously at all. This did, nonetheless, leave the option of *two*-year degrees for them all, as he and Sharleen had originally considered for the Business course, but he decided to move that one onto the back burner, until the rest of the menu had tempered a little.

★ ★ ★

Following discussions in The House, a bill was passed that a degree had to take at least two years, leaving the second option open, but scotching any possible lure of the putative sesquiennial Business degree. Since the market for business students was already saturated nationally and could not be milked further, and no more students could be siphoned from the States; however skilfully Sharleen manipulated the source, the whole venture was a disaster. Sharleen went back to The Midwestern Baptist University in a huff, and the other EEU departments all had their budgets slashed in order to cover the bill of close to £10 million that had been rung up by the whole fiasco.

5

"**O**ch. An office, you say? I'd not considered that one. And a lab? You'll be asking me for a new building next!"

Charles was staggered. The man had not thought at all beyond getting him there. To EEU. There was no concept of *how* he was actually supposed to do the job he'd been appointed for. It was rather like a Sunday league football club who, by some miracle, had got their hands on a star striker without it occurring to them that he needed a pair of boots to play in. Hamish could read the consternation in the man's face, and his stance softened.

"I'm sorry, Charles. It's just that you're the first person we've ever appointed at professorial level. All the rest of us have come up through the ranks, as it were. I guess we're all on a steep learning curve." He smiled, and Charles felt reassured again.

"Sorry, Hamish. I'm just keen to make a start. This has all been a big move for me, and I want to make sure it was a good one."

"Well, I'll see what we can do. You know Tommy Wakefield, don't you? He's in Poland just now, so why don't you use his office. I'm sure he won't mind."

"What's he doing in Poland?" Charles was genuinely curious.

"Och. He's working at the University of Warsaw. He has a long-standing collaboration with the Institute of Theoretical Physics there. He usually goes over for a few weeks during the summer to write some papers."

Charles was reminded that at least there was Wakefield in the department. Someone with some credibility, out of the rest of them. But, as he sat in Tommy Wakefield's office, things did seem rather subdued. The place was like a graveyard: not the peace of respect and reflection, but the absence of living bodies. Where was everybody? Not even the lights were on. There was no one at home. It had a truly depressing air of decay.

"Where is everybody?" Charles asked Hamish.

"Och, they're on holiday. It is the summer, ye ken?" Hamish seemed puzzled by the question, or awkward, or both.

"But what about their research?" Charles persisted.

"When you've settled in a wee bit, I'll take you to meet the vice-chancellor…"

Charles felt he understood the answer.

★ ★ ★

Once back from their summer-long holidays, the rest began to rumble. Mutterings down the corridor.

"He's never here. He doesn't do any teaching, you know. I don't know why they appointed him."

Disappointed shakes of heads. It was a terrible shame, to be sure. Scurrying off to give yet another lecture, run another practical class, attend another meeting, or just to go home early; Charles Rae was a threat to the numb security of that world. Tarquin Tupper, reader in Industrial Physics and, along with Tommy Wakefield, in charge of research in the Department of Applied Physics and Astrology, was the most threatened of the lot. He would lose this tin badge of authority once Charles Rae arrived in the post of professor of General Physics, which must outrank all other posts, including his own.

On the face of things, Tarquin behaved affably toward Charles, seeking him out from his billet in Tommy's office. It was a ruse to gain his trust, but Charles was reminded of his misgivings on their first meeting. There was something sly in his manner, which conveyed the impression that Tarquin did not have Charles' best interests at heart.

★ ★ ★

"Och. I'd hoped to avoid having to give you any administration." Now Hamish was the latest visitor in the procession of tourists that came to gawp at Charles, as though he were a rare animal in the zoo. Charles was never very fond of paperwork, and his heart sank in the forbidding promise of Hamish's remark.

"Oh yes?" Charles cast him a suspicious glance.

"Now, it's not a big job…" Charles had heard that one before.

"What is it?"

"Industrial training. I've been talking to Tarquin Tupper. He is currently our industrial training liaison officer, but I think that would be an ideal job for you."

"Why?" Charles smelled subterfuge. It was obvious Hamish had been nobbled, but not obvious to Hamish himself, who now thought it was all his idea, and a bright one at that. One of his better ones, of late.

"It'll mean you having lots of involvement with local industry. You'll be in constant contact with them. You'll be on the phone on a daily basis, arranging placement of our students with companies for the third year of their degree. You'll be going out to visit them in their workplace. There are about forty students altogether, so this will give you ample opportunity to meet with potential industrial partners, and... who knows... you might be able to set up contracts with them for short courses... and even research!"

Hamish bowled in the latter point swiftly, to reassure Charles his essential role remained as advertised: that of a *research professor*, before adding, "Ah yes, that reminds me: short courses. I'm afraid the department's finances are rather in the red. I should perhaps have mentioned this before... probably on the day of your interview, in fact... but it must have slipped my mind. The fact is, I can't pay the staff salary bill on the income from our current student numbers. Recruitment has been especially low recently in Applied Physics. So the only way is to bring in additional income, say from short courses. I'd like you to coordinate this, and liaise with your colleagues to decide what kinds of courses we could indeed run for local industry... and, well, anyone else you can think of, who might want them," followed by a nervous laugh.

And on this jaunty note, Hamish tripped out of Tommy Wakefield's office, leaving Charles Rae head in hands, in the realisation that not only had he been conned into taking a job in a shithole, it was a bankrupt shithole to boot.

* * *

Hamish Humble looked grey. A grey man on a grey day. He caught his breath at the top of the stairs, and leant, head on forearm against a flaky painted wall. He looked ill. Charles would have asked if he was all right, had he known him longer, but instead held back awkwardly in Tommy's office doorway. At last Hamish walked on once more. That was a relief, thought Charles: at least he hadn't dropped dead. There was even a trace of colour in those ashen cheeks. What could be wrong with him? A shock, perhaps?

Maybe some bad news?

★ ★ ★

On the following morning, the cause became clear. The Department of Applied Physics and Astrology was indeed bankrupt, and the vice-chancellor had called an emergency meeting with Hamish Humble to tell him that "with regret, I have no financial option but to close your department forthwith".

That was it. Hamish was stunned. Poleaxed. Blood draining from his face, he turned away; he'd failed. No one had wanted to become head of department; not of Applied Physics and Astrology, anyway. Hamish, as the only professor, drew the short straw, from a choice of one. He'd done his best – he was sure of that – but the events that transpired were entirely out of his control.

★ ★ ★

Charles thought Hamish was looking better. A grave earnestness still over-shadowed him, but the sickly pallor had gone.

"Aye. Better sit down, Charles. What I've got to say makes the rest of the agenda a wee bit superfluous."

Six pairs of eyes focused on Hamish Humble with an unusual attentive-ness. He pushed the sheet headed "Departmental Strategy Meeting" to one side, with a resigned deliberation, marshalling his words.

"We're going to be closed down."

The hush of a funeral congregation, before the "amens" and in between the prayers, straining at the vicar's voice pronouncing the deceased in the promise of a better life beyond this mortal dimension. As on such occasions, it was not clear where their new dimension lay; what plan existed, if any, for the staff of the Department of Applied Physics and Astrology beyond its closure.

"Well. You can imagine how I feel!"

Charles Rae was stunned, but he would learn that life at EEU was a collection of stuns, like electric shock therapies used to subdue the men-tally institutionalised, along with Largactil, Valium and other tranquilising agents. Tarquin Tupper gave him a false look of profound sympathy, actually thinking along the lines of "Oh well. I'll probably get early retirement. Serve this young whippersnapper right if he ends up on the dole. Two 'undred publications? Professor? He's only a bloody kid! That'll learn him!" But he didn't volunteer these sentiments out loud.

In contrast, Hamish felt genuinely sympathetic toward Charles, as well he might, since the whole fiasco was fruit from his brightest ever idea. It was Hamish, after all, who had worked so hard to convince the vice-chancellor to release the funding for Charles' appointment, despite the impending bankruptcy of the department, which had been realised in the short period of only six months.

★ ★ ★

While the fate of the physicists rode on the vacillating scales of resolution, Hamish fretted. In a well-rehearsed routine, he paced the floor, and then sat on the edge of the bed, head in hands and groaning, while his wife lay awake, concerned for the wellbeing of a man long from youth. This had become a nightly scene, going back for well over the past year, as he read the diminishing departmental accounts in dismayed impotence.

He knew the situation was bad, but later the calmer view of his retirement brought to him the absolution that no one could have expected it all to bottom out quite so abruptly. His hope had been that Charles Rae's research funding would bring in a fresh piggybank, upturning the fortunes of the department, and which could be broken open if they needed its contents fast.

"Why, oh why?" he implored. "What's to be done?"

Curiously, the astrologers, under Mervyn Omen, the professor of Astrology, appeared in a safe position, even though their own undergraduate recruitment record was far worse that that of Applied Physics, and currently negligible, with only three students in total registered to study that subject. Being a more adept politician than Hamish, Mervyn had already anticipated the shortfall, and ingratiated himself with Stirling George, and more expediently with his wife, Mrs Angela George, a well-known Evergreen psychic and clairvoyant.

The incongruous match of Astrology and Applied Physics was the demonchild of Norman Rayle, dean of the Faculty of Technology, who engineered the metastable subject arrangement in order to destroy both Astrology and Physics, whom he despised with equal rancour, though for different reasons. As an observational biologist, an authority on the reproductive endeavours of the mallard duck, Norman considered himself a serious scientist, and so he voiced the rhetorical question of "What the hell is Astrology doing in the Faculty of Technology?" loudly and often.

In contrast, his antipathy toward the physicists stemmed largely from an inability to comprehend the subject as a schoolboy, which had seated in him a deep sense of intellectual inadequacy and inferiority. "Bloody Physics! What's the point of the damn subject, anyway. Obscure and of no practical relevance," he would rant; and more dangerously, "It has no place in an institution of this kind." This was real polytechnic fighting talk, and especially dangerous as duck counting and most other activities in the Faculty of Technology were relatively cheap, even at the research level, while Physics, lock stock and barrel, cost a bomb.

Since neither Applied Physics nor Astrology could recruit students, Norman surmised that chaining them together would secure each as a millstone for the other, ensuring that their collective department sank without a bubble on the surface. Mervyn Omen could read the portents, and realised that if Applied Physics sank alone, Astrology might be made buoyant, so he began to drop stones in its pockets.

As university pro-vice-chancellor for research, Mervyn was in frequent and interactive communication with the vice-chancellor and the University Executive Strategy Team. He was able, therefore, to divert attention from the disappointing performance of Astrology by badmouthing Applied Physics, aided by the fact that Physics, never represented on any level, had no chance to fight its own corner. It was, however, meeting Mrs Angela George that lent determined power to his arm.

She was well known, indeed respected by some, in Evergreen as a psychic and clairvoyant, and keen to prove a credible link between the spirit and astrological realms. Stirling George was more mainstream in his beliefs, though devoutly Christian within his own interpretation of the faith, but respected his wife's interpretation of it. How in any case, if she was right, did that not square with the hand of the Creator? His was a liberal view of matters spiritual.

Mervyn's background started in psychology, even researching in the field, but he switched to astrology, following the flow of public conviction away from science, and from organised religion too. Astrology, he reasoned, presented a fertile middle ground.

The star of Mervyn Omen had started its ascent when Stirling George attended a conference on The Future of Higher Education in the US, where he seized upon the rising popularity of astrology among potential undergraduates there who wished to study it as a degree subject. On his return to EEU, he called an emergency meeting of the faculty deans and Letticia Jolanda.

"I've just had a *wonderful* idea!" he enthused.

Silence. What pieces of idiocy would need picking up this time? They each weighed their budgets mentally, wondering how they might absorb the costs of another failed "Business School" type venture, or something of the kind. Even in his manic optimism, Stirling could not ignore the sense of palpable apprehension which pervaded. It felt like a solid wall of mistrust and incredulity, and it was Letticia, with no real fiscal accountability as assistant vice-chancellor, who tapped at the first brick.

"Yes, Stirling. We are all ears. Is this connected with your recent US education conference?"

"Oh, Letticia. You are a mind-reader! That's just it! Why the long faces? Talking to some of our transatlantic colleagues has been truly an inspiration! I would never have thought of it otherwise! Honestly, we are all so stick-in-the-mud here, but it's all the rage in the US... astrology!"

The assembled shifted uneasily.

"Yes, Stirling, what do you have in mind exactly?" prompted Letticia helpfully.

Stirling switched on his avuncular manner. "As you probably know, I am always amenable to new ideas..."

This much they did know.

"And where better to find innovation than the *US*, especially in matters of education. It is no secret that the traditional subject bases are currently under threat. Chemistry, physics, modern languages, and the like... well, frankly, no one wants to study them any more. Engineering would have closed here *years ago,* were it not for all our international customers – Malaysians and Greeks, mainly. Trouble with them is because they've paid a hefty overseas... international," he corrected himself, "customer fee, they expect us to award them a degree even if they fail the course! Sorry... I'm digressing... but the point is that in the US they have the *same* problems. *Exactly* the same. So what do they do about it? Well... I'll tell you. They diversify! They cater to their market!"

Although it had begun to dawn what was coming next, the details needed to be confirmed explicitly, so Letticia stepped in again. "I'm sorry, Stirling, perhaps I'm being a bit slow today... but where does *astrology* fit into all this?"

"But that's the whole point, don't you see?" Stirling went on. "This *is* their up-and-coming market. So what, if no one wants to study the traditional science subjects, modern languages, computing, etc. There are always popular alternatives! And astrology is a very popular subject in American universities at the moment... especially in the State of California. So what I say is, if it's good enough for California, it's good enough for Evergreen! Not a bad slogan, now I come to think of it. Letticia, perhaps we could put it on the front of our undergraduate prospectus, for next year?!'"

"Yes, Vice-Chancellor. I'll contact the Corporate Publicity Team."

Stirling continued. "Now I realise this *is* a rather novel idea. As far as I'm aware, there is no other university in the country offering a degree in Astrology, which is all to our advantage!"

Then Norman Rayle exposed his neck. "If I might ask," he ventured, cautiously, "which faculty do you think would be best suited to *host* astrology, as an academic discipline?" This was the question that was on all their minds – who would pick up the tab?

Stirling beamed. "Yes, Norman. Practical as ever! That was my next point. Let's first consider what faculties we have. In terms of a simple list, there is:

(1) Business and Legal Studies.
(2) Education, Society and Hotel Management.
(3) Applied Health Sciences and Drama.
(4) Media.
(5) Built Environment and Dance... and last, but certainly not least...
(6) Technology."

Each drew a mental bargepole, but they knew it would have to go somewhere. When Stirling George had a bright new idea, he could not be dissuaded from it, but by the time the consequences of its impracticalities hit the fan, the notion itself was forgotten. It was then somebody else's fault for handling a golden opportunity so badly.

Stirling frowned in deep thought, and then lightened, raising both hands in a *eureka* gesture. Was this a papal blessing or an albatross fanning its wings? Probably the latter, going on past experience, but they held tightly onto each word that would follow, just to make sure. Pleasant surprises did happen sometimes, didn't they?

"Now, I do know of *one* man who's doing *research* into astrology, although there is no *teaching* component. He is... if I remember correctly... based in the Department of Psychology at one of our sister universities. Begins with an O. Olwen? Owen? No... Omen. Yes, that's the fellow! Omen. Mervyn Omen. He was on TV the other night... don't know if any of you saw him?"

No one had, as it was a graveyard slot.

"If we could get *him* here, then he could set up the whole show for us. Wonderful!"

Then Stirling gave a more thoughtful frown. "That still leaves the question of where to host the new venture. Mmm... Ha... of course... it's obvious. If he is currently in a department of Psychology... well, we have one, don't we? Let's put him in there... on a nominal basis at least... then we just see how the show goes off. Norman, I believe Psychology is part of your empire, isn't it? The Faculty of Technology. So, I'm leaving you to keep a general eye on things..."

This was a great comfort to all, and surprisingly, had they all only known it, that included Norman Rayle himself. He knew astrology was a complete non-starter, and that almost nobody in their right mind would enrol on a degree course to study it, no matter how glossily it was packaged. It was another of Stirling's fads – a flash in the pan, but with potential issues, which he could bend to his own advantage.

"Yes, Vice-Chancellor, Psychology is part of Biological Sciences, so the relevant academic director will be Professor Patrick Walker, the current head of that department. I shall liaise closely with Pat on this one. I'm sure he will be entirely receptive to any suggestions I may have regarding the launch of the new astrology degree. There are resource implications, of course: staff, space and overheads, which will need to be diverted from current budgets... unless the university proposes to put up a separate pot of money to pump-prime the new venture?"

Stirling's expression indicated stony ground. "Sorry, Norman, the university's funds are fully stretched. There really isn't any slack left in them, short of laying off existing staff, and we've always fought shy of that. Pride ourselves on it!"

Then, more confidentially, "Maximum employment is, as you know, an Evergreen tradition. They'd have made good communists, what! Ha ha! Hmmph... yes... well, when a worker proves himself unsuitable for a particular role, we prefer to move him to another one, rather than getting rid of him, or simply rely on natural wastage. That way they get a good pension. We may, however, require some revision of this policy now we are independent of the local authority. Time will tell, but to answer your question,

Norman, no, there's no extra money."

Norman cast an inscrutable glance. His was the face of a natural poker player. "I'll see what I can do, Vice-Chancellor. I'm sure Pat and I can come up with a plan. As I see it, the main cost would be salary. At what level do you think we need to make an offer to this chap... Mervyn Omen... in order to attract him here? Do you know what position he holds currently?"

"No. Not offhand, but I would guess lecturer."

"Then we need to offer him a readership at least, don't we... and probably a couple of PhD studentships to go with it."

"Why do we need to offer him funding for any PhD students?" Stirling looked genuinely perplexed. The plan seemed to be getting more expensive by the minute!

"Well, if he's as good as you say, then he'll want to do *research* here. He won't be satisfied with just teaching an undergraduate course in Astrology, and doing the admin for it. I would imagine his career aspirations go some way beyond that, and we have to convince him that coming here *is* a good career move. He would see it as a statement of our commitment to the new enterprise."

"Yes, Norman. Yes, of course, you're absolutely right. Don't want to spoil the ship for a ha'peth of tar now, do we? We need to come up with the complete package. OK, you're in charge. I leave the whole business of making the appointment in your eminently capable hands! Ha ha. I look forward to a favourable result! Capital!"

★ ★ ★

By pruning his allocations to the various departments within the Faculty of Technology, Norman managed to garner a reader's salary piecemeal from the overall existing faculty budget. Two research studentships were also funded from the Vice-Chancellor's Research Student Support Fund for Newly Appointed Lecturers (VCRSSFNAL) by not allocating them to newly appointed lecturers as would be normal practice. Thus, Mervyn Omen arrived at EEU to face a fanfare of undisguised consternation and resentment. Mervyn was, however, a sanguine politician, and distanced himself from it, amused to play dog in a manger, observing the rest of the pack chew out their ranking order around his unassailable vantage point.

As Norman had sagely anticipated, recruitment onto the new-flung Astrology degree flopped embarrassingly, and well below Stirling George's wild projections. Evergreen was not California, after all. The result did not surprise Mervyn either, but establishing a thriving undergraduate Astrology degree course was not his main purpose in moving to EEU. Rather, he wanted a firm foothold to build a research base in the subject – a platform from which to promote himself as the country's leading astrologer. And when he was promoted – as Stirling George had intimated strongly that he would be...*soon* – the title "Professor" would do no harm to his image, and in all likelihood add credibility to him as a "proper scientist". Then, astrology might be taken as a serious science, as a new imperative, planting roots in the rich ashes of smouldering establishment science and organised religion, since the hopeless need to believe in the green springs of hope, whatever crop may ultimately be yielded.

★ ★ ★

During the next twelve months, Mervyn worked diligently ("shamelessly", bitched his envious colleagues, biting at the manger's edges) at self-promotion, both within and outside the university. This proved a well-considered strategy, since Stirling George embraced publicity with a passion. He loved good publicity, anyway, although he was battle-hardened in dealing with regular slatings of EEU in the media. This other kind, more often termed notoriety, passed well greased over unruffled feathers.

"It'll take more than those buggers to sink me," he reassured Mrs Angela George, the worthy woman behind this great man.

★ ★ ★

Mervyn appeared on Radio Evergreen... "where it's at, on 94.7 MHz, sponsored by our very own EEU" (actually sponsored to the tune of fifty grand, supplied from Randolph Epstein's non-existent legacy). There were sound-bites broadcast on regional TV stations, featuring "Professor Mervyn Omen, Astrology Expert", as sage and guru. Pieces appeared in the local Evergreen Gazette – then the *coup de forte*: Mervyn Omen became its resident astrologer, precognising the daily fortunes of the citizens of Evergreen in a morning horoscope.

In this prestige, Angela George divined an ally. She was well-recognised herself in Evergreen psychic circles, but could not deny that matters of the spirit world lagged well behind astrology in terms of credibility, and that

Mervyn Omen was making the latter appear more nearly respectable by the day. If she could latch her clairvoyance onto Mervyn's coat tails; as he rose, so would Angela.

"We should invite him over to dinner, Stirling." Angela placed her book, spine up, to her lap, against a counterpane spread on sheets and blankets. Duvets did not feature on either of their twin beds.

"Sorry, Dear?"

It was a honking horn, sounding out amid the white noise of routine traffic.

"He seems a most personable young man," she continued, unfazed, knowing that Stirling had connected subliminally.

"Dinner? Yes, why not? As you say, he does seem a decent chap… adds a spot of colour to the place. What!"

★ ★ ★

The card arrived in Mervyn's pigeonhole, addressed to "Professor Mervyn Omen, Astrologer", written in ink in a neat hand. "RSVP". RSVP? How could he refuse such an invitation? He took his own pen – a biro – but hesitated after writing the word "Dear". There is always a slightly awkward point of etiquette on such occasions. If he were opening the batting, it would be "Dear Mrs George" but she had naturally signed the card *Angela*, so "Dear Mrs George" seemed too formal; and yet "Dear Angela" smacked of familiarity as he had only met her once, at his inaugural professorial lecture, which she insisted on attending, the two of them merely exchanging a few polite words over the finger buffet that followed.

"Dig in! You've sung for your supper!" Stirling George laughed heartily, adding, "Have you met my wife Angela?"

The show was a proud occasion, officiated by Stirling George in person. His introduction still echoed in all attending minds, most in disbelief.

"This is the future! We are a modern… forward-thinking university. It is our mission… to look toward the less traditional subjects, in order to expand our customer base. Where better than… astrology! Our future is written in the stars! It is my very great privilege to introduce Mervyn Omen, our newly fledged professor of Astrology, on this auspicious occasion of his inaugural lecture. Mervyn, my dear boy, the floor is yours! All our hopes are with you!"

And thus, Stirling gestured in the proceedings, fingers pointing skywards, from the pyramid of the Evergreen Polytechnic, projecting like the Egyptian god Ra, toward his own star in the heavens.

6

If astrology could star centre stage, with Mervyn Omen in a top hat and cape, might not Angela be his glamorous assistant, ushering in a supporting cast of psychic phenomena? Forged together, such lone elements would be assembled into a campaign of military precision and consequence, where all was fair, no love being lost at any point.

"How have you settled in at the university, Mervyn?" Angela clucked over him, hatching her plot.

"Oh, very well, thanks." He smiled, in turn at her and then the vice-chancellor.

"How long *have* you been with us now?" Stirling's question was a genuine one.

"About eighteen months," Mervyn replied.

It was a month after his inaugural lecture, and the promised "dinner" had arrived, *chez* George.

"Do you think you'll stay at EEU?" Angela's question hit, disarmingly sudden and direct, and she analysed him closely for all traces of reaction. But Mervyn maintained a glacial advance.

"I don't see why not. I would like to diversify, though..."

"In what way?" Angela drew him on.

"Do you remember our brief conversation after my professorial lecture?" Mervyn asked her. "You mentioned your own interest in the spirit world – psychic healing and clairvoyancy." Angela nodded. "I've been thinking more about this," continued Mervyn.

He then shifted his game toward the vice-chancellor, playing the full hand.

"While I still have every faith that the Astrology degree course *will* take off, our initial recruitment has, I admit, been disappointing..."

Stirling was impressed by the man's candour, and merely nodded in empathy. Clearly Mervyn Omen could roll with the punches and face the unexpected blow on the chin.

"Nonetheless," he continued, "there is still an enormous interest in astrology within Evergreen... I have mailbags full of letters and requests for personal readings, which are prompted by my daily horoscope in the Evergreen Gazette. Quite a large number of those who have written in want to become astrologers themselves, although studying for a three- or four-year degree in it is out of the question for them... given their financial and family commitments, etc."

"You mean they are *mature students... customers...* potentially, at any rate. Not the usual eighteen-year-olds?" Stirling stepped in to clarify the point.

"Yes, exactly," Mervyn confirmed, picking up the next card. "I know you have a policy to recruit *more* mature students, and... well... those from less traditional backgrounds, on courses at EEU..."

"Yes. Absolutely. And I am always looking for new ways to get them here."

"Then I have the perfect mechanism..." Trump card on the table. "We run short courses... a week or a fortnight, long weekends... evenings... we become completely flexible to fit our customers' requirements... whatever they need. Why not ask them what they need?! Let's advertise locally... *Why not put an advert in the Gazette?*"

Stirling made to interject, but Mervyn reigned in full flight, flapping an open palm to halt him. "Sorry, Vice-Chancellor, but that's only the start..." and here was the next stroke. "Why stop at astrology? There are clearly other... shall we say *sibling* disciplines..."

"Angela?" Mervyn had divined the situation well: he sensed in their first encounter that Angela George would love to have the university underpinning her psychic activities, enhancing them in both profile and credibility. Mervyn seemed to Angela a likely champion, if she could get him on her side. In truth, how could he not want her on his side: what more perfect ear to the vice-chancellor than she, and so to the support Mervyn needed to drive his own ambitions home?

"What do you think is the level of interest in Evergreen regarding psychic phenomena: healing, clairvoyance... séances, even? All of it, really."

Angela swallowed, then took an even breath.

"A lot. A real lot!" she answered. The reply was unequivocal.

"Right. I'm pleased to hear that's the case, since it brings me on to the second part of my plan..." Mervyn tuned his cool wavelength to match Angela's radiant elation. "...I think Angela and I might join forces."

The dial then rotated back to Stirling's own hailing frequency. "Why not open a suite for *Alternative Lifestyles*? That would include topics such as astrology, psychic phenomena and healing, clairvoyance, perhaps séances , as a practical application. The only problem appears to be *space*. Where are we going to physically fit it all in?"

"There's always a way," Stirling reassured him. "What about the space available within the main Faculty of Technology building. Couldn't it just be used... more effectively? I could talk to Norman Rayle. He is the dean, after all. I'm sure he can offer some suggestions."

"Yes, thank you, Vice-Chancellor..."

"Oh please, call me Stirling!"

"Yes...Stirling. That would help, but I also plan to build up the astrology *research* base. We'll need room for research assistants, desks, computers, astral charts, pentagrams for the floor. I imagine that Angela has in mind a research component for psychic phenomena too." She hadn't thought of this, but nodded a supporting affirmative anyway. Where Mervyn went, she went – and *vice versa* in this Faustian scheme.

"It seems to me that Astrology has no place with Applied Physics, in this future plan." Mervyn cranked up the odds some more, aware that once he was free of the physicists, he could move ahead more or less unimpeded. He was fed up with their unhelpful chafes and chides, which always seemed deliberate and mischievous obstructions to his will. *Scientific Method and all that nonsense – bloody reactionaries!*

★   ★   ★

As the essence of "the scheme" and its ramifications reached Norman Rayle, Stirling George's voice rang as music to him. "Yes, Stirling. I *do* see the problem. I have been giving considerable thought to finding a solution finally for Applied Physics. In the current climate, they have no viable future as they are. Neither they nor Astrology can recruit enough customers to support their staff salaries.

"Ah, yes, I see. Well, if you have particular plans for Astrology, then the simplest solution is to split Applied Physics off from it, rather than being a drain on them. If we cut back the space allocation for Physics according to the number of students they are actually teaching... yes, well, that would leave them with a room about the size of the gents toilet – probably minus the cubicles. Yes, I agree – too draconian... so we'll double them up, two to an office, and that way the lot of them can be contained within one side of a single corridor. The rest of their current space can then be given over to Mervyn Omen and his show. Then we need to decide how to best deploy the Applied Physics staff. Early retirements, transfer to other departments... if anyone wants them that is... redundancies even? In the first instance, however, I shall need your official ratification as vice-chancellor to formally close the Department of Applied Physics and Astrology."

★ ★ ★

Hamish Humble was surprised that his secretary hadn't knocked first... but panic overtook her natural deference.

"Professor! Have you heard...?!" Eileen Traylor's agitation was more than usually apparent.

"Eileen. Now calm yourself, dear. Whatever's the matter? Please... sit down now."

Her arthritic knuckles whitened into marble, tremulous on the surface of the desk, as she eased herself down painfully opposite him. Seated, she felt calmer, and her breath restored.

"I've just heard from Sandra in the typing pool. She overheard it from her supervisor, who got it from Norman Rayle's secretary. The Department of Applied Physics and Astrology's going to be closed!"

"No, Eileen. That can't be right. Och, it's just another silly wee rumour, that's all. Just a rumour. Where do they get them from? Some folks just don't seem to have anything else to do but stir up trouble." He chuckled reassuringly. "Now, Eileen, I'm the head of department. Do you really think if they were going to close it down, no one would have told me?! Och, away with you... whatever will you come up with next?!"

★ ★ ★

Whatever might become of the rest of the Applied Physics staff, Stirling George knew he must hang onto Charles Rae. Charles regarded the current crisis as a final hiatus in the entire appalling litany of his appointment at EEU, and he wanted out of the whole business. Stirling George remembered Hamish Humble's plea, that creating a new position at professorial level was the only way to raise the Physics RAE grade above rock bottom of the national pile. Since the university's submissions for the next RAE were now due in only twelve months, Stirling was under no illusions that appointing someone else in time for that, were Charles to leave, would be highly unlikely, and someone of his calibre all but impossible. Hamish had put an edge to the situation in emphasising Charles Rae's marketability and that he had already been offered another job.

In truth, he hadn't, though there were vague approaches made to him, which at the mere mention of them, Hamish's troubled imagination cast into wings that would bear Charles Rae out of EEU and from their glory of him. Nonetheless, assuming the information as correct, Stirling George decided on a swift pre-emptive manoeuvre.

★ ★ ★

Eileen Traylor's voice lapsed hysterically into a broad Evergreen vernacular, which Charles was as yet unused to.

"Charles Rae… It's Eileen, Professor 'Umble's secretary. I've been trying to get 'old of yer. Yer've left yer voice mail off again!"

Christ! Here she goes again, he thought… then Charles interrupted, "Yes, OK, Eileen. What is it exactly?"

"It's the vice-chancellor!" This time, she did sound about to wet herself.

"The vice-chancellor?"

"Yeaah! He wants to see yer!"

"Mmmm. Any idea what about?"

"Nooo! He just says will you phone his secretary to make an appointment."

The call was transferred almost immediately.

"Charles?" It was the man himself.

"Yes, Vice-Chancellor. I'm just returning your call."

"That's fine. I told my secretary to put you through the moment you phoned back. Look. I'm sorry about all this curfuffle, but I want to reassure you that none of it need affect you. It's all just part of a general restructuring. I shall be visiting the Faculty of Technology tomorrow morning, and if you're available at, say, ten o'clock, I would like to discuss your future here with us."

Echoing from the recent shocks, this seemed marginally comforting, and at the very least, Charles thought it worth hearing what he had to say: this was a vice-chancellor, after all!

★ ★ ★

Charles drank a lot that night. When he awoke he wondered where he was. Perhaps it was all a bad dream. No. Perhaps he had passed away. No. He was sure the dead didn't feel as bad as this. Where was he, anyway?

"Charles, would you like a cup of tea?"

He wasn't in his flat. Ah, yes, it began to trickle back to him now. He was on the floor of the back bar. Decided not to try and make it home.

"Tea?"

"Oh, yes, thanks."

"Are you OK?"

"Mmm. Yes, what time is it?"

Piss holes in the snow. Red-eyed, like a cheap Polaroid, he moved windingly to the Gents, and surveyed the damage in the mirror.

"It's nine thirty."

"Shit!"

He was due to see Stirling George in half an hour. He felt sick. He was sick. Copiously so.

"Are you all right, Charles? Ah well, better out than in!"

Who was this guy? Ah yes, he must be the landlord. Nice chap. Very generous. Remember him passing out first. Head on the bar – snoring. Helpless as a baby... Must get myself together. What did the V–C say? Something about "discussing my future"? It was like a dream – some surreal film, *L'age D'or*, but that was anti-Catholic. Would that work here? Stirling George was a well-known pillar of his church. But which church did he go to?

Head under the tap, sip of tea. Improved, much improved...

★ ★ ★

"He's here! The vice-chancellor! He wants to see *you* first..." It was Eileen. "Not the professor, I mean."

"You mean the *other* professor," Charles laughed, encouraged by the moment.

"Yes..." Humour was not Eileen's forte. "Well, he's on his way now."

"Thanks, Eileen... Ah, sounds like he's already arrived!" Charles replaced the handset to a purposeful tap-tap on the outer door. It was a vice-chancellor's knock.

"Hello, Charles. I'm glad you could make time to see me."

"Please come in, Vice-Chancellor." Charles pulled up a chair for him, and positioned it opposite his own, both sideways-on to the desk, and facing one other.

"Yes, Charles, as I said to you over the phone, you have nothing to fear about your position here at EEU. Of all the Applied Physics staff, your job is *secure*. I can't stress that enough." That did sound good, but it begged the broader matter, which Charles decided to broach delicately.

"Thank you, Vice-Chancellor, but I wonder if I might ask... what do you intend to do with the Department of Applied Physics and Astrology overall?"

Stirling George nodded amicably, and then gave Charles a deliberate stare. "That's a fair question, and one I *am* prepared to answer, but I don't want this going beyond these four walls."

"Yes. Sure," Charles consented.

"We have discussed the matter within the university at the most senior level. Tony Naismith the bursar and I have been at it for weeks with Letticia Jolanda." Even under the gravity of the situation, Charles found himself suppressing a schoolboy smirk at the thought.

"Our decision is not to make the physicists redundant. At least not at this stage. Your own position, as I have stressed, remains unaffected by any of this, and absolutely secure. We intend to separate Astrology from Applied Physics... we have a different agenda for Astrology... and to then attach Applied Physics to Leisurewear, making a new 'Department of Leisurewear and Applied Physical Sciences', or LAPS for short. Rod Shine, the current head of Leisurewear, will take over as head of LAPS."

"Leisurewear and Applied Physics?" Charles was incredulous, but maintained his composure. "I'm sorry, Vice-Chancellor, but this seems a pretty incongruous mix, doesn't it?"

Stirling looked him face-on, and his voice hardened. "To be completely frank, no one wants the applied physicists, but Leisurewear is the only department bringing in enough revenue to absorb the cost of their salaries. So there's absolutely no choice in who I pair them up with. Otherwise I *would* have to make them all redundant."

"What about Hamish Humble?" Charles asked him.

"Ah, yes. Good old Hamish... he's been with us – first at the polytechnic and then the university – for a very long time. Thirty-four years to be exact – 'man and boy', you might say!" Stirling chuckled. "Well, we've decided it's time for him to put his feet up. I'll give him two years to wind down his research, and then a full enhancement on his pension, so he'll get the same as if he'd stayed on for another three years until he was sixty-five. I can't say fairer than that!"

Turning as he left, Stirling added, "I've heard on the grapevine that you've been offered another job. We can't afford to lose people of your calibre. Make me a list of what you want the university to provide to make your stay with us more *comfortable*. I fully intend to make it worth your while."

★　★　★

Charles felt some sympathy for Hamish. "Poor old sod, he's been shafted too," he muttered, picking up the phone again.

"Hamish? It's Charles...

"Yes, the vice-chancellor's just left me. Anyway – although he's sworn me to secrecy... well, I hardly trust the bugger after all this – I thought I'd put you in the picture. He'll doubtless make it official in his own good time... well, I suppose he will... you know him better than I do... but, apparently he plans to split Astrology off from Physics...

"Hmm. Yes. He wasn't forthcoming with any details about his plans for them, and I was more concerned with what he intends to do with *us*, so I didn't press him about that...

"Indeed. Yes. It seems we are to be merged with Leisurewear – 'attached to Leisurewear' were his exact words, to form a new 'Department of Leisurewear and Applied Physical Sciences', LAPS for short. Makes me think of lap dancing, somehow. The head of LAPS is to be Rod Shine. What's he like? I haven't met him yet...

"It sounded more like a stay of execution, though no redundancies 'at this stage'. He went to great lengths to assure *me* that *my* position is safe here... more than that, actually, he asked me to make a list of my requirements, I suppose as a sweetener to keep me at EEU."

"Screw him for all you can!" came Hamish's reply, in a less than Humble rattle of the claymore.

★　★　★

That weekend, at home with his wife, Charles Rae raised pen and paper, and began his list. It was a very long list. Charles decided to approach the negotiations as though opening a deal with a Moroccan carpet salesman. He knew what price limit made EEU definitely a worthwhile proposition, and accordingly stretched out his wish list, maximising his own worth without overplaying it. Charles decided to ask for both equipment and personnel.

The major equipment request centred upon the purchase of a small particle accelerator, at a cost of £10 million. Human resources came out cheaper: a couple of post-docs and a couple of PhD students, plus support costs, amounting to a comparatively trifling £100K.

"Let's see what he makes of that one!" Charles laughed, and experienced a growing sense of confidence that all would turn to his advantage, ultimately. He had only to ride out the wave. As he licked the envelope marked "Office of the Vice-Chancellor", and let it drop purposefully into the sack marked "EEU Internal Mail", Charles felt a slight pang he may have overplayed his case. He was, however, testing Stirling George's resolve: one of either serious investment in him if he stayed at EEU; or empty rhetoric and false promises to keep him there, with no further costs beyond his salary. Which was it?

The answer seemed refreshingly clear:

> *Dear Charles,*
>
> *Many thanks for your note. My initial reaction is that your request is entirely reasonable and quite within the university's budget. There are, nonetheless, a number of operational issues, since the monies will need to be devolved from within existing preallocated budgets. I have delegated Professor Rod Shine to resolve these matters, since he will be formally your Departmental Director, once your post has been transferred to the new Department of Leisurewear and Applied Physical Sciences, when this is fully operational.*
>
> *Perhaps you would liaise with Rod regarding these details.*
>
> *Kindest Regards,*
>
> *Professor Stirling George, OBE.*
>
> *Vice-Chancellor and Chief Executive Officer, Evergreen Epstein University*

It was indeed *on*.

★   ★   ★

So many voices, new faces, new names. Whose was this?

"Ah, yes. Rod Shine. Of course. Nice to hear from you."

"Charles." The tone was reassuring – a soft, educated Evergreen accent. "The vice-chancellor's passed your list to me. Seems I've got to sort it all out. OK, I'm on to it. Now... the personnel you asked for: that's the least issue... I'm sure we can sort that out later. The main capital outlay is for the machine... the... *particle accelerator*... is that right? Ha ha. Not much call for one of them in Leisurewear, you know! Well, anyway, that's what I'm working on now. I don't know offhand where we're going to find ten million quid for it, but... I'm sure we will. I'm seeing Letticia Jolanda about it later, and I'll keep you posted on any progress. Bye now..."

7

Charles could scarcely believe the figure that transfixed his attention, hovering at the end of the corridor. Possibly a tramp, wandered in by mistake; lost perhaps, or at the outside, a Computer Science lecturer? Beard. Sandals. Filthy feet, he noticed as the lumbering apparition shortened its distance toward him. And "Ah yes, leisure pants," he mumbled, resigning himself, though incorrectly, to the latter identity. Elasticated. Great belly distending beyond the belly bands of decency, and unlovely handles of flesh rippling over the sides in kinetic concertinas.

"Charles Rae?"

Astonishingly, it seemed to know him?

"Mmmm." Charles responded curiously.

"I'm Bob Bates. Professor of Leisurewear Dynamics." The leisurewear was indeed dynamic, thought Charles, suppressing a sudden, if currently rare, urge to laugh. Leisure pants, presumably bought at a special bulk discount from the "Shine Leisurewear Chain".

"I've been hoping to meet you. You've caused quite a stir since you've been here, at least so I've heard from Rod." It was one of those loaded remarks, at once offhand yet inviting a response, which Charles denied in instinctive distrust.

Bob Bates' promotion was a very recent culmination, having been effectively on the ultimate lifelong learning course at EEU. He had joined the polytechnic aged eighteen, completed a degree programme in Leisurewear Studies, scoring a reasonable 2:2, then stayed on for a PhD in Leisurewear Dynamics under the supervision of Rod Shine, his erstwhile undergraduate tutor. As a vacancy appeared for a lecturer in Leisurewear, Rod saw to it that Bob was appointed, believing strongly in the abiding polytechnic code of "better the devil you know". Bob then completed his PhD work while working on the staff of the Department of Leisurewear, and in the fullness of time had been promoted to a readership and finally a professorship in Leisurewear Dynamics.

Although his lack of ever having been anywhere else rendered a crass naivety in him, Bob was extremely dangerous to Charles, whom he envied with a profound and focused vengefulness. And because he had never left the polytechnic/EEU, he knew all its ways, and he knew all of the "old guard", most of whom had never worked or studied anywhere else either, and some rarely left the city of Evergreen, apart from odd "awaydays".

He was also the sole representative of the University Research Strategy Committee for Leisurewear and Applied Physical Sciences since Charles Rae's displacement from it when the original department to which he had been appointed was closed. Bob could thus withhold essential information from Charles, and brake his progress in administrative treacle, or not tell him about some vital and urgent tasks he should complete, and then slag him off among the worthies and elders of EEU for not doing them, until the name Rae became Mudd. In this campaign, Bob was amply assisted by the far more draconian and bureaucratic procedures that prevailed at EEU than Charles was familiar with at his old university.

"He's completely uncooperative. It's exactly the same in the department."

Bob's voice matched his bulk. Loud and ponderous, but with a curious whine that heralded the ending of his sentences in a trumpet of portentous self-importance. "I don't know ... Why on earth was he ever appointed here?" (And Charles Rae asked himself that very same question each morning as he approached the seething concrete shithouse that was EEU.)

★ ★ ★

Rod Shine did the rounds himself, knocking on each door with the message, "Pass it on. It's Charles Rae's inaugural lecture tomorrow evening – make sure you all attend. We must get as many in the audience as possible. Stirling George will not be best pleased if we don't have a good turnout for him. Hmm... especially after all the trouble he's had, with the Department of Applied Physics and Astrology being closed... and him just appointed as the new professor of General Physics ... tut tut ... It doesn't look good, and the V-C is trying to make it up to him."

Rod was worried, as he had been left to sort out with Letticia Jolanda where the hell the money was going to come from exactly to pay for all the rash promises Stirling George had casually avowed to Charles in order to keep him at EEU.

"We simply can't afford to lose someone of his calibre," he had stressed to Rod emphatically. "You look after him, and give him what he wants. He's a good lad, Charles!"

Stirling George handed Rod the wish list Charles had sent him, and half turning with his usual buck pass dismissiveness declared, "Sort it out, Rod!"

The particle accelerator was a particular source of angst. Rod and Letticia stared dumbfounded at the quotation for it — stargazers into a black hole from which neither the light of reason nor resolution would emerge. It was hopeless.

"How much?! What's he trying to do? Ruin me?!" Rod nearly wept. "Didn't he have any idea...how much it would *cost*? Even if we can pay, where the hell are we going to put the bloody thing? We'll need a new building! Oh God!"

Letticia recovered some stoicism. "Oh, Rod. Don't take on so! Come on. Let's consider the matter logically. Now it's *Stirling* who's made the promise, not you. Nor *me* for that matter. If we can just *delay* things for a while... well, it might just *go away*. You know what Stirling's like. By next week, he'll probably have forgotten *all* about it."

"I hope so, Letticia. My God! I certainly hope so." Rod dabbed his brow, suddenly somewhat restored, and flashed a weak smile.

But Stirling George did not forget. His was a finely capricious memory. Exactly a week later, he reiterated verbatim his previous side of a one-sided conversation.

★ ★ ★

"Rod. Glad to catch you. Have you made any progress on that ... that piece of kit for Charles?"

"You mean the particle accelerator?"

"Yes. Yes, of course, the bloody accelerator."

"But, Vice-Chancellor ... it's ten million ... just for a small one..."

"Well. Well. Yes. I didn't think it was going to be cheap, but you're an entrepreneur, aren't you? I mean ... a man of your commercial enterprise... you built up that chain of leisurewear shops, didn't you? Then there's always the departmental fund. You can dip into that a bit, can't you?"

"Vice-Chancellor. I hesitate to mention it but..."

A blank shark-stare formed in Stirling's eyes; a hundred and fifty million years to evolve into the ultimate unswerving purpose of a vice-chancellor.

The quarry trembled. "I mean… would it be possible for the university to…take out a loan maybe… we just can't find that kind of money…"

("Never tell the vice-chancellor any bad news", so Hamish Humble had warned Charles Rae on his first day at EEU, "he doesnae like it", which was pretty sound advice.) The word *loan* made him flinch – he was still paying off the Business School debts.

"Rod. If you *don't* find the money…" Then Stirling softened, unexpectedly, "I'm sure you can find excellent use for a particle accelerator in Leisurewear. I've been reading about all this stuff… what is it now? Yes. That's it! Strings! Physicists are always going on about strings these days. String Theory! Yes. Well, you have *strings* on sale in your leisurewear shops. G-strings and the like… well, so I've heard … hmmph … That's the connection: the accelerator will unify the two sections of the new department, in a common thread. Leisurewear and Applied Physical Sciences – LAPS! Ha ha. LAPS and strings – excellent! You all have more in common than I realised! Capital! I knew I could rely on you, Rod! Well done!"

"Oh God!" Rod's viscera hump-backed beneath a queasy pallor.

"Are you OK, Rod?" Stirling gripped his arm.

"Yes. Yes. Never better, thanks."

"Good. Well, time to take our seats now."

Rod Shine's torso slumped gratefully onto the firm bench seat, which supported his rear more confidently than his legs alone had promised to. Stirling and Rod occupied front row seats, and theirs were the first faces Charles Rae saw as he stepped from behind the curtain onto the stage, to be introduced by Letticia Jolanda, who presided over the occasion as a shining Valkyrie, resplendent in her full regalia as assistant vice-chancellor of EEU.

Stirling George regarded the inaugural "professorial lectures" as a showcase series, and it was rare if he missed one of them. Today's feature was special, though, as without his personal persuasion, Charles Rae would no longer be at EEU to deliver it. In Stirling's eyes, Charles was the corpus of his own intervention: the pure body of divine will.

Charles did not disappoint. It was one of his best lectures. On such occasions, the audience is supposed to be on the side of the speaker, who is demonstrating in a modestly gentle way why they deserve to be a professor. An inaugural lecture is supposed to be a public performance too. Not heavily detailed in the jargon of the few, but accessible to all. Charles threw into this spirit, and managed to raise flickers of smiles from staff in most of the major subjects present, including astrology; and especially from the vice-chancellor. There were no questions at the end, contrary to the traditions of most lectures, just a session involving Charles, Letticia, Stirling and Charles's wife, posing for a glossy record of the occasion made immortal by the EEU resident photographer.

Stirling threw his arm around Charles' shoulders.

"That was excellent, Charles. I hope everything has calmed down now, and you can get on with your work. I've told Rod to get you your bit of kit, so you should be well away. I'll bet you're glad you stayed with us now."

The promise was made, and in the bonhomie of that hour, pleasant words all around, with wine and a finger buffet, Charles felt perhaps he had fallen on his feet at last.

★ ★ ★

"Charles? It's Jasper. I just wanted to tell you how *terribly* sorry I am to hear of your ... er ... unfortunate predicament. I did try to warn you, you know? But you wouldn't listen."

Charles' free fist clenched in his pocket, his left turning white against the handset. "Supercilious Bastard!" he thought, but decided to play along.

"Sorry, Jasper. I'm confused. What *have* you heard exactly?"

"Well ... that your department's been closed, and how you're unemployed."

A moment's delay, and then, "Look. Your old job here hasn't been filled yet. Obviously, you're not worth a professorship. Ha ha... But, I've spoken to the vice-chancellor and he agrees with me that we could do you a favour and reappoint you, say, as a senior lecturer. We do have some other candidates, who are at *about* your sort of standard – I mean, *nothing special* really – so we could consider an application from you, along with theirs."

"You mean I would have to formally reapply?"

"Yes, of course, dear boy...ha ha...and you *do* realise that the honeymoon period is over, don't you? You'll have to take on a *lot* more teaching and administration than you were doing before. I've been talking to Dudley about it. He'll be only too happy to accommodate you."

"And what about the salary?" A sense of the absurd began to descend on Charles.

"Oh, well, you'd be on a *little* more – a couple of thousand perhaps – than you were as a *lecturer* here."

"I'm sorry, Jasper, but you seem to have your wires crossed. It's true there has been some reorganisation here. In fact, Applied Physics is being merged with Leisurewear, but the vice-chancellor has offered me a number of incentives to stay at EEU. He has even agreed to take out a loan to buy me a new particle accelerator. And, naturally, a pay rise…of four increments on the *professorial* salary scale. So, I'm sorry, Jasper, it's thanks but – you must be joking! Ha ha! By the way, I hope you do finally manage to replace me, although your university is not in the most salubrious of *inner-city* locations. Bye, now."

Jasper knew this was true. In his smug complacency, he imagined that replacing Charles Rae would be easy. He'd done the fellow a favour getting him there in the first place, from a poly after all. Jasper laughed at Charles as a man moving back down in the world – the subterranean world he imagined of such institutions as EEU and all the other new universities (bloody ex-polys, as he privately referred to them). But the sands had already started to shift, and his department was no longer much regarded, as it once was. They found themselves having to readvertise, and even the second time around the applicants were dire. None of them remotely approached Charles's research record. So, although he couldn't afford to lose Charles, his pride, dented by what he saw as Charles' ungrateful temerity in leaving in the first place, prevented him from offering the man his worth.

If Charles was going to work for him again, Jasper would rub his nose in it: "Hello, Professor! Oh sorry. Ha ha." (Charles could just imagine it.) He would bait him and make him crawl up through the ranks: senior lecturer, reader… then keep him there for as long as possible, refusing to endorse any application from him for a professorship. Since he chaired the university's promotions board, Jasper could do this; he could turn him down, summarily. And being turned down for a Chair in one of the older universities was almost permanent: often there would be no second chance. But as Charles was later to learn, the possibilities at EEU were rather more flexible.

8

The various shenanigans leading to the creation of the new Department of LAPS had cost valuable time, out of time that was short at the start. The RAE submission was due in by the following March, and September was already reaching for its overcoat, ushering in the prospects of a new academic year. They were left with six months to make a case good enough to score above the grade 1 which had prompted a desperate Hamish Humble to implore the vice-chancellor in sanctioning the appointment of the first external candidate as a professor at EEU. Hamish emphasised the need for new blood; rather than seniority based on length of service or senior management responsibilities, secured via internal promotion, irrespective of academic calibre. (Sensibly, he avoided explicit reference to the latter point, which would have disqualified both himself and the vice-chancellor.)

In truth, Charles Rae had been on a hiding to nothing from the outset, as hindsight would disclose. Were it possible that a single person could arrive brandishing a magic wand, dispelling the entrenched crassness of EEU and turning it into a major league research university, the transformation would require far longer than the eighteen months which were finally left for that purpose. Hamish first broached the vice-chancellor three years ahead of the RAE deadline, but was not taken seriously, as sadly, he rarely was. Undaunted, he persevered, even enlisting Letticia Jolanda the assistant vice-chancellor to help in the campaign. Letticia became a vital pivot for Hamish's efforts, since, once fixed, Stirling George was intractable to shift from any particular position. Of all his staff, he trusted Letticia, who in a funny coquettish way could cajole and tease him into changing his mind; especially when the idea was basically sound and he only needed to be finally convinced that it was.

"OK, Letticia. Let's let Hamish have his run." Stirling removed his glasses, and twirling them, placed them deftly on top of the day's remaining agenda. "I know you're keen on this, and I've been awaiting sight of the Applied Physics and Astrology department's books before making my final decision. On paper, it's not all beer and skittles, quite frankly – they are well in the red. However, Terry Mason is about to retire, so if we simply substituted him with someone else at the same level – of professor – they wouldn't be any *more* in the red than they already are. Moreover, as I recall Hamish's argument, by bringing in someone of top quality – from *outside* the university … new blood – the vastly improved RAE rating he predicts, and the money that will come from it, will more than offset any costs to us. The new appointee will need lab space and probably a few other things. I think it will also look rather good for the university to make such a senior appointment. We should make a big fuss about it … whole-page adverts…"

Letticia stemmed the effervescent flow at source, prompting a more modest tributary from Stirling, who continued, "Well, yes. OK. Full page in the Evergreen Gazette. Then something a little more modest for the 'nationals'. But advertising for someone with an exemplary academic record … what would that involve…? Yes. That's it. An excellent record of published work in internationally acclaimed academic journals. Prizes…? What else…? I know. Why don't you scan the job adverts from other universities? The big players. See what they're looking for in a professor, and we'll simply word our own ad similarly. Capital!"

And so a heavy net was hauled in, holding one large Rae, and a handful of tiddlers who hit the water again without a splash.

Now all eyes were suddenly turned upon the Rae in expectation of it to work a magic spell, like a mermaid.

★ ★ ★

Tarquin Tupper knocked at his office door.

"Charles? What grants have you got?"

Charles looked nonplussed, so Tarquin explained his new role.

"Ah'm in charge of the new LAPS *ree*-search committee. And it's mah job to make an inventory – an *inventory*, mind you – of all grants and publications of staff in the new department."

Charles kicked himself later for not replying immediately with "Well, Tarquin, what grants have *you* got?!" knowing full well what the answer would have been. "What grants have you got?" It was exactly the same bloody question from Tarquin at his interview, Charles mused ruefully. But at the time, Charles simply reeled off the list of them all, and printed off the roll of his publications, to get rid of him. Odd that Tarquin didn't want anything written down particularly? It was just a four-in-the-morning Stazi style visit, telling carefully selected candidates, on a shortlist of one, that Tarquin was watching them, and that he had the ear and approval of power.

In reality, this was a non-job, intended to keep him from forever knocking on Rod Shine's door and interrupting more lucrative business with an incessant volley of trivia.

"I'll have to call you back…

"Yes, Tarquin, what is it now?!"

"Ah say, Rod. Ah've been doing a bit of thinking about *ree*-search in the new department…"

"What the fuck does he know about research?" Rod unwisely confided to Bob Bates. "I've read his CV and the man's an arsehole!"

But Bob could see a loop in Tarquin, a snare to foil unfamiliar prey. A large Rae possibly, if the wire could be kept hidden.

"Look. Bob. I'm not suggesting you take Tarquin under your wing, exactly… Yes, life *is* too short, and he *is* too ingrained for reprogramming, but can't you just find the idiot something to do, that keeps him out of my hair?"

So, Tarquin became the departmental research assessor and chair of the Departmental Research Committee – a man dutifully ticking boxes on a clipboard.

"Well, Bob. Ah've done like you asked, but look…there's only Charles Rae I can put anything down for…! and Tommy Wakefield's published a couple of papers. But that's it. Haven't you got anything, Bob? A grant, or anything published, ah mean?"

Bob felt a similar irritation that Charles had, but unable to deflect the facts, ducked under them instead.

"Yes, Rae. There he is with all his grants and papers published in internationally recognised journals, but I'm one of the old poly boys." Bob began to adopt a tone of pious sincerity. "I don't know why they appointed him … off the record," he whispered. "To me, research has always been in the service of the local … *parish*, for want of a better word. Our role is to serve local industry and benefit the Evergreen people… Now we have him here, he just puts our true cause into a bad light …" Bob shook his head sadly. "It's simply not possible to quantify everybody's contribution so easily as Rae's. No. I don't have the grants or the publications … but I have the goodwill of

Evergreen ... a wonderful, proud city with a strong sense of its history..."

"So that's a *no* then," surmised Tarquin flatly, his thick skin dully impervious to Bob's rhetoric.

★ ★ ★

"Och, Charles, we've got to start thinking about the RAE submission." This would be Hamish's last job. His legacy to the institution, passing on the mantle of his vision in the hands of Charles Rae.

"Yes. I've been a little confused about this," Charles replied. "Letticia Jolanda seems to think it would be better to enter me on my own... She mentioned it first at my professorial lecture...but I'm not happy with the idea. I think the Physical Sciences Assessment Panel will want to see some kind of united front, perhaps with me as the major player...but not the only one! That would merely give the impression no one else here is doing any research! Who else should we include though?"

"Aye, that's a good point. Last time, we were advised to put in as many staff as possible ... but then you know the results of that." Hamish frowned at the thought of it.

"As far as I know, to be included at all in an RAE submission," Charles continued, "someone needs to have published a minimum of *four* papers. Bob Bates seems quite certain of that, and it's not a bad guide. Let's face it, anyone who is at all research-active should have managed four papers in five years!" Charles spat the rider with tacit contempt for those who did not.

"Aye, well that does weaken Tommy Wakefield's case a wee bit."

"Why?"

"It's not that he's unproductive, exactly ... as you well know..." Hamish grimaced at the irony, as no one worked harder than Tommy, doing as much teaching and admin as Tarquin and the others, and his research on top of all that.

"But," Hamish continued, "because most of his recent research is funded by the defence industry ... and well funded too...he can't publish any of the results. It's all hush hush. Nerve gases, and the like. There are internal reports he's written for them, but these probably won't see the light of day for another thirty years. So he *is* a bit low on actual papers in the journals."

Worse was to follow.

"Then, there's myself. The Japanese are very interested in our results on lard oxidation ... and they're no' shy about putting their hand in their pocket, either … but I'm sworn to secrecy too, and so I've no publications at all… other than some chapters in books that I've edited myself, so they're not strictly peer-reviewed exactly…if someone wanted to press the point."

Charles kicked himself again, this time for not checking the publication output of the EEU physicists before applying for the job there, but once more, reality had taken him unawares. Possibly in the unconscious but unrealistic hope of a miracle, or more probably in denial, Hamish left the final form filling until the day of the deadline.

"Might be better if we missed it altogether," Charles confided to Tommy despondently, but they had to make their show. In a last-minute cast of dice, it was decided to include Charles Rae, Hamish Humble, Tommy Wakefield and three fairly recently appointed lecturers, emphasising their future promise, in the hope the Physical Sciences Assessment Panel would give their new blood a fair run, rather than clotting it in their veins.

★   ★   ★

"Charles. You'd better come on up." It was Rod Shine, in a rather flat, faceless tone.

"I'll bet you're disappointed with your grade…" came a call along the corridor. "We got a *4!*" This was unnerving.

As he passed, all eyes were on the Rae, who swam a blind gauntlet, realising the news was bad, but not knowing exactly how bad. "Must be a *2*," Charles consoled himself. "Well, it's not a *complete* disaster…"

When he arrived at Rod's office, the door was left open for him, and as he walked in, Bob Bates handed him a piece of paper, which he scanned rapidly. Applied Physics … grade 1. The lowest possible score … *again*. His appointment there had made no difference. But, on looking higher up the list, he read: "Leisurewear … *grade 1*". Thank God! They'd got the lowest score too!

★   ★   ★

The mutterings started up again; tones haunting the dumb corridors. Maybe they'd never stopped. Voices drifted into his office, but fell silent as he appeared outside it. Charles could detect his name in their murmurings – or thought he could. At least their grade 1 languished in parity with Leisurewear, so they couldn't be pilloried for that; but the rules rested in their hands, being the senior partner of LAPS, and Charles' own position had been dealt a body blow.

"If he's so good, how come they only got a 1?" Bob began to hone the number into a weapon, starting at the next meeting of the university research management team, and diverting attention from his own failure.

"I know we're just the old poly boys..." the next sentence opened, "... but Charles Rae is from the *old university* sector. Why have they turned their back on him? What's he done *wrong*? There must be something we don't know about."

"At least he brings the grants in," volunteered Letticia, who was one of Charles' champions. "And he has got us a lot of *good* publicity. He spoke very well on the news the other night. Stirling was very *impressed* ... and that *is* an achievement." She laughed, diffusing the moment, while Bob seethed, but regrouped tactically, knowing if he maintained the volley, sooner or later Charles would be brought down.

"At least in Leisurewear, we still have the student numbers, and that is keeping all of us afloat – including the physicists, whose recruitment is still very poor."

No one could argue with that, including Letticia.

"Yes. There is some restructuring still to be done with LAPS." Letticia glanced at a rather heavy diary. "Oh. I see that I have a meeting with Rod about that next. There are *issues*," she noted guardedly, stressing the word with a subliminal nod in Bob's direction.

This was the key. He could catch up on all the details with Rod, later on.

9

"*Jawohl*, Herr Professor Lederbauer."

Although he had worked for him for over twenty years, Hanns-Peter practically stood to attention in his presence.

"I'm afraid I find myself no longer able to support your position here. You must seek a post in another university."

Hanns-Peter stared at him wide-eyed, in disbelief. "But, *why*, Herr Professor?" he pleaded.

"It is sufficient that you know this fact," he replied, and turning away impassively, Professor Helmut Lederbauer stepped toward the doorway, leaving that little bombshell to fully detonate in Hanns-Peter's brain.

Hanns-Peter slumped into his chair, and stared at the desk, surveying the memorabilia of his life. Pictures of his wife and of his six lovely children; of his election as an elder in his Fundamentalist Church; the Leibnitz medal of the *Physikalischgeselschaft* (Physics Society), only recently awarded to him.

Why was Lederbauer treating him like this?

The agony and confusion of the situation rolled over and over in his mind, as he tossed and turned, unable to sleep. He looked at his watch … 4.30 … and got up. He wrapped his dressing-gown around him and went downstairs, trying to disturb his wife as little as possible.

But she was awake, anyway. "Where are you going," she asked.

"Try to sleep," he kissed her. "I must talk to Lederbauer later, and try to get to the bottom of this. Then you and I must talk, this evening."

★   ★   ★

"I have decided that it will be best for your career, if you get a professorship in your own right, at another university.

"You are now well past the age of forty-five years, which is the normal maximum for such an appointment, so you should manage this as soon as possible… Therefore, to encourage you in this effort, I will no longer undersign your grant application forms here. Since I am head of this department, without my signature any applications for funding from you will be invalid."

Hanns-Peter stared at him, dumbfounded, and dumbstruck, only superficially comprehending the words that bounced past him.

"You have the choice: either stay in Wuperbaden and take a teaching post in one of the technical colleges here, or get a Chair elsewhere and continue with your research work. I hope you choose the latter course, but I am not anyway prepared to discuss this matter any further."

Helmut Lederbauer's cold impassive gaze betrayed no emotion beyond his polished steel-framed spectacles as he ended his speech, "Now, I am busy."

Hanns-Peter had felt secure at the university, after more than twenty years there, but now he was thrown off balance by the unbidden abruptness of this change in management policy. But there it was. Suddenly, like the flick of a switch, he was out.

He wrote to Charles:

> *I am sorry, but I am no longer able to participate in our European project. I have lost the support of my boss. I am living on his money, and I need his signature on any grant applications I make. He refuses this, and if I fail to find another position, I will be out of science before the year is over.*
> *Yours sincerely,*
> *Hanns-Peter Krankenpfleger*

This was a terrible blow. Charles and Hanns-Peter were good colleagues, and had published more than twenty papers together; more than that, they were friends.

"What a bastard Lederbauer is," thought Charles.

He reached for the phone and dialled, then listened, finally hearing "Allo".

"Hanns-Peter? It's Charles. I've just received your letter, and I'm shocked. Why has Lederbauer done this to you? Have you fallen out with him?"

"No. Sorry, I can't talk now. I'll phone you back."

He seemed very strange, quite unlike himself. Then Charles guessed why. Lederbauer was probably in his office, standing next to him.

And there he was, urging along Hanns-Peter's imminent departure from Wuperbaden. "There are resource implications. We have a new professor of Physics arriving within the next few days, who will be moving into this office. I have to ask you to move out by the end of the week. Yes, I know it is already *Mitwoch*, but there is of course always the weekend. The technical staff will find you a desk which you may use in the corridor outside, until you are ready to finally leave the university. You can move your papers and other belongings out there forthwith."

★ ★ ★

Bertie Bantam was a distinguished academic, or at least distinguished in his own narrow field of boson physics, which numbered about half a dozen other distinguished academics, worldwide. Following a BSc and then a PhD at the most prestigious of British universities, he had gone West, to post-doc in the United States. But this was in the late '60s, at the end of the expansion phase of the UK university system, by when all the lectureships had been filled – mostly by the students and protégés of the established order, in days when formal interviews for university posts were unnecessary, and lifetime tenured posts could be had on a wink and a nod.

It was at this time that Bertie found himself exiled.

Unable to return to Britain in a permanent academic post, he accepted a second, but also temporary post-doc at the University of Wuperbaden to work with Herr Professor Helmut Lederbauer, and there he met Hanns-Peter Krankenpfleger, who was doing his PhD under Lederbauer's supervision. Bertie Bantam had chanced upon a theoretical breakthrough: a new mathematical description of the quantum boson, which pointed the way to the detection of three such particles in an enormous tank of cleaning fluid, which Lederbauer had installed in the basement of the Physics building at Wuperbaden University.

A seminal publication arose – Lederbauer's grant was renewed, and Bertie spent another five years in Wuperbaden. It also sealed Hanns-Peter's PhD (*summa cum laude*). Bertie and Hanns-Peter had both traded on this discovery ever since; steady adaptations of which led to Hanns-Peter being awarded the *Physikalischgeselschaft* Leibnitz Medal almost twenty years later. Meanwhile, Bertie had gone "back West". He had found a tenure-track assistant professorship position at The Midwestern Baptist University, got tenure, and then ultimately been promoted to a full professorship – in Quantum Boson Physics. Now, he was a proud member of the "brain drain". To hell with that "old country": if they hadn't room for him, it was their loss. He was too good for them anyway.

Bertie began to adopt various trappings of a colonial academic. A penetrating "British" accent, and an even more gratingly "British" manner. He would attend every research seminar, sit at the front and then grill the speaker at length, interrupting them and picking on small, but irrelevant details. His mode of dress also became colonial. White suits and a Panama hat; white gloves and sandals; a cravat and a kidskin briefcase.

Bertie didn't like Charles Rae – who returned that sentiment fully. The main problem was Bertie's sense of self-importance; while, contrastingly, Charles thought Bertie was of no importance. Actually a bumptious little sod. In return, Bertie thought Charles was an arrogant young upstart. Charles' success got under Bertie's skin. He scanned the scientific journals: "Another paper by Rae! He publishes *far* too much!"

Bertie would have liked to dismiss Charles' work – and Charles himself for that matter – but the volume of it, and it's quality too, simply couldn't be ignored. There were mutterings among his peers: "Mark my words. Charles Rae must be in line for a Chair sometime soon".

Bertie seethed at the thought, and then the news broke. Rae had been appointed at Evergreen Epstein University as professor of General Physics. Bertie was stunned. He had expected it, but resented the prospect so much that he put it from his mind – in denial. However, the news was unequivocal.

"Bertie. It is Hanns-Peter. I thought you should know that Charles Rae is now a professor."

Hanns-Peter was stunned too, and avoided phoning Charles himself, to congratulate him. A strange lapse from a friend, but Hanns-Peter's condition remained critical, and highly uncertain beyond the surety that Lederbauer would force him to leave Wuperbaden by any means. When he replaced the receiver, Bertie's mind began to revive, and he fumed. He, Bertie, had been to the country's top university. He had done the "North American postdoc thing", which was almost obligatory to getting a lectureship. But he had found himself exiled – excluded from the establishment of his own land – when he was the spawn of its establishment. They should have taken him in with open arms.

Then there was bloody Charles Rae, who had attended a *good* university, it had to be admitted, but not the best. He hadn't gone to North America, but got a UK lectureship anyway, run up a huge list of publications, and then been appointed to a full professorship – without even going through the intermediate levels of progression of senior lecturer and reader. It was outrageous! How old was Rae, anyway – about thirty?! This was too much.

If it was the last thing he did, he would teach Charles Rae a lesson, and put him back down in his rightful place.

★   ★   ★

Word had got round – mainly from Charles Rae, who wanted to help him – that Hanns-Peter Krankenpfleger was being forced out of Wuperbaden by Lederbauer, and that he was looking for a Chair elsewhere; anywhere! Because of the narrow and esoteric nature of Hanns-Peter's research, finding and securing one was proving very difficult. So, Hanns-Peter, in keeping with his status as a church elder, began to invent spurious "applications" of great importance to humanity, that might be achieved using the quantum boson. It might have profound benefits in cancer research, to industry, in helping to avert climate change. No one believed any of these claims, but eventually, through a friend of Lederbauer, he managed to secure a professorship at a small university in Southern Saxony.

His wife, however, refused to move away from Wuperbaden on the grounds that: (a) she would miss her mother, (b) she didn't want to uproot their six children from their schools, and (c) she didn't want to give up her job. Wuperbaden was the most conservative of the country's regions, and in whose society women played highly traditional roles. They were expected to be highly visible in various activities of their church; to have *at least three* children; to be good *Hausfraus*; and to instruct their community's young girls to *become* good *Hausfraus*, in their course. And Regina loved instructing the girls, which was not a job she would find in the more liberal south.

So, on Sunday, Hanns-Peter, having bought an inflatable mattress, which he carried under one arm, and with a suitcase packed under the other, headed for the main railway station in Wuperbaden. On arrival, he bought a return ticket and headed for the station: Southern Saxony (University). He had arranged an unfurnished apartment, literally around the corner from the university, where he proceeded to activate the air-bed. He lay it on the floor, and attached the nozzle of the foot pump. It surprised him how much air was needed to inflate it; he must have pressed two hundred times – puff, puff, puff – then, finally, it was done. Sweating slightly, Hanns-Peter sat down on the mattress, and unpacked the sandwiches his wife had made for him: cheese, ham and gherkin. Looking out, seeing the twinkling lights of the city – the evidence of other lives, mostly going on normally, in family apartments – he suddenly felt very alone.

★   ★   ★

Hanns-Peter did not sleep well. Hardly at all, in fact. He was in that proverbial *strange bed*, strange surroundings, and alone. He had been a happy family man; and then, without warning, Lederbauer had turned on him, casting the dice of unrolling destiny. Driven by the fundamentalist part of his soul, Hanns-Peter justified to himself that Lederbauer was a demon, sent to test his faith. And he, Hanns-Peter, would overcome him, proving ultimately that his was the true and hence surviving faith.

Clearly, God had decided that Hanns-Peter, an elder in His one true church, was of a soul that would transcend into spiritual eternity; whereas Lederbauer would *descend* into such vile pits of tormented and visceral endlessness, as depicted by Heironymus Bosch. And by the example of Hanns-Peter, he, Lederbauer, would be reminded of his demonism and unworthiness; hence his fall into Hell. Perhaps in Hell, there would be others condemned in rank by the true church; but in that other, exalted place, the perfect spirits of the chosen few would reign in a true perfection of their spiritual purity, perhaps even led by Hanns-Peter, their *spiritum messiah*.

Hanns-Peter bathed his face, then looked for a paper towel, but finding the dispenser empty, instead used toilet paper to dab away the beads from that fervour of faith. Gripping the cool sides of the basin hard, he felt calm once more.

★   ★   ★

Hanns-Peter became increasingly brittle. As the various stresses he found himself subjected to stretched him in their different directions, he was drawn inexorably toward his elastic limit. Finally, he must snap completely, but meanwhile, little pieces of him would break off in curious outbursts of word or action. Then immediately he would feel ashamed, and act apologetically; at least insofar as a man could, who was imbued with a divine sense that he was never truly wrong.

So he would not say "Sorry. I'm a bit stressed" or something of the like, but he would act humbly and say something kind, and then those who had felt the sting of the outburst would remember the "old" Hanns-Peter and recall their affection for him. But as one accidental flick from a rubber band is easily forgiven, the constant insults of it are not. His colleagues and even his friends who bore the brunt of his increasing irrationality recognised his advancing mental fragmentation. He was unstable and dangerous, and better avoided.

In fact, Charles' circumstances were similar to those of Hanns-Peter. Not a family man but fond of his home, and married, with a cat. His wife *would* have moved to Evergreen, although she didn't relish that prospect particularly. But, trapped in his own twilight nightmare – the *Alptraum* that was EEU – Charles felt unwilling to set his roots too firmly in the soil of Evergreen. So he spent his nights alone, constantly awaking from shallow sleeps, wondering how the hell he had been drawn into the living horror that emerged when he awoke, without even the cat for consolation.

10

As Charles waved to Hanns-Peter across the conference hall, it was not a happy face that reacted. The man looked glum, but raised his hand back heavily, managing merely the suggestion of a smile.

"Hi, Hanns, good to see you," Charles greeted him. "How's it all going in Southern Saxony?"

"It's OK." They shook hands as usual, but he looked tired, and even for a man of his large frame, somehow weightier than normal.

Charles felt sorry for him, and touched his arm saying, "Come and have a drink."

There was an awkwardness between them, which Charles had never felt before, in all the time they had spent together. So, mainly the conversation skirmished around work; the organisation of the conference – who was to speak; enquiries as to the wellbeing of their colleagues, past and present; and some of the recent developments in particle physics; both of them skirting around the palpable business of what was the matter with Hanns-Peter. There was a pain in him that just couldn't be ignored.

When they went in to dinner, the venue was lavish. The waitress approached them, proffering a silver tray.

"What would you like to drink, sir?"

"Oh, thanks. I'd like a gin and tonic," Charles replied.

"Yes, the same for me, please," Hanns-Peter responded, as she turned the tray toward him.

They had one more each, and then, following the sound of the gong, replaced their glasses on the tray, went into the dining room and sat together at the nearest table.

It was the most prestigious meeting of the world's academic physics community, and part of a series of conferences which were hosted only once every four years. Both Charles and Hanns-Peter had been invited to give main lectures at this one, which was an impressive plume in each of their caps.

To host such a meeting was also a source of considerable pride, and many universities in many countries vied with each other for this privilege. Mainly under the threats and influence that Professor Helmut Lederbauer was able to wield from his "top dog" vantage point on the major international policy and funding committees for particle physics, it had been agreed unanimously, and well in advance at one such committee meeting, that in this year the conference should be held at the University of Wuperbaden. The event would celebrate Professor Lederbauer's long and distinguished reign there, and mark his forthcoming retirement. The rumour was: he was running down his research group.

It also marked the approval of continued funding for the international megagigatron accelerator, (a further five hundred million euros, and topping the total budget to 1.2 billion euros), which was already providing preliminary data that challenged the most sophisticated and groundbreaking theoretical models of how nature was supposed to behave at the limits of the universe, whether it knew it or not. The conference was additionally a great honour for the University of Wuperbaden, chaired by one of its senior professors, Helmut Lederbauer, and for the Wuperbaden region of the country. It was, moreover, an honour to the entire nation, and so, in their meticulous planning, not only the regional government of Wuperbaden, but also the national government, had pulled out all the stops to ensure the fineness of its quality.

The venue itself was beautiful, set high in the Wuperbaden mountains. In winter it became an exclusive ski resort, but now it was summer, yielding rhapsodic views extending for miles, of the sierras in the lower ranges, beyond which the vista then uplifted to the highest snow-dressed and permanently luminous peaks – the whole a floating landscape of inquisitive red and orange shadows that traced the ebb and flow of each day there. The buildings were splendid too. Annexed to the original *Schloss*, a ski village had been constructed from local pinewood, formed around floors and staircases cut from marble blocks, hauled up the mountain via the funicular railway.

The main business of the conference, however, was conducted in the *Schloss* itself; wherein, in its main dining room, brightly illuminated by an array of gilded electric chandeliers, sat together Charles Rae and Hanns-Peter Krankenpfleger, who was patently not himself. The meal was sumptuous. As each course followed the previous one, one Russian delegate, who

83

was sitting at Charles' left, would remark almost in disbelief, that this was the finest food he had ever tasted. It was probably true.

"Poor bugger," Charles remarked to Hanns-Peter. "I expect he's been living on beetroot and potatoes most of his life."

But this was good, by anybody's standards. And, as each course was served, a complementary type of wine would be served too, the *Schloss* having a famously fine cellar, with a perfect and constant temperature, hewn fast into the temperate body of the mountain. As these proceedings progressed, Hanns-Peter became more than usually vibrant. Big booms of laughter would erupt from him, displaying a rare mood of humour.

He began to tell jokes that were actually funny (and even a little rude in places), rather than his usual Sunday school style stories with a moral undercurrent.

"What a good chap Hanns-Peter is," Charles thought, laughing along with him at the latest punchline. He truly was the life and soul; seemingly gone was the stuffy sadness that appeared to suffuse him earlier.

"Perhaps he was just a bit tired?" Charles wondered, beckoning to the waiter to pour them both some more wine.

The meal was concluded with a bottle of fine Armenian brandy, which Charles remarked was "better than cognac, according to Winston Churchill!"

Hanns-Peter agreed that "Churchill was probably right. But we should have some more to be sure!"

And in the inner collective glow of the evening, one of the basking voices recommended, as someone always does on such occasions, "Let's go on somewhere else."

"Do you fancy it, Hanns?" asked Charles.

"Yes, why not?"

And so a group of the collective, as interactive as a hill of termites, maintained their convivial momentum, and headed for the Schloss Bar (which was actually, the only "somewhere else" in town). But a drink or so later, at least well past the stage when a mental tally is kept running, the quantities only disputed with the barman later on when the account has to be paid, the earlier phantom of melancholy began to possess Hanns-Peter's frame once more. They seemed isolated from the others, his pain forming a screen around them, which Charles found disquieting.

"Hanns? What's the matter?" he demanded. "I've never seen you like this before."

The brittle surface abruptly fractured into an outpouring of woe.

"Oh. It is terrible.

"I miss my family so much.

"I am in Southern Saxony almost full-time.

"Even at the weekends.

"I only get home to Wuperbaden once every month or so.

"Then my wife doesn't talk to me.

"She cooks dinner, but she says nothing.

"I am sure we will be divorced.

"My children now are strangers.

"They feel I have abandoned on them.

"I am no longer an elder in my church, now I am in Southern Saxony most Sundays, and never there during the weekdays.

"But it is a good university."

The latter bullet point sounded more as a question: a supplication for reassurance – that at least something worthwhile remained of his life, now utterly transformed of its former values. It was almost a plea that Charles could read in his eyes, imploring an affirmation of self-worth; the way a child sometimes looks to its parent, and occasionally the other way round. But here, Charles was the grown-up.

"Yes, of course. There are some very good young people there, and the quality of its facilities for particle physics is well known," Charles attempted to reassure him.

Indeed, Charles felt a pang of envy in the latter respect; his mind suddenly cast back to the homeland, to EEU, the monstrous concrete shithouse full of staff who would never have been employed anywhere else, and where he should never have been appointed himself; its feeble facilities and activities bobbing about haphazardly like turds in a cesspit. It should be the Cesspit Epstein University, (CEU). In fact, Charles felt pretty sorry for the hand both of them had been dealt, but there it was. At least Hanns-Peter had a decent job, and hadn't been conned by the University of Southern Saxony. He knew what to expect when he went there; that was something to buoy him up at least.

★　★　★

As the following morning swept its luminescent shadows over the dawn of his consciousness, a miniature metro system began to trundle its carriages through the pain-tunnels in Hanns-Peter's brain. As he rose, half upright, the amplitude of their vibrations ramped unsteadily into the pit of his stomach, and he lurched, vomiting into the sink. Having disgorged its acidic cargo, the fully erected frame collected its reflections in a morning mirror of moral approbations. He had got drunk. But what else? Who was he with? What had he said? Had he let himself down?

Ah, yes, he was with Charles, whom he had always felt a rivalry toward. Charles was good – instinctive rather than analytical. More an artist than a scientist, who took chances and paid contempt for the orderly but restricting rules and mandates that had held his own life firmly by the balls, ever since he could recall. Church, family, analytical but pedestrian rules of scientific etiquette, an effectively arranged marriage to a "good girl" who would make a good *Hausfrau*.

All of that. And in the alcoholic disorder of the previous evening, he had dropped his guard, revealing weakness to a rival. Yes, he had let himself down – an elder, both to Charles, and in his Fundamentalist Church – to Charles, a drunk and a sinner. The bar of the fulcrum had to be weighted back in favour of his own moral gravity. This conclusion possessed him, and, as it was the last morning of the conference, and Charles had an early flight back to Evergreen City Airport, he would not have to face him, shamefacedly; both paddling around in the shallows of his unhappy situation.

Charles had sympathised with him too, since his own personal situation was not so much different – away in Evergreen during the week, but with the knowledge that he'd been lured into a nightmare situation, which he was desperate to escape – and that made it all the worse, since it implied a parity between them, and from which Hanns-Peter had to lever the upper hand.

★ ★ ★

When he checked his pigeonhole on the Monday morning, Charles immediately recognised Hanns-Peter's handwriting on the envelope. But, on sight of its contents, it was a stranger's voice that stunned him. He began to read the words again, but a single reading had already branded them on his mind.

> *Dear Charles,*
> *I was shocked to hear stories of your having to be taken to the airport. This is not the first time I have heard stories about your alcohol consumption. This is not my picture of a professorial candidate. I suggest you change your*

life before seeking a more prestigious Chair, even though you are the good scientist you sometimes are.

I cannot, therefore, act as a referee for you, as we discussed.

I realise this letter is hard to take, but this matter had been on my mind. You may rest assured that only you and I know of its contents.

Yours sincerely,

Hanns-Peter Krankenpfleger

Taken to the airport? What was he talking about? What reference? The man had flipped! It seemed as though Lederbauer had got rid of him just in time.

11

Michael Moynihan almost shat himself. Fucking Jesus, here was that liability, Dai Davis, screwing up his chances again. Jesus fucking Christ! Here was Davis sounding off at Charles Rae, the erstwhile chairman of the National Physics Society. What was his game? Professional suicide for both of them?! His fat mouth had fallen open again.

"NO! It's not supposed to be about self-aggrandizement. Quite a few people round this table..." the mouth went on.

The room paused, but Charles decided not to rise to *that* moment. He had begun to doubt the worth of the research group, whose application for a national scientific facility he had recently supported. A national centre of excellence. Especially as run by Davis, a jumped-up technician, but Charles had to look into the details of this. A slanging match was too crass. On the receiving end of the peer review system, Charles had learned the hard way that he could use his influence to inflict a more deeply wounding castigation at a later stage. And as far as he was concerned, this fat wanker and his side-kick were fucked from here on in! But unbeknown to Charles, the two were not the best of friends.

"How the hell had he got there, with that bastard nosing through his desk; trying to find any faults in the minding of his business," thought Michael. The source of the problem being that Michael Moynihan was a threat. At least, that was how Dai Davis saw him. Michael gave him an irksome sense of his own inferiority, and so he wanted a few negative points to equalise the score some. Dai had been there a long time: twenty-five years, whereas Michael was a yearling lecturer; a stripling to Dai's mighty oak.

Since he was an experimental officer, Dai was not formally an academic but a technician, and that lent an uneasy friction between them. Dai had joined the department as an MSc student, working on a research project supervised by John Jenkins, a senior lecturer in Physics. He had done well,

88

and so, when John found some money available through his head of department Lewis Roberts to support the salary of a technician, he appointed Dai to the post. Dai had then registered as a part-time PhD student with Jenkins, working around his other duties, and consequently had taken ten years to earn the title "Doctor" Dai Davis. Meanwhile, there had been some bad feeling toward John Jenkins from Lewis Roberts, who described his work as "too pedestrian".

This had two outcomes. Firstly, Jenkins had never risen above the rank of senior lecturer, and secondly, Dai Davis, whom he referred to scathingly as "John Jenkins' technician", was deliberately kept on a technical grade, rather than being himself given a lectureship. Dai had always felt a bitter resentment for this, and indeed confronted the head of department to demand redress. Since he had done this in the form of a written message, he received a written reply:

Dear Dr Davis,

I have given a great deal of consideration to your surprising letter, in which, among other matters, you give the reasons why, in your opinion at least, you should be elevated to a lectureship in this department, rather than remaining here on a technical (experimental officer) grade. My responses to your specific points are as follows:

(1) I agree, your name does appear on a quite lengthy list of publications, which extends to more than 100 articles. However, how many of them were actually written by you? Clearly none, as they have the hand of Jenkins all over them, who has in reality merely acknowledged you for your "technical assistance" i.e. you may have operated the equipment, but provided no intellectual contribution; or sufficient at any rate that you should really be a co-author. Your name should have appeared at the end of most of the papers among the "Acknowledgments".

(2) Regarding your academic qualifications, I see that you had originally technician's qualifications, which you obtained while you were working in industry. These you attempted to aggrandize up to an MSc, which was awarded to you by this university, and that Jenkins was your project supervisor. Again, I question what precisely your intellectual input was, since your MSc thesis again has

Jenkins' hand all over it. The same goes for your PhD, which you obtained part-time while working as Jenkins' technician.

In order to be appointed to a lectureship in this university – in this depart-ment certainly – you would need a good, i.e. a first or at the very least an upper-second class degree (MScs are then always unnecessary); a PhD carried out in a credible fundamental academic field (not Jenkins' applied rubbish!) followed by a post-doctoral fellowship in a decent university and supervised by someone at professorial level and at the cutting edge of their field, and with evidence that the publications resulting and their intellec-tual content are substantially your own work.

(3)   I remain sympathetic to your situation following the sudden death three years ago of John Jenkins, who was a greatly valued colleague and a close personal friend, and I appreciate your efforts in holding together his research group until all its PhD students had completed their studies. Nonetheless, the above still holds.

If, however, you remain seriously intent on being appointed to a lecture-ship, I suggest you apply to one of the polytechnics, whose standards are likely to be somewhat less rigorous than our own.
Yours sincerely,
Professor Lewis Roberts
(Head of the Department of Physics)

Well, that was that. Dai liked it where he was – he felt a part of the furniture – but he also thought some acknowledgment of his efforts was overdue. After all, he was the only one sufficiently versed in John Jenkins' research, even if bloody Roberts did consider it as "applied rubbish", to have got *their* research students through their PhDs. But it was not to be, as his academic pedigree was not deemed good enough. Then along had come Michael Moynihan, an upstart, in his first year now following his appointment as a lecturer, and with exactly those credentials that Lewis Roberts had so cruelly made clear were lacking in himself. No. Of course he wouldn't apply to a polytechnic. "A poly?" he thought. "Roberts was a bit out of date there, 'new-univer-sity' now!" But Dai was a snob too, so an element of him could nonetheless sympathise with his sentiments.

★ ★ ★

When Charles Rae had been appointed as a professor at EEU, Dai sent him a warm letter, whose sentiments at the time had been sincerely meant.

"Congratulations on joining the scientific peerage!" he had written, but what that really meant was that he wanted to be on Charles Rae's good side, as he was now quite likely to get their grant application to review.

Since then, the word had got round that Charles had hardly fallen on his feet. In despair and over a surfeit of red wine at the last conference, Charles confirmed the dire circumstances of his appointment, with the result that his esteem had crumbled in Dai's estimation.

"You've been sold a pup there, haven't you!" he lilted, smirking.

Charles was growing increasingly suspicious of this line, believing it to translate into "You're nothing special! I don't have to treat you as a professor any more, do I?!"

Charles expected trouble.

While Dai still wanted to score some points from Michael and did not desist from rummaging through his desk in the casual routine of a village bobby on the beat, Dai's tongue remained in firm protrusion to the anal-ring of the Establishment. And in all honesty, he acted as though he was a member of that Establishment – an associate member, anyway. A sergeant-major to the officers, and he had by now decided that Charles Rae was no officer. Plainly a pretender, a usurper to its glory, and he, policing its grounds, was duty-bound to bring him down to his rightful, lowly level.

Charles Rae should be prostrated at its feet and made to submit to its mercies. He would need to bide his time, though, for Charles was the present president of the National Physics Society, the fact of which appalled Dai utterly. However, as Dai was secretary of the latter, he not only had to work closely with Charles, but also ingratiate himself with him, especially as he and Michael Moynihan together had a grant application riding for £3 million, and Charles Rae's word could thumb the outcome "up" or "down" in the award of it or not.

It was his legacy from John Jenkins. In going through the personal effects in his office, Dai had found the grant application written by John shortly before his death. This was his true bequest to providence; really to Dai, who was incapable of conceiving the idea of the project for which it requested funding. But if they got the money, Dai would become the director of a major national research facility, and a full member of the Establishment, and for this elevation he needed Charles' support and goodwill.

Dai retyped the application, substituting the name Michael Moynihan for John Jenkins as "principal applicant". He also added the name Dr Dai Davis into the box marked as "co-applicant" on the administrative form that had to be submitted along with it. He was doing Michael a favour in one way, but really it was the *only* way, because only Michael, of the two of them, had an "academic" post. As a technician, Dai was formally ineligible to be the principal applicant, which would preclude the application from being considered. Michael was delighted, albeit he had reservations about getting into bed with Dai, but as every one of his own grant applications had been rejected thus far, he deferred to the wisdom of going along with it.

If awarded, the grant would be accounted against his name on the departmental research income tally. And *£3 million*, in the first year of his appointment too, that would be a real feather in his cap! It would also allay the continual remonstrations toward him from both Lewis Roberts and the departmental research coordinator:

"Michael! You must *get that first grant*! What are you doing wrong? There must be some fault in your research proposals. Sloppy presentation, probably!"

"We took a chance on you, you know! We could easily have appointed from a better pedigree than yours. Simon Meddows, for instance."

Simon Meddows. That name had been fashioned into a prong for their goad. Simon Meddows had worked with Professor Conrad Connory (FRS) at the country's finest university. He then post-doc'ed at the University of Wuperbaden with Professor Helmut Lederbauer. But when he and Michael had been interviewed together, it was the name and establishment of Conrad Connory that was Simon's ace in the hole, and which he played remorselessly, name dropping it into the game at every opportunity.

"When I was with Conrad Connory..." he would announce superciliously, lest anyone even momentarily forget his pedigree.

Michael's teeth flinched with each flick of the card.

"Arrogant Bastard!" he seethed inwardly.

"Meddows wouldn't have any trouble getting a grant." The needle was driven home. And it was probably true too. Connory would have thumbed up his applications, and the committee would not have dared to dissent, particularly as he chaired that particular awarding body and could put any dissenters out of business themselves. This was a key point, not lost upon the appointments committee, who realised that Simon Meddows was, as it was put at the time, "money in the bank".

But Simon turned them down, realising that university life was no longer all it was cracked up to be. Indeed, Conrad Connory had advised him against accepting the position, as although the address was "quite respectable" it was "hardly the best", and even with his help, getting funding would, overall, be extremely difficult. At grade 4, they were at base level to be considered for research funding, and if they dropped a grade in the next RAE it would be curtains. Quite likely, Conrad stressed, in that event the department would be closed down and Simon would find himself out of a job.

"My advice, Simon, is, either get in somewhere *good* – Effington, for example, although I'm not aware of anything coming up there. Otherwise, forget it. Just forget it! A better option might be to get a research position in industry." And that was what Simon had done, leaving Lewis Roberts no choice but to appoint Michael Moynihan. Lewis Roberts had taken Simon's snub rather personally, still in denial of the new realities that now prevailed against the universities. This was unfortunate for Michael, upon whom the sting of his scorn was visited from day one, and to add to the sense of unsettlement this imbued, he had to endure the daily ministrations of the village bobby – Dai Davis – whom Lewis Roberts held in abject contempt, as "John Jenkins' technician", his association with whom weakened Michael's esteem further in Roberts' eyes.

★   ★   ★

Once Dai was satisfied that Charles Rae would support it, the grant application was duly submitted to the Research Council. The office dealing with physics research funding applications received it safely, along with almost a hundred applications from various universities around the country, including one from Professor Charles Rae, asking for only £100K to upgrade the small facility at EEU, rather than the £3 million Dai and Michael had requested to establish the far larger facility at their own university, which was supposed to provide a national service available to all the country's universities.

This was a good sales pitch toward the grant awarding committee, as the zephyr of prevailing politics had steered the cargo fleet toward only certain ports, in the intention that research provision should be centralised through facilities hosted in a limited league of just fifteen universities out of the one hundred and four that existed altogether. Academics in other universities would then be eligible to apply to use each facility in a kind of timeshare arrangement, but with the host institution withholding 80 per cent of the consequent available resources to support its own research programme. A nice little earner, in anyone's book! Funding through the back door. The host university gets the cake, from which it flicks a few crumbs here and there, if here and there makes the effort to apply for them.

The applications were gathered together in the coordinating office. Any late arrivals were allowed a couple of days grace, but beyond that were simply returned to sender along with a remonstration that the deadline was strictly observed, and that posting the application a week or so in advance of it was highly recommended. Dai's application had, however, got there well ahead of time. The next step was to activate the mechanism of "peer review", in which the expert and impartial opinion of a "peer" reviewer is invoked, the peer being a specialist in the particular field pertaining to the subject of a given grant application, and a member of a university other than that of the applicant.

In order to assist the assignment of an application to someone suitable, a new box had been included on the administrative form entitled: Suggest names of up to three possible reviewers. (See note 6 of the enclosed 'notes for guidance of applicants'.) Dai had put Charles' name at the top of the list: (1) Professor Charles Rae, Department of Leisurewear and Applied Physical Sciences, Evergreen Epstein University, Evergreen.

"Mmmm... I wonder who else I can put down," he mused.

Then it occurred to him. "Why not put down a couple of *past* presidents of the National Physics Society?"

After all, he'd been secretary of the society for fifteen years, and he knew every one of them pretty well. There was Conrad Connory, of course. Good old Conrad – Dai felt sure he could rely on him. Conrad had always been especially attentive to Dai, who, as a bedrock of the society, could manipulate its committee to ensure that he, Conrad, would be asked to present a main, plenary, lecture at its conferences. (Not every year, obviously – that would be too embarrassing – but every other one.)

"Well, he is Conrad Connory, after all," Dai would lilt, much to the aggravation of the other committee members, who were only too well aware there were dozens of other physicists in the world who had done much more than Connory had; but somehow, it always seemed rather churlish to object to the idea, especially as Dai's heart was so set upon it. So, Conrad would appear every other year, whereupon he would present precisely the same lecture as he had the year before last, never having any new material, as he was by now fully engaged in politics rather then research. And this was the real basis of any wish to avoid churlishness: the fear that Dai would feed back to him the facts and faces of any miscreants and objectors.

"Well, Conrad, I tried to get them to invite you, *see*, but it was..." (Fill in the gap with their name.)

Objecting to Conrad's name going forward among those of the plenary lecturers for the next conference was professional suicide, since he chaired the Physical Sciences Research Funding Committee, and could cut them off without a penny – forever. He wielded the proverbial sword with two edges, both lethal in his hands. It had been the same when the committee had to select a name for the recipient of the prestigious Newton Prize, this country's equivalent of the Leibnitz Medal awarded to Hanns-Peter Krankenpfleger. "Well, I think Conrad Connery's our man," and again no one dared suggest otherwise.

The village bobby surveyed their faces, until even the most resistant of them acquiesced into a bland unanimity.

"Well, Conrad, I've got some good news for you, see...off the record, mind. But, anyway, you know the Newton medal? Well, of course you do, don't you? The committee voted at the meeting yesterday, and it's yours, see. Unanimous, it was!"

"Thaaaank you, Dai. Eeeexcellent, I shan't forget this..."

Dai glowed, in his imagined shared warm glory of the moment, while Conrad calculated with his cool blood, and uncoiling slightly, his voice became a slow rattle.

"Well, one good turn deserves another. What was that application of yours about again? Ah, yes. three million isn't very much. A trifling sum, really. No problem!"

He would make sure they got it. It was in the bag. But Conrad's motives had an ulterior dimension. True, it was worth his while to keep Dai sweet. A faithful hound whose loyalty he hardly had to whistle for, but if necessary whom he could command at will. Conrad had been charged with the task of rationalising the costs of the nation's university physics departments; and to commence this exercise, the national funding for physics research needed to be pruned rather closely, and across the board.

Natural wastage helped enormously. The massive shortfall in the numbers of students who wanted to study physics at university reduced the income of most of the smaller physics departments to the level of unsustainability, where job losses were threatened. Vice-chancellors around the country had fought shy of closing them down outright, and instead adopted interim measures in which the physics staff were merged with other departments more abundant in undergraduate numbers, and hence cash, such as Leisurewear, while Science courses closed. Indeed, many universities were now opening departments of Leisurewear to bolster student numbers in the sciences. This had a knock-on effect: the physicists became unwelcome pariahs; parasites who began to drain the previously healthy resources of the single department, e.g. Leisurewear, who resented these intruders.

The draining taxed the vitality of the combined collective, until in desperation a V-C would finally have to "let the physicists go", cutting out the cancer so the main body might continue to live. They each expressed their regrets at doing this, but with the Government's bums on seats style funding policy, there was no alternative. Only the very large departments – the "big boys" of physics – could survive, because only they, at RAE grade 5 or 5*, could pull in enough income both through the exercise itself and their consequent eligibility, being of the top grade, to secure very substantial research council funding. Some of the largest grants that could be awarded were likely to be for the support of national facilities, national centres of excellence, where a particular specialist technique was available.

So, by supporting Dai Davis' application and establishing a centre in his department, Conrad Connory could divert a large chunk of the total available research funding away from other, smaller departments, such as that of Charles Rae at EEU. If he could drive the "smaller boys" out of town before the next RAE, all he then had to do was lever downward the RAE grades of the intermediate level departments at grade 4 or less, to leave them swinging on the gallows. The final fifteen or so that remained – the "big boys" – would then be viable within the financial constraints that had been indicated to him. He would have achieved the outcome charged to him, "And probably a knighthood too?" he surmised.

If Dai's department did suffer a gallows fate, it mattered not one iota, as the Centre could simply be relocated in one of the other departments elsewhere, which would roll on, invulnerable throughout the entire exercise.

The choice of the third reviewer had been a little more circumspect. Dai had done an exemplary job as the Physics Society's secretary, and accordingly he had earned a sincere spirit of gratitude and goodwill from the other members, mainly because nobody else wanted to do it. They were only too pleased to re-elect him every three years in a one-horse race, and he had just now been restored to the position for a sixth term. Dai considered carefully the past presidents of the society, and then it struck him: yes, there was some-one else who owed him a favour – Alistair Blakeley.

12

A few years younger than Conrad Connory, Alistair Blakeley had joined the university as an undergraduate, when Conrad began his PhD studies. Conrad had achieved the adulated rank of a celestial iconic beacon, toward whom each gaze, including Alistair's, was drawn in an inexorable seduction. Dai felt this too, although he had been more enlit by the candle of Alistair; but then you know what they say about rugby players. Alistair had later begun his PhD with David Mason, who was a reader in Theoretical Physics. This was in the 1960s when in the "white-hot heat of revolution", to quote a prime minister of that age, the first batch of "new universities" was created. David Mason was headhunted by one of them, with the duty of establishing the freshly budding Department of Physics there. He had taken Alistair with him, and although his PhD was as yet incomplete, appointed him directly to a lectureship, recognising that he would serve him well as a loyal lieutenant, before shortlistings and formal interviews became mandatory.

In a way, Alistair's PhD was never completed, since he traded upon the selfsame topic of it for the next thirty years, juggling only subtle permutations and combinations of its elements. But it was a floor show to be repeated endlessly, on and on into the realm of irritation, at least in all other eyes but Dai's, whose normally clear vision was smeared in their moist worship. And Dai never tired of the performance. Like a girlie wrapped up in a cosy cardigan; a fluffy, pink bunny, waiting to watch her favourite weepie chick flick, Dai would always ask the conference committee "Why don't we have Alistair Blakeley?"

"Well, no, sorry Dai, but we had him last year. He can't speak two years in a row, now, can he?"

Dai would look instantly sorrowful, but of course that objection would not apply the following year, when Alistair would then give the same verbatim performance of two years previously. The whole business did, if truth be told, rasp against the backbone of Charles Rae, whose nerves were beginning to flake off in shards. It occurred to him that Alistair Blakeley and Conrad Connory were rather like the Mr and Mrs in a toy weather house. Who was Arthur or Martha was another matter, but either way, on alternate years, one would appear in a summer dress, with the other wearing gumboots and bearing an umbrella. Exactly the same dress or the same umbrella would be unfurled shamelessly each time, the edges of both worn unignorably frayed.

Following David Mason's death, Alistair Blakeley succeeded to the Chair of Physics in the department, and later became its head. His career had been productive. Although his footfalls never strayed beyond the beaten path of his PhD subject, he nonetheless notched up over two hundred publications. This was impressive by anyone's standards, and was the official justification Dai would offer up, before anyone asked him, for his repetitious invitation of Alistair as a plenary lecturer. No similar explanation could have been found for Conrad Connory's performances, other than the eminence of his political influence and that of his university, but none was ever sought. It was simply "taken as".

When Charles Rae received Dai's grant application to review, he was pleased. He noted the name Michael Moynihan as principal applicant, Lecturer in Physics, and that of Dai Davis as co-applicant, experimental officer. Then a mild sense of ranklement entered Charles' mind, which was no fault of the applicants, both of whom he was on good terms with, as far as he knew; but of their head of department, Lewis Roberts. When the vacancy had arisen, which Michael Moynihan ultimately filled, Roberts had approached Charles Rae, hoping to headhunt him. But Roberts was minding his pennies, and gambled on Charles being so desperate to get out of EEU, as Dai Davis told him, that he could short-change the appointment.

"Well, I mean, it's not like you're a proper professor, or anything, is it, mun? Some of these *new* universities, places like yours I mean, just about *anybody* can be a professor these days. It's a joke! So, no, I think we might be able to consider you for, well, not a readership probably, but a senior lectureship, anyway. Are you interested?"

Of course he wasn't bloody well interested, not on those terms at any rate, and he said as much.

"No need to be like that, mun. I'm only trying to do you a favour, see!"

It had all the shades and reverberations of that unforgettable conversation with Jasper Totter (at least Charles had never forgotten it), trying to con him into taking his old job back, and that really stung. But that was hardly Michael and Dai's fault that Lewis Roberts was a tosser – indeed, he pitied them for having an idiot like that as their head of department – and so Charles remained willing to lend them his support.

The application was part solid and part speculative. It had been constructed so as to emphasise Dai's experience, but also Michael's youth and promise. The solid work of John Jenkins' group provided an historical precedent, while Dai was the anchor man, supporting Michael amid his novel approaches and adaptations of the bedrock into which he had been set. Moreover, it was to be a national facility, a beneficiary for all, and therefore one that the Research Council could crow about while making its supplications for more seed to be injected its way from the loins of the Government.

It all looked OK. Charles was glad to help Michael, especially in his fledgling year, to get started, to get his name around, some research money, and indeed whatever else he could do for him. For the past several years Charles had felt almost alone among anybody who could be considered even remotely as representing youth in the field, and it was encouraging to have some new blood to keep it alive. Charles read the main selling points of the plan, and bought the job lot in its entirety. Dai was, it has to be said, a good salesman, and he had primed all: Charles, Conrad and Alistair, to bring about a safe conclusion. And so it was, the grant was awarded, a feather in a cap, shared, share and share alike, between Dai and Michael; but really it was Dai's, who would never let Michael forget the point of true possession. Charles, however, was less fortunate.

Dear Professor Rae,

We have now received reviewers' reports on your recent grant application. I am sorry to inform you that both recommend against supporting your research project. The science is sound, but unfortunately your department was rated as grade 1 (the lowest possible) in the recent research assessment exercise. This means, unfortunately, that no application from you can be seriously considered for funding.

Moreover, surely you can simply do all your work using the National Centre, hosted by Dr Michael Moynihan and Dr David Davis.

Yours sincerely,

Martina McDonnel

(Research Grants Coordinator)

So that was it. In supporting Dai and Michael in all good faith, Charles had cut his own throat. What was he supposed to do now? Stirling George had let him down on all fronts. The accelerator never materialised, nor any of the other equipment, which was why he needed this grant now, and now the research council and their reviewers had shafted him as well. He had PhD students to look after, but without any working equipment available for them, how would they finish their projects? It was a pretty pickle indeed.

The Research Council's policy seemed to Charles to be doomed to self-defeat, as holding such a line would simply drive the country's research groups out of business, and then there would be no requirement for the National Centre, either. But that was exactly the plan: Conrad Connory had been handed freely a scythe with which to chop down all physics research on the periphery of the field, leaving only himself and Alistair Blakeley as central players in the game. At grade 4, Dai Davis and Michael Moynihan's department straddled the whetted blade of viability; their vice-chancellor had warned that if they didn't make it up to grade 5 in the next exercise, it would be curtains for them. And in that event, Conrad decided, the Centre would be handed over to Alistair Blakeley, who coincidentally had mean-time become its director; rather than Dai, who bestowed his cherished bless-ing upon the event.

A key rider on the arm of the next RAE for them was, in fact, the Centre. If they didn't make a go of it; if there was insufficient use of the facility both in-house and more widely, since it was supposed to be a *national* centre of excellence, the amount spent on it (£3 million) would stick in the craw of the Assessment Panel, word would get round, and the award of the grade 5 was then most unlikely. So, although his self-interest had been largely inno-cent, Dai had in reality jeopardized the future of his entire department, by playing into the hands of the Connory–Blakeley political Mafia, who would fully sell him down the proverbial river, if their purpose so demanded – which it did.

Not that this occurred to Dai, as his tongue still massaged the great and the good, believing them above reproach, unlike "that pretender Charles Rae, who needs taking down a peg or two, he does!"

This was rather sad, and a very bad move, as of the three: Rae, Connory and Blakeley, Charles was his only sincere ally. But there he was, the unwor-thy, and Dai was shouting his mouth off at him, much to the chagrin of Michael, who was considerably more astute than Dai. This was the first meeting of the National Physics Society since Charles Rae had stepped down from his three-year tenure as its president. While he held that office Dai, as secretary, regarded him as unassailable, but now the gloves were off!

★ ★ ★

"NO! We're not having *you* as a speaker. What have you ever done?! You're nobody! It's not supposed to be about self-aggrandizement! Quite a few people round this table..." Self-aggrandizement? He could talk! Jumped-up bloody technician!

The sentence levelled off, without finding its metre, and then, "Why don't we have Alistair Blakeley?" Dai's eyes brimmed in the ecstasy of anticipation. It was like a loop tape.

Charles said nothing, believing in the adage about revenge tasting best as a cold dish. But that was it. No more support from him to Dai or Michael; and rather the converse! Michael could read those tacit sentiments in the unforgiving promise of his face.

"Bugger him! He's nothing! Not like Conrad Connory or Alistair Blakeley; they're proper professors, not like that upstart!"

Such had been Dai's response when Michael tried to remonstrate with him on the train journey home.

But Charles was on his own train back to Evergreen and in his heart he vowed revenge.

"I gave them that bloody centre, and I can take it away again." He recalled Alistair Blakeley phoning him with a message of thanks for supporting funding of the application. "Coming from the National Physics Society's president, your words carried a lot of weight. Thank you."

Charles had been genuinely pleased to help, but then it had cost him his own grant. Then that jumped-up technician had appreciated neither his efforts, nor his own loss, and then treated him like shit, to boot.

"Well, let's see how good he is, if he thinks he can talk to me like that!" Charles muttered, typing the name *David Davis* into the search box and pressing "return".

There was a mistake, surely – the last ten years' publications didn't appear. The last entry had John Jenkins' and David Davis' names, from ten years ago, but nothing since. Then the truth dawned. Since Jenkins' death, Dai Davis had published nothing. He really was just the monkey, not the organ grinder; the technician, not the originator of any ideas. Charles realised immediately he had been conned into giving his support, and this, along with the other offence, demanded blood. In his mind, Charles began to whetstone the gelding knife, laying low, ready to unman any of Dai's or Michael's appeals for further funding. It was easily done. Charles had been on the receiving end of this kind of treatment so often himself, that it was practically like breathing.

Pouring the festerings of his own wounds into the rising weals on Michael's white corpus, Charles consigned the next five of their applications to oblivion. The initial application which sought £2 million Charles made sure overshot their coffers and fell miserably into the trash bucket. Michael's heart became ashes, but rejection is always hardest on the young.

At ten years older than Michael, Charles had been made punch-drunk, and by now was only dimly aware of the blows that impacted continually down on him, his sensibilities passing through the charnel house toward the ossification of their buried remains. Grant applications being turned down; great steaming cartloads of teaching; job insecurities; "friends" and colleagues stabbing him in the back, writing nasty reports about his publications; begging bowl held out to industry; and ah, yes, there was of course EEU, just for added rapture.

What a wonderful life it was being an academic. He could almost weep with the joy of it all! At least Michael and Dai had their funding for the National Centre of Excellence, for now anyway, while Charles waited to sever its stem. It was not, however, a great success, which lent conviction to Charles that cannoning them out of the water was justified, and not merely a petulant act of singed pride on his part. There was no real national demand for it, not even for the 20 per cent of its support which was to be made available publicly while Dai and Michael kept the 80 per cent balance for their own research activities. The situation was all the more dire because they found little use for the equipment in-house either. It was rather a tainted chalice, whose metal would chime in the death knell of their department. It was dead in the water already, and that reality only needed to be spelt out to discredit the whole enterprise.

While he lay low, waiting for the main assault of an "end-of-grant period review" of the Centre's effectiveness, Charles used his reviews of other grant applications from Dai and Michael to snipe at it with dead precision:

"How can the applicants seriously expect to get more research funding when their national facility for excellence is grossly underutilized, and at a cost of three million pounds? They should be made to demonstrate their competence to use their existing resource from the Research Council effectively before they are trusted with more. There is no national need for the facility whatsoever, the whole exercise being a construct to fund their own research through the back door."

With money tight, this was the kiss of death to any application, and dropped it dead in a single blow. It also ricocheted into the armour of the facility, denting its increasingly fragile mettle, as tongues began to waggle and ears listened to their rasp, especially those attached to the charge of Conrad Connory, which pricked up urgently.

★ ★ ★

Lewis Roberts gathered wind of the climate shift, and he began to regret signing the administrative form promising, as was formally required of him, that his department would accept the grant in the event of it being awarded; but given his lowly opinion of Dai Davis, he had voiced aloud that its successful outcome had "a snowball's chance in Hell! Ha ha, stupid bloody technician. Who does he think he is, eh?!" How wrong, how wrong! The ruts of his face no longer recounted as much as the trail of a smile. If the Centre went tits up, the RAE panel would crucify them, pummelling the shafts of a grade 3a probably (or a 3b, oh God, even worse!) into their flailing limbs, whenceupon, their own vice-chancellor would plunge his own shaft disconsolately into their quivering flesh, allowing for a decent period of supplication from the forsaken corpus. Conrad Connory knew all of this too, and in his cold venom he had already calculated their fate. Charles had merely identified the splinters of their execution, but which Conrad would confirm from the lethal pointers to that end.

Conrad had advanced his name as chair of the review committee for the Centre, which pleased Dai enormously, believing him to be a bosom buddy, a bum-chum, a rugger-bugger. Michael, in contrast, had grown suspicious of Conrad, believing Charles Rae to be the truer man, at least before Dai had let his big fat trap fall open. Indeed, Michael suspected that it was Charles who had shafted all of their grant applications for the last two years since then, and he was in no doubt as to what the reason was, either. There it was, in full evidence, nosing through his desk again.

★ ★ ★

On the appointed day, Conrad had been affable. He shook hands with both Dai and Michael, and engaged in the usual badinage. "Yes, the journey was excellent, thank you" and all such pleasantries. Then the meeting was convened. Conrad Connory, Alistair Blakeley, Lewis Roberts, Dai Davis and Michael Moynihan were all in its attendance, along with the secretary of the Physical Sciences Research Council. The chair cut to the chase. "We have received a number of reports from reviewers whom we enquired of regarding the efficiency of the Centre. I must say, they are scarcely flattering, and *one* is particularly condemning."

Dai's face fell, and Lewis Roberts began to observe both him and Conrad Connory closely.

"So, what's the trouble, then?" Roberts asked him.

"Well, essentially, it all boils down to this: they've been given a grant of three million pounds— "

"Yes, I know that, of course," he interrupted.

"But, they've not *delivered*," Conrad continued, unfazed. "Nobody outside this university has made any use of the Centre at all, and no one has even *applied* to do so! The in-house research work, which remains the only conceivable justification for it to exist at all is, well...how can I put this? *Pedestrian*, at best! Especially as compared with the highly innovative results coming out of the rest of Europe and the States just now, and actually some rather nice work that has just been published from Russia."

Pedestrian. The word hovered among them. It was exactly how Lewis Roberts used to describe John Jenkins' work – "Applied *Rubbish!*" – which Dai remembered only too well. Lewis could also recall it quite clearly, and tripping from the lips of Conrad Connory, he felt vindicated in his opinion, and restored in his contempt for Dai Davis.

"Well, can't you just beef up the quality of your research, mun?" Lewis turned his attention toward Michael, now ignoring Dai. "Take some tips from your European or American colleagues, or the Russians even? And try to *promote* the facility more widely – make the rest of the country believe they can't do without it!"

"We've tried," Michael admitted, "but it is just such a difficult and esoteric technique that no one wants to know."

Dai's eyes flashed angrily at this breach of confidence, but then, "So why was it ever proposed that the facility should be set up as a national facility for excellence?!" Conrad demanded.

"Well, we've got plenty of supporting letters from various research groups around the country saying they wanted to use it, but none of them have. They've all let us down!" Dai grizzled.

"In fairness, though, quite a number of them have disappeared from the scene during the recent cull of the national university science departments," prompted Alistair Blakeley. This was a good point, but it challenged saliently the viability of any *national* centre of excellence once the required critical mass of its users has been lost. It began to dawn even on Dai that the forecast was none too bright.

"We simply can't throw more good money after bad," Conrad interjected. "You've had a fair run at it. You've got the equipment now, so consider yourselves lucky! It's a shame it cost three million quid to discover there was actually no need for the facility in the first place!" Alistair nodded in assent of this, both he and Conrad looking reprovingly at poor Dai.

"Our only option is to limit the damage by cancelling all future funding to you," Conrad continued. This was the *coup de maitre*. They were shooting fish in a barrel, and in a Romanov style execution, would continue until the job was done.

"You can't mean *all* our funding, can you?" Lewis Roberts' voice rang out an alarm.

"Yes, until your department demonstrates its competence with its existing awards," Conrad replied firmly.

"But that will probably *lose* us a grade, *at least*, in the RAE," Lewis implored. "The vice-chancellor has threatened to close us down if we don't go *up* to a grade 5 next time, let alone go *down* a grade."

"I am also the chair of the RAE panel for Applied Physics, and will bring the whole matter to its members' attention, so they can make a fully informed decision in allocating an appropriate grading for this department," Conrad promised flatly, his face firm and unforgiving.

Dai's jaw dropped upon his chest, drooling like the village idiot.

He couldn't believe it: *Here were both his heroes – turned on him, they had!*

Michael was less surprised, recalling Charles Rae warning him when they first met, what a pair of rattlesnakes they were and not to be trusted, but he had believed Dai instead. And when Conrad presided, he was faithful to his word, delivering them a 3b, and passing the elliptical ball back to their vice-chancellor for the final drop goal. Over the bar it sailed, and them into touch.

The Centre had to go somewhere, and so Conrad proposed, "Why don't we give it to Alistair Blakeley?"

Poor Dai. He might have said this at one time too, but now he had more pressing matters – cashing his redundancy cheque.

But Alistair, regarding Michael Moynihan as entirely blameless in the whole business, and potentially a good and loyal lieutenant, offered him a new home, to run the facility when it was installed in his own department.

13

Simon Meddows had met Charles Rae at a conference of which he, Charles, was the chairman. At the time, Simon was working as a post-doc at the University of Wuperbaden with Professor Helmut Lederbauer, but was imminently due to take up a position in industry, apparently abandoning the academic world. His record was of the good, solid kind, approved of by the university establishment. First a PhD with Conrad Connory: a Fellow of the Royal Society (FRS), and politically the country's most eminent physicist. This had much more to do with where he was than what he'd actually done and, scientifically, there were many better than Conrad, but he remained as the master puppeteer, and few dared to cross his path or turn their back on him.

Then had followed a most respectable initial post-doc in Southern Saxony with Herr Professor Max Moeben. Max Moeben was an ex-student of Helmut Lederbauer's and recommended Simon Meddows to him unreservedly. Indeed, the appointment process was perfunctory, and was arranged over one of their frequent and amicable telephone conversations. Max was in no doubt that Simon would do a good job in Wuperbaden, and neither was Lederbauer who, in the interests of protocol, had also contacted Conrad Connory, whom Simon also named to be approached for a formal reference, and which was similarly glowing. The post-doc in Wuperbaden did indeed prove successful, both academically and in that it gave Simon some breathing space to decide what his next move might be.

Back home, the scene of university physics, and science generally, was gloomy. Conrad Connory had recommended that if he couldn't get a lectureship "somewhere good. Grade 5 at least", finding a research post in industry would be a better option than settling for a department even at grade 4, and definitely not less than that. Simon also met Hanns-Peter Krankenpfleger, over whom the clouds were gathering in Wuperbaden, and by the time

Simon had left there, so had Hanns-Peter – for a Chair in Southern Saxony. The latter had been arranged by Lederbauer with Max Moeben, who was now head of the Department of Physics there. Lederbauer was positive that Hanns-Peter would make a good choice. He was up for grabs, and after all, considerable difficulties had been incurred in filling the post during the past few years.

Hanns-Peter was also a safe bet. If Southern Saxony made him the offer, he would accept it genuinely and not mess them about, trading a Chair there against a more prestigious one somewhere else, or in obtaining an internal promotion in his existing university. The latter was not an option in any case, Lederbauer stressed to Max, as in his opinion it was time for Hanns-Peter to fly the nest and make his own mark somewhere other than Wuperbaden, where he could build up his own independent research group with his own funds to support it, rather than living off his, Lederbauer's, grants.

It was "tough love", he assured Max (Hanns-Peter's little wings flapping furiously on the windowsill, while Lederbauer slammed the window fast behind him). He realised it would be difficult for him after so many years in Wuperbaden but, at his age of almost fifty, if Hanns-Peter didn't make the move now, he would never establish his independent reputation, which Lederbauer was certain he could do very well, and he hoped Max Moeben would afford him whatever support was required.

There *was* truth in all of this: he did wish Hanns-Peter the best of luck, but most of all, Lederbauer did not picture him as his natural successor, and probably he did not want a successor, preferring to burn the boat that he had built, like a Viking warrior's burial ship. Someone else could make their own way, if they were good enough.

The percolation of these matters formed the wisps of conversation between Charles and Simon, who was aware that Charles was a friend of Hanns-Peter, and had visited Wuperbaden on many occasions, and that he consequently knew Lederbauer fairly well. As it turned out, Simon's new place of work was actually based in the outreaches of Evergreen City, and so it seemed reasonable that he and Charles might maintain contact, and perhaps devise a joint research project; ideally supported by some funding from Simon's company being paid to Charles at EEU. The latter prospect seemed highly desirable to Charles, but obviously Simon *knew* that it would. He knew that although the chances of getting a research grant were not too bad abroad; in his experience, back home they were vanishingly small, particularly if one was in the "wrong kind" of university, and the wrong kind of department, i.e. grade 4 or less, and at EEU the Department of Applied Physics was grade 1, as Charles reminded him: QED.

Simon could smell the fragility of Charles' predicament, and so it was quite apparent he could get away with throwing a few small crumbs in the direction of EEU, in return for a useful allocation of time on their equipment. Of course Rae would go for it. What choice did he have, with nothing else on offer? If the project looked promising, he could then take it to a more prestigious university, although he certainly wouldn't be too candid with Rae about that! These elements formed the case he presented to his directors, in which he emphasised the advantage to them of his academic connections, and how strapped for cash most universities were, and open therefore to "...Well, exploitation is too strong a word, but in our dealings with the universities, 'he who pays the piper', and all that...we *do* have the whip hand!" Conrad Connory couldn't have put it better.

"How much are we talking about? For the preliminary work at EEU, I mean?"

Simon found himself being taken seriously, and smiling disingenuously, he named his figure. "Five thousand."

"Five thousand? Is that all? God, we couldn't get a *couple of days'* access anywhere else for that! Not at commercial rates, anyway. Are you sure it's enough?"

"I reckon we'll get a good ten days' worth for that, which is more than enough to test my basic hypothesis. I can probably try out a couple of other experiments too, and then we'll know if the project is worth taking further."

The proposal met with nods all around. How could they refuse a deal like this, in anyone's conscience?

Charles was perfectly happy with five thousand, grateful even, since he had something of a cash flow crisis. He still had to find travel costs for himself and a couple of his research students in order for them to run some experiments on the international megagigatron accelerator, and then they would need to attend some conferences to present their results, but the EEU conference budget had just been axed on the grounds that "it's conferences or salaries". So, he accepted Simon's offer and was indeed quite generous with the number of days he allowed him: twelve in all.

As far as Charles understood, the project was simply "a piece of consultancy work, internal to the company", as Simon had assured him at the outset. It came as a surprise then, when, after hearing nothing from Simon for about a year, an envelope arrived in Charles' pigeonhole. Its contents though, provided the real surprise, along with a covering note:

> *Dear Charles,*
> *I thought you would be interested in a reprint of my paper, which was published in the latest issue of the Physics Journal.*
> *Yours sincerely,*
> *Simon Meddows*

Charles felt stung, and that Simon Meddows had made a mug of him! It wasn't just "a piece of consultancy work, internal to the company": the bastard was working on publishing a paper. That was *not on!* It is an unwritten rule in any scientific collaboration that publication of the results was a matter for all parties involved. Even though Charles didn't necessarily want his name on the paper, Meddows should have made his intentions clear at the outset; or even later, once he had decided to publish, he should have at least let Charles know! This truly was worthy of Conrad Connory.

"Well, OK, we won't have anything further to do with the bastard," Charles resolved to Tommy Wakefield. "At least the five grand has been useful."

Useful, and revealing too, as the next conference Charles attended, supported through its emolument, provided unexpected developments in the tale.

★ ★ ★

"Hello, Charles. I see that Simon Meddows has been doing some work with you." It was Michael Moynihan.

"Yes, that's right. It was a piece of consultancy work. How do you know?" Charles answered him, sounding a little surprised.

"Well, he's been over to see us. It seems he wants to fund a post-doc for two years to take the project further. We've been working out the costs for it."

This irked Charles considerably. If Meddows wanted "to take the project further", why didn't he want to support the post-doc in Charles' lab? Why go to Michael Moynihan and Alistair Blakeley? Especially since EEU was only a few miles away from him, not a couple of hundred? Didn't he think Charles was good enough to supervise the work? It was rather annoying and perplexing. Also, the funding for a post-doc for two years would be worth having…at about £100K, including a 40 per cent overhead, plus £30K or so for other running costs… Charles made that automatic mental tally.

"Oh, I haven't heard from Simon for a while. He did send me a reprint of a paper that he's just published from his work in my lab though," Charles responded, thin lipped; and Michael understood his annoyance as Charles continued, "As a matter of fact, it's a few months since I last spoke to him. When I get back from the conference, I'll chase him up to find out where we are with it all."

Michael glanced away, feeling rather embarrassed, realising that Charles had been shafted. It was an apt moment to change the subject, which was prompted by the arrival of another figure, Manfred Hemming. Manfred clapped Charles warmly on the back, and they exchanged pleasantries.

"Have you met? Michael, this is Manfred Hemming. Manfred, this is Michael Moynihan. Manfred works at the international megagigatron accelerator facility … you know, where we do most of our experiments, these days."

Michael nodded.

"Actually, Charles, I have moved from the megagigatron. I am now working in Southern Saxony with Hanns-Peter Krankenpfleger. My contract ended at the megagigatron as it was only temporary, and I was out of work for some months, but Professor Krankenpfleger has just got two years' funding for a post-doc, and he has given me the job. It was quite lucky."

There was a sudden unease, from which both Charles and Michael suspected the answer before Charles had asked the question. "Where, in fact, is the funding coming from?"

"Ah, yes. That is also lucky. Do you know Simon Meddows…?"

Oh yes. They were beginning to know him pretty well. Michael cornered Charles later in the bar. "The bastard! So he came along to you and did the preliminary work."

"Then published a bloody paper about it without telling me what he was up to," Charles followed the story on, indignantly.

"Right. Then he came over to us, and got us to do the work of costing the full project. And now he's taken the money off to Southern Saxony. Fucking Jesus!"

"That's about the size of it," Charles concluded grimly. "We've both been treated like shit!"

"But, hang on. Isn't Krankenpfleger supposed to be a friend of yours?

Didn't he mention that the project had ... well ... *moved?*"

"He didn't say anything about it ... but then he's not the man I used to think of as a friend." Charles' breath caught in his throat as he spoke.

Michael was immediately curious. "Why?" he asked.

Charles sighed, his shoulders crumpling in a sad exhalation; head bent, focusing his gaze downwards in a combination of regret and consternation. He shook his head, this time breathing in, and looked up at Michael again.

"Ah, I'm sure it's all down to the stress and strain of his circumstances."

"What do you mean?" asked Michael, still puzzled.

"Oh. Don't you know? Well. He was in Wuperbaden for twenty-odd years with Helmut Lederbauer. Then... I've never got completely to the bottom of this ... but I suddenly received a letter from Hanns-Peter saying that Lederbauer was no longer prepared to support his position there. He kicked him out, basically! Hanns-Peter doesn't seem to know why. I mean – it's bizarre! Apparently there was no falling out between them, according to Hanns anyway, but one day Lederbauer just told him to go."

"I agree, it does sound bizarre. But Krankenpfleger is quite well known. Does Lederbauer have the power to ... well... just oust him like that?" Michael was intrigued.

"Apparently he does," Charles answered him. "Wuperbaden is in the old style of Teutonic universities. The professor's power is practically absolute – almost like a god! There was an internal inquiry into the whole affair, and the university's High Commission concluded that actually Hanns-Peter's recent publications were of far better quality than Lederbauer's, but because of some statute going back to the 1300s – when the university was founded – the professor has complete control over his staff; including whether he wants them there or not."

"And he doesn't want Hanns-Peter there any more?"

"It would seem not."

"That really is curious," Michael concluded.

"Yes, it is. Anyway, there he is most of the time in Southern Saxony, with his family back in Wuperbaden."

"They won't move?"

"No. They have six kids, and they don't want to uproot them from school. Also, his wife has a rather special job – training young girls to be good *Hausfraus*. Yes, really! Wuperbaden is a pretty reactionary sort of place, and such a job wouldn't exist anywhere else in the country! She loves it, apparently. Also there is their church. Well, yes, Hanns-Peter is a church elder, and his wife is very active in it too. She is pretty annoyed with Hanns-Peter for buggering off. She is threatening to divorce him, which would be a great disgrace in their local community.

"His kids are none too happy, either. They feel that he's deserted them. As I recall, they seemed a really happy family. Apparently he could have stayed in Wuperbaden and taught in one of the technical colleges there, but no. His research work is what really counts to him. I find that a bit curious since he is so devoutly religious. You would think the family would come first. Well, what do I know? I'm not very religious myself, but Hanns has always been the great moral majority – always quick to present examples of moral turpitude in others, and to castigate them for it."

Michael smiled. "A bloody hypocrite, in other words. There are a few of them where I come from too," he laughed.

Charles' face became sombre. "Anyway, there he is in Southern Saxony. He's got grief from his family, who he hardly ever sees these days. There's all the stress of getting grants, teaching and building up a research group. I just think it's all taken its toll on his mental state. Sadly, this places him vulnerable to political manipulation. He was always a bit naïve at the best of times, even when I first knew him in Wuperbaden. He seems to have been stirred up in some kind of vendetta against me by Bertie Bantam."

"Who's Bertie Bantam?" asked Michael, once again puzzled.

"Oh, the joys of university politics," Charles replied laconically. "He's some guy in the States, at the Midwestern Baptist University."

"Never heard of it."

"Well, no, you probably wouldn't have. Anyway, he thinks he's king of the pile. I think the problem goes back to a conference we were both at, years ago, when I first got a lectureship. Well, perhaps being new into the game, I probably didn't know the protocol. Nobody bloody tells you, do they?!

"Anyway, Bantam was one of the organisers. I wrote up a couple of papers for the conference proceedings, which were published in a pretty obscure journal, but I hadn't realised that I was supposed to produce a poster presentation for each of them – otherwise they wouldn't be accepted. I know someone else who ran foul of this some years later: he was seriously ill, in fact, which was why he couldn't attend the conference to present his results in person, but Bantam bounced both his papers, just the same.

"However, I did have two posters of some other results which I wanted to present at the conference because I thought they were quite good, but I didn't want to relegate them to obscurity in the conference proceedings, but rather to publish them in a decent journal, which is what I did eventually. But Bantam started berating me, accusing me, really, of dishonesty: that it went against the 'spirit of the thing'. I don't see why: results are results, surely? I got a bit annoyed with him, told him to get stuffed and that if it was such a big deal I would produce the desired posters – I handwrote them, actually, and stuck them up on the wall. I think Bantam felt that a young upstart like me should have treated him more deferentially, whereas actually he's lucky I didn't punch him.

"He's an annoying little bastard! Those kid gloves, the Panama hat, all of it! However, since then, he's done the usual stuff: tried to reject my papers, stamp on my grant applications, and so forth. I could deal with that, as I would simply point out the unreasonableness of his typically stupid and uninformed remarks and insist on an adjudication, which invariably would decide in my favour. Now, though, with Hanns-Peter cracking up, Bantam has managed to convince him that I deserve all manner of attacks, and to support him in making them.

"The worst came last week. I received an email message. Well, I could see who it was from, and I realised that coming from Bertie Bantam it was hardly likely to be good news. And it certainly wasn't. It was entitled, 'Complaint' and addressed to 'The Editor' of a journal that I am on the editorial board of. We published a paper in the journal. Anyway, the letter made all sorts of allegations of malpractice on our part. Mainly that we had failed to cite some earlier papers by Bantam and by Hanns-Peter."

"Is that true?" Michael asked.

"Well, yes, but for the simple reason that they were entirely irrelevant to the matter in hand. Even so, when Bantam slings mud he does it in volumes. So although, really, there is no case to answer, by kicking up a huge fuss, he creates the illusion that there is. And, of course, the letter was signed by both him and Hanns-Peter, which adds credibility to the lie. I emailed Hanns-Peter immediately to ask him what the hell he was playing at. I said, 'How long have we known each other?'"

"What was his answer?"

"Well. I got a further tirade of abuse from him. That I don't care about the work of others. I was unprofessional. He is personally insulted by my lack of care. Etcetera, etcetera. It really didn't sound like the man I used to know. Hysterical almost. Anyway, I had to get all the papers together to see whether I *should* have cited them or not. That was a real hassle, considering the shit quality of our library, which has cancelled all but three physics journals, 'due to financial pressures within the university', so the vice-chancellor's newsletter assured us recently. And at the end of it all, as I said, they were completely irrelevant! You could see the whole business was a vendetta against me by their reference to the paper by 'Rae *et al*'. Of course it should be 'Chambers *et al*' but you can see who the damage was intended for."

"Raymond Chambers? Your old post-doctoral mentor?"

"Yes, that's right. That was how I got into the whole situation – through Ray. I was trying to promote our area of physics somewhat, so I wrote to the editor of the journal and suggested that we produce a special issue, with me as the guest editor. He agreed, and I wrote around to everybody in the field, including Bantam and Hanns-Peter; however, Ray sent me a handwritten manuscript, which was pretty awful, actually. He's getting on a bit now, and his health isn't too good. Apparently, he picked up some parasitic infection walking through infested water in Egypt, and he can't get rid of it. But the manuscript bore no relevance to the subject area of the special issue, but something related to it. I didn't want to hurt his feelings, but luckily, or so I thought, we were scheduled some time on the megagigatron accelerator the following week, and I slipped in a couple of extra samples, and then rewrote the paper including the new results, which were relevant to it.

"I suspect Bertie Bantam has had something like this in mind for a while, but has waited for his moment, and the fact that I was both the guest editor of the special issue and a member of the editorial board for the journal is a real double whammy – an opportunity he couldn't pass up on. The editor is by no means happy about it all. The annoying part of it, from a personal point of view, is that Hanns-Peter has done to me, in reality, exactly what he falsely accuses me of."

"In what way?" Michael frowned out an air of palpable curiosity.

"About five years ago," Charles recounted, his gaze heaving abruptly upward, as often happens when one tries to connect with past events whose memories are uncomfortable, "I came across a paper by Hanns-Peter. It was around the time of his move to Southern Saxony after Lederbauer had kicked him out of Wuperbaden. The topic was one that I had done a lot of work on. However, he didn't cite any of my work, just his own, and more annoyingly, papers by others which I had already shown to be wrong. I published a major review of the entire field – it took me months to write – but he didn't refer to that either. It's not as though he hadn't seen it either, as it was published in a book that I edited, which I sent him my personal copy of, when his got lost in the post. I was really quite hurt, in fact, but of course I didn't write a letter of complaint to the editor about it. In fact, I didn't even mention it to Hanns-Peter.

"I suspect that his real motive in not referring to my review is that, in it, I suggest that some of his own results are probably wrong, and he would rather it remain buried. Hanns-Peter is never wrong – even when he is. Especially when he is! However, I gave him the benefit of the doubt that he probably had rather a lot on his mind, what with the move, and also the rather upsetting circumstances if it. I know how tough it has all been for him. He practically cried on my shoulder about the whole business – Lederbauer, family, church, etc – at a conference recently. Ironically, the conference was held in Wuperbaden, with Lederbauer as its chairman. It must have felt rather strange for him to be back there. We'd had a few, and I think that is part of the problem. He probably feels that he dropped his guard a bit. Which is a pity, because if he can talk to anyone, he can talk to me. But he now seems to have turned against me – particularly with Bantam stirring things.

"I think Bantam hoped that I would be sacked from the editorial board of the journal, as he made some remark in the letter about how embarrassing it was that 'Dr Rae' was a member of it, and this 'tarnished the good name of the journal'."

"*Doctor* Rae?"

"Yes. That was another little piece of spite. But of course, in the US all academics are addressed as 'Doctor', even if they are full professors like me, so that is all part of his amusing little game. I know what he was implying though. That this 'unprofessional' man doesn't deserve the rank of professor. And he has big, stupid Hanns-Peter to back him up. He really is like a big child. Rather like your man Dai Davis. What's he doing since they made him redundant, incidentally?"

"Ha ha. He's going to become a magistrate!" laughed Michael.

"Good God! God help the poor bastard who comes up in front of him!" Charles guffawed.

"I know. I'm going to have to watch my drink-driving," Michael mused.

14

The disaffected physicists at EEU were now fully attached to Leisurewear in the new Department of Leisurewear and Applied Physical Sciences (LAPS). Despite the apparent merger between them, Leisurewear, with its healthy undergraduate recruitment, still went its own way as the dominant partner. Applied Physics (reduced to "Applied Physical Sciences", in case further restructuring might dilute them even more weakly with other refugees from within the Faculty of Technology) remained as an unwanted body, which Leisurewear wanted lanced painlessly, like a sore boil on its bottom. Leisurewear was not a true academic discipline; but it did bring in money to the university.

Leisurewear were a proud department; they could trace their origins back to "The Evergreen Corset and Shoe Company (Est 1823)". It was, indeed, all cobblers, as Charles would often remind himself. Since there were only ten departments of Leisurewear in the country offering degrees in that subject, their market was a safe and lucrative niche. They didn't need to recruit actively either, because the students came to them in a ratio of four applicants for each place they had to offer, and regularly turned away hopefuls with grades most science departments would give their eye teeth for. In contrast, Applied Physics carried on scraping a shallow barrel.

Rod Shine, the head of the Department of Leisurewear and later on LAPS, was a decent fellow to Charles, as he was required to be. Stirling George had told him: "Good lad, Charles. Look after him, or else..." So he did. Rod was a shrewd businessman. He owned a chain of successful leisurewear shops in Evergreen. "He's a millionaire," it was often said. Perhaps he was, or wanted to be, and the two careers began to stretch him by their demands, beyond the bounds of one man. While, in his role as head of LAPS, he was good to Charles, an unwritten dossier was presented to him on a daily basis, like the Chinese water torture.

Rod had too much on to deal with the rapidly burgeoning admin load himself, particularly since the merger, so he created a *deputy* head position. The post was advertised internally following formal procedures, but in truth, Rod expected only a very few candidates to apply. It would have to be someone familiar with the Department of Leisurewear – Applied Physics didn't count. For most people, it would appear an unattractive job, apart from the small pay enhancement which it offered. Cutting through the verbiage, the specifications of both "person" and "job" called for someone who was prepared to take on all the department's major admin tasks, double for Rod at meetings and other university events when he found himself called elsewhere, and keep him up to speed on what had happened there, and still carry a substantial teaching load. Really, it was "a shit job" and "who in their right mind would do it?" Rod tut-tutted the matter over with Bob.

There was one man. Thomas O'Grady. An unexceptional man. But that was his strength. He had published one scientific paper – thirty years previously and arising from his doctoral thesis, but nothing since then. Devoutly Catholic, he believed that Rod's business activities were nothing less than a gift from God unto him. Until now, he had been a nobody. Rather a joke. Comments floating down that whispering corridor had stung him. A boring ineffectual little man with polished steel-rimmed spectacles, an eye for detail, and a boredom threshold as high as Everest. But now he had a little power.

Thomas hated Charles Rae – Charles was salt on that one paper and the thirty barren years since – and was receptive to any point of criticism about him. Following the RAE result Charles' position was weakened, and Bob rapidly encouraged Thomas to collect whatever dirt he could find, and feed it back to Rod.

"He's never here. He's not a team player." Bob and Tarquin said the same.

The drops dripped from his lips onto Rod's forehead, tormenting him daily, making Charles an irritation in his mind.

Thomas undermined Charles with his physicist colleagues. The finger always pointed, whatever its cause.

"I'm sorry, but we simply can't replace Applied Physics staff – the *problem* is your professor, who does very little teaching!" Dog in a manger. Said enough times it becomes believable; at least in minds that want to believe it.

As pressures and tensions – the daily strains of increased workload – built, a scapegoat was found for the oppressed. "Yes, Thomas is right. Bloody Charles Rae – leads the life of Riley."

Charles could feel their resentment, and it hurt him. He remembered the vice-chancellor of his old university warning him, "Well, my boy, you must do as you see fit, but I can't help feeling you're too good for them!"

"Bloody snob!" Charles had remarked, repeating the story at home, but now he understood the meaning of those words. Oh, yes – only too clearly. Young ambition – how naïve he had been. He realised just how much he had been appreciated there: A good example of an up-and-coming academic.

"Why can't you be more like Charles Rae?" his only marginally younger colleagues were told. This earned him slight resentment, but of the right kind, and much respect. At EEU his talent made him anathema.

"I don't see how we can continue carrying Charles Rae," Bob Bates ventured thoughtfully to Rod. "What with the grade 1, I think he should be doing more to earn his keep. Look how little *teaching* he does – only about 100 hours a year."

"That's what they promised him, apparently, when he was being interviewed – otherwise he said it wasn't worth his while coming here. He needed the rest of his time to do research," Rod commented.

"They? Hamish Humble you mean?" Bob asked. The two exchanged a knowing smirk.

"I don't want to take him on directly," Rod reviewed the situation aloud. "He still has the support of Letticia and the vice-chancellor, and they don't want to lose him." Rod shook his head contemplatively and continued, "Now there's another point... What about all the equipment and the personnel I'm supposed to fund for him? Am I still supposed to do it? After his RAE result? That, at least, seems to have cooled off a bit. I get the impression that Letticia is actually quite pleased that we delayed it all, until *after* the RAE ...

"I said to her, I don't want to throw good money after bad, but a promise is a promise. What can I *do*?

"Then again, Stirling wants to keep his word. He's sent Charles a handwritten note after the RAE result was announced, assuring him that the university would make up its own mind about pockets of excellence.

"So it's still on! But I don't have the money. Simple as that. And Rae keeps coming back to me. He says if he hadn't been messed about so much, and the university had kept its promises from the start, the RAE grade would have been better, and we're lucky he's still here at all. If he'd known we were going to welsh on the deal he would have gone back to his old department.

"Try telling that one to an industrial tribunal ... it's *tricky*!

"Anyway," Rod gestured with his open palms turned upward, "Hamish is on his way out now, so I've asked Jake Parr to be head of physics teaching. He wants a replacement member of staff for Hamish, but I've told him, what with the poor recruitment of physics students, my hands are tied." Rod raised them again to make sure, continuing, "He doesn't know the half of it though. I was looking at the department's books with Letticia, earlier. We shall need to let at least three more physicists go – that's *after* Hamish, I mean."

"Who?" Bob asked him.

"That's easy: Donald Smallpiece, Paddy Bowens and Neville Farmer. They're all over fifty-five, and who would miss them, let's face it."

"What about Tarquin Tupper?" asked Bob.

"No. Tarquin refuses to go. He wants his full pension, and he's only fifty-three. The university won't wear the cost of a full enhancement – not for the equivalent of twelve years – to take him up to his full pension at sixty-five. So we're stuck with him. Tommy Wakefield's only fifty-one, but he's useful. We don't want *him* to go. And Jake Parr is fifty-three, the same as Tarquin. All the others, including Charles Rae, are well under forty…he's still only thirty-four, in fact." Rod checked the summary of staff details on his desk, and continued, "It's hard on them, I know. Five staff doing the work of nine. Well, *four*, if you don't count Rae. When Parr comes back about this lot, I'll just tell him to make more use of Charles Rae. That way we'll get round this '100 hours a year teaching' nonsense, and the wedge will be in, thin end first! If he leaves, he leaves! The good news is the Department of LAPS overall is in the *black*. Leisurewear recruitment is *booming*! So, although we won't replace these posts with more *physicists*, we can still make new appointments – hire more Leisurewear staff and recruit even *more* students. We'll be *rolling in it!*"

Rod's hands rose, his arms now fully outstretched, palms facing upwards. There was nothing he liked better than making a good deal. It was in his blood, and he literally rocked in ecstasy at the prospects ahead of him. This was the driven shrewdness that built the Shine Leisurewear Chain. Rod really didn't need too much hassle from EEU just now, as he wanted to concentrate on lengthening the chain. He had inside knowledge about a rival franchise that was going under, no longer able to compete with "Shine". The business had reached a crucial phase, and Rod needed to move carefully. If he put up his money too fast, they might rally; too slow and the business wouldn't be worth touching: property only. He needed a nice, smooth take-over of a viable business, which he could repackage at minimum cost, making himself a fortune, and creating an empire: SHINE. He could do without too many distractions.

Pulling off this scheme was his ticket out of EEU, and he wasn't about to let anyone disrupt the workings of the machine. Someone else could deal with the redundancies, and day-to-day crap, while Rod dealt his talents where they could best serve his own interests. Providence, however, had provided Thomas O'Grady. He, of all men, would run the department uncomplainingly, and attend to the necessary paperwork, while Rod concentrated on his master-plan.

It was a good deal. Better than he could have dreamed of. Not that Rod slept long enough to dream much of late, the machinations of it all draining his nights like a bawling child. Out of the blue, another offer was thrown on the table. Rod needed the money quickly, but didn't have all of it. He could get a loan against some of the existing business, but that would take time. Someone – he wondered who – was offering cash. He was short by about half a million. The bulk they could have tomorrow if necessary, but he needed the rest by Friday.

Why hadn't he thought of it before? An amber light began to shiver in the fugue of his protracted consternation. Could he get away with it, even?

The light hovered on red. But…losing the deal…the deal of his life. It felt almost what he had been born for. His purpose. A promise to his grandfather, before they put him in the ground, to shine forth an empire from Evergreen, where the family had settled, and it would SHINE – the world's biggest leisurewear conglomerate. Worth millions! The highway now glittered a purest green: emeralds above rubies. He could put it back again. After all, it was just a loan. Who would know?

★ ★ ★

"Congratulations, Professor Robinson!" Both men exchanged smiles.

This was truly the proudest day of Rob Robinson's life. After twenty years of loyal service at EEU, promoted through the ranks: lecturer, senior lecturer, principal lecturer, reader (a brief spell as acting head of department), and finally, the pinnacle of *professor*. Everyone was pleased for Rob: he was a popular man, liked equally by his colleagues and by his students.

The vice-chancellor placed his hand warmly on Rob's shoulder, looked into his eyes and announced, "Well done!" then confidentially, so that just he could hear, "Rob, no one deserves this more than you."

Stirling George addressed the assembled audience.

"It is a real pleasure to welcome Professor Rob Robinson, at this, his inaugural lecture, as professor of Statistics at EEU."

Rob's heart glowed. As he delivered the lecture, the audience seemed to absorb each word. It was one of those rare lectures when both the lecturer and the audience are as one, and both revel in the flawless flow of concepts and communication. It was a good lecture, given by a good chap, and everyone felt warmly toward him.

After all, Rob Robinson's research record was excellent – one of the best in the university. He had included a list of over a hundred papers, published in internationally regarded journals of statistics. He was honoured as a visiting professor in the University of Wuperbaden. He currently served as the chair of several important statistical committees. The inclusion of all such honours had made his application for promotion to a "personal Chair" uncontestable, and Stirling George had proudly endorsed the award himself, as vice-chancellor of EEU, rather than leaving the paperwork to Letticia Jolanda, as he usually did.

The university publicity team were instructed to contact the Evergreen Gazette, asking them to carry an article about Rob Robinson, as part of an ongoing effort to promote the local public image of EEU, ever with its eye on "good publicity", to help boost their undergraduate recruitment from the youth of that city. A happy day.

Rob bought a copy from a news stand to take home to his wife. She was proud. Her husband was quite a man: an early night, and one more passionate than either could recall.

The article was also posted on the EEU web page, where it did rather stand out, amid the other features describing the university's bureaucratic structures, donations to the local media and any number of equally academically bereft matters. Now here was a hero. A local man, Evergreen born and bred, and an academic star of the university. But, alas, in this electronic age, the web posting of Rob's credentials was to render his glory ephemeral.

"Allo. Is that Herr Professor Stirling George?

"Ja. Gut.

"I am Professor Helmut Lederbauer, of the University of Wuperbaden.

"I have your website on my computer.

"Ja. There is some confusion in my mind.

"Why say you that a Professor Rob Robinson is here?

"Here, I mean, as visiting professor of Statistics, in Wuperbaden.

"No. He is not. I have consulted with our rector here, who has no knowledge of who is he.

"I am further confused. It says on your website Professor Rob Robinson has published a hundred papers, more than.

"I have checked on the web database under 'statistics' papers. I can find ten articles, just, with 'Robinson, R*' as author.

"This is highly misleading. It is, of course, your business but we want no implications to this man, here. I ask you kindly to remove all mention of our university in Wuperbaden from your website."

Stirling George was ashen: mostly grey, like the pre-wash on the canvas for a portrait painting of a sick man, before the colour is added, but with green shades below the eyes, and sloping furrows, tracing the laughter lines toward the corners of his mouth. But as he replaced the receiver, there was no trace of laughter in his face.

As they subsequently discovered, it was true. Rob Robinson was a fraud. No wonder Wuperbaden had never heard of him, as he had never been there! Then there was his extensive list of publications, in fact the most flagrant piece of academic fabrication in history. He had literally made them all up, taking a genuine statistics journal, then inventing page numbers and volume numbers; and even a title for the "article", preceding the authors' names: R K Robinson along with a liberal sprinkling of his colleagues' names, as co-authors, making them unknowing accessories to his deception.

Nobody had ever checked, and so the fabrication of Rob's house of sand had trickled from year to year into a formidable edifice. This was bad enough, but in the full inquiry Stirling George found himself forced to instigate in order to cover his and all other arses at EEU, worse was to unfold. As it transpired, on his appointment as lecturer in Statistics at Evergreen Polytechnic, *Dr* Robinson did not in fact have a PhD – he had made that up too. Indeed, he had neither an MSc nor a BSc, although he claimed both.

As Stirling George dredged further down the murky records of the Evergreen Municipal Technical College, which later became the Evergreen Polytechnic and then EEU, he found an entry on a list of qualifications awarded: R Robinson, Ordinary National Diploma in Statistics, 1970. But nothing later, anywhere.

"Oh, God! A technician's qualification. The man didn't even have A-levels!"

By the time the news broke in the national press: "Bogus Prof Sacked!"

and "Scandal of EEU Worthless Professor!" Rob Robinson's desk was empty.

And Charles just knew that back at his old university, reading his morning paper in the senior common room, munching a chocolate biscuit, Jasper Totter would be laughing: laughing at EEU, but mostly at him, Charles, for being there.

★ ★ ★

Jasper cooled his forehead against his fists. He had fought the battle since the previous research assessment exercise – fought the Good Fight – but it was all over now. The battle was to keep the Department of Physics open, despite their poor RAE rating, against the vice-chancellor's will to close it down.

The historians whispered in the V-C's ear, "Those physicists...they take anyone... two Es at A-level...whereas in History we can get students with four As...and their research rating...3b...we got a 4 !"

Water on a stone...drip drip...steadily eroding his patience with "the physicists".

"Professor Totter? It's the vice-chancellor. Will you come to my office? I've come to a decision about the future of Physics here."

Jasper's heart bounced in his chest; fists in his pockets.

He went into the Gents to bathe his face, and rubbed cool water over the reddening heat of his neck. He had already had one heart scare. Jasper breathed slowly – as the university stress management counsellor had shown him.

Placing her hands on Jasper's back and chest:

"Now, in and out, Professor.

"Sloooowly.

"Think caaaaalm thoughts.

"Imagine you're by the seaside.

"That's it!

"You're feeling better, I can see!"

He *was* feeling better too. And he was even thinking calmly as he knocked on the door of the vice-chancellor's outer office.

"Yes, please take a seat, Professor. I'll just check the vice-chancellor is ready for you."

★ ★ ★

"Yes. Totter. About Physics. Well, that RAE rating is just an embarrassment – the lowest grade in the entire university. A 3b, eh? No research income from that one, eh?

"I've consulted the Academic Board.

"Oh, it was that meeting you missed last week…

"You didn't know about it?

"Oh well, sorry. It doesn't matter anyway… but you're closed…

"Just needs the official stamp to confirm it. The registrar should be doing that … about now." He looked at his watch.

Jasper's neck reddened.

"But, Vice-Chancellor … don't you see … our low RAE grade is due to years of underinvestment in Physics here.

"Our building is in a desperate state of dilapidation … the rain runs in over the high-voltage power supply, and so we can't even keep our particle accelerator running full-time. The repair bills are astronomical!

"What we need is investment … a new, purpose-designed accelerator … building … a complete overhaul of the accelerator itself … some bright, new, young staff. With this level of support and commitment from the university, we can really place ourselves firmly back on the centre stage of world physics!"

The vice-chancellor liked this idea. As Jasper talked, he viewed him quietly, taking in his every word. Jasper was very convincing. He had contemplated running for politics in his younger days, but decided on physics instead, and then slaked his youthful ambitions by involving himself in university politics, in which he became highly skilled.

The V-C was convinced.

"Very well, Jasper." His hand reached out to clasp the politician's shoulder in a reassuring grip. "The university does not have the necessary resources – I can tell you that without looking at the figures – but against our collateral, we should have no trouble in borrowing the sum of ten million pounds. Physics on the map again? Wonderful! That will rub their noses in it, at our rival universities!"

Duly, the new accelerator building was built. Other departments, particularly History, surveyed its rise upon the skyline with scornful envy. The accelerator itself was fully refitted, and installed in the purpose-designed basement. It now ran for twenty-two hours out of every twenty-four, allowing for the weekly shutdown on Wednesday evening for essential maintenance. They had done well in their recruitment, too, as the recent closure of half the nation's physics departments led to an employer's market, and from that glut, six new lecturers were appointed. All specialists, with PhDs and post-docs from among the world's most prestigious universities – lean and hungry – bellies aching to carve their notches in the annals of the world's leading physics journals. (Such is the naked ambition of post-'70s youth.)

Undergraduate recruitment was also buoyant, due to the plummeting availability of Physics courses in other universities that had closed them. As the next RAE deadline rose upon the horizon of the year, Physics was buzz-ing – the humming of the high-voltage power supply to the accelerator, and the frantic mental and experimental vibrations that would get them a grade 4 at least, maybe even a grade 5! But a critical term had been factored out of the equation during these calculations, namely, the composition of the RAE Assessment Panel for Physics.

The V-C had been right. His investment had rubbed the noses of their rival universities "in it". But now those same noses were poking through the RAE submissions for Physics, and particularly at Jasper Totter's department.

"Mmm. A 3a, I think." The panel were in full accord. Just one notch up from the 3b they were awarded last time: still not high enough to bring in any research money, and to begin paying off the £10 million loan. And it was more than £10 million – the costs of the building had meanwhile escalated, so now the debt was almost double that. Thus £18 million had to be paid back – and the interest on it too – none of which would now be recouped from the Physics Department.

So, Jasper sat with his head held low. Physics were closed, and their building was given up to IT and business studies – subjects that were cheap to teach and had plenty of students. The accelerator was dismantled before being ignominiously sold off for scrap. And the bright young staff? Some with mortgages and families to support, were each given a £5K severance deal, to help support them through their retraining as school teachers; sub-ject-qualified science teachers being in very short supply at the local inner-city comprehensives.

And Jasper, having reached the age of sixty-five, was put out to grass – onto the bowling green, where his mind would wander, retracing the green pathways of happier days.

15

Sandra was a smart girl. Without an O-level, she joined the Evergreen Polytechnic typing pool, and set her eye on the new guy, Dr Patrick Walker. An Evergreen girl, she was going places her family never had, and shrewd enough to look for help in getting there. A tall imposing figure, Patrick Walker was appointed lecturer in Human Biophysics, to head up a new, sexy-sounding course, unique in the country, that would put the poly on the map. There was talk they would become a university one day soon, and Peter's one paper, published in the world's most prestigious scientific journal, it was argued, must surely secure him research funding too, although it never did. At thirty-five, he was in any case pushing it to get a university lectureship, but the poly had a more foggy image of an ideal candidate for one of their lectureships. More sensibly, they just wanted to hire someone of good potential, regardless of their age or pedigree.

Not that anyone could criticise that either, as Patrick had got a first from Oxford, stayed on there for his DPhil, and then done a post-doc in Switzerland at the ETH Zurich. But his timing was out, being born in 1947. On finishing a second post-doc in 1977 back at Oxford, only a blank horizon faced him, as all the university posts were filled by appointees from the '60s boom, most of whom were only in their mid-forties, and unlikely to go for another twenty years. He managed instead to secure a five-year research fellowship from the Royal Society, or rather his post-doctoral mentor had, being a fellow of the society itself: an FRS. Patrick regarded this as a holding position, but once again, as he approached the end of this temporary contract, there was not so much as the word on the grapevine of a permanent position anywhere, and certainly nothing advertised. Then the poly had cast its net, and caught him in it; the biggest fish they could have wished for. It was not exactly what Patrick wanted, but it was, he thought, a bolthole for a year or two. Then the axe swung with a vengeance – a single deliberation by a Bodicean prime minister of the moment. Cuts! Cuts! Cuts! And suddenly there was nowhere else for him to go, even had his age allowed it. At thirty-six he recognised the end of a one-way street: he was stuck at the poly.

Sandra was to provide the perfect stimulus to coax him from the dejection which enveloped him. When he went into the typing pool, she caught his eye in a familiar way. He felt flattered by her, and that warmed his day. She was only eighteen, "Half my age", he mused. He wondered what she would be like, and found his mind increasingly simulating the various prospects, none of which seemed at all disagreeable. He shifted in his seat.

Did she have a boyfriend, he wondered, and how could he find out without showing his cards prematurely?

They began to strike up short exchanges of words over the various handwritten pages Patrick submitted into the pool for typing. Sandra watched the door from the corner of her eye, sensing the vibrations of prey in her peripheral vision. She recognised the sound of his footsteps, saw the door handle move, then snapped into an inviting smile, drawing him into the scent of her nectar, as alluring as a Venus flytrap.

"Hi, Sandra." His voice betrayed hesitancy.

"Hello, Patrick. What can I do for *you*?" she looked at him knowingly, almost like a "Carry On" film character; teasing him gently.

"I think I saw you walking to work this morning, but you were too far ahead of me to call out to you. In any case, I would have looked a bit of a fool, if you'd been someone else." His eyes were warm, as though he'd been plugged into her; a juice flowing into him and urging him closer.

"Maybe. Where were you?" She was genuinely curious.

"It was about halfway up St James Street, by the Nat West Bank. The car's at the garage, so I walked in today."

"Yeah. I walk in that way from the bus stop."

"Perhaps I could give you a lift, tomorrow. I'm collecting the car later, so I should be driving in to work at about the same time tomorrow morning."

"Yeah. Thanks very much. That'd be nice."

This was perfect. Sandra's gaze saw him walk toward the door, then turn and smile before leaving the room.

The script then ran its usual course. The gladly accepted drink became dinner. Since he was divorced and now lived alone, there was no reason not to take her home with him. She accepted that invitation too, warm cups growing cold on the coffee table, undressing in front of a man for the first time. His mouth was dry. Hers was not.

"Come on, Patrick…"

He looked, and understood immediately but unexpectedly, a true first time. He said nothing, but felt the unknown tenderness of this special experience. He kissed her with a unique gentleness, as though washing all past pain from himself in her purity. A true bud, which he must not violate, but draw it open preciously, into the light.

It had been a while for him too. Not since well before the suitcase in the hall, and the door slammed with no backward glance of regret. As he pressed into her, he could feel a small resistance, which yielded into urgent invitation; the first acts of an unfolding play. She had allowed him possession of her most valuable piece of merchandise, saved for the highest buyer (*caveat emptor*). Sandra saw the matter as a simple act of trade, and she expected a return in kind. Patrick was more than willing to reward her. It was a renewing sensation to enfold her nakedness in a shadowy, surreal dawn; a combination of unsurpassed wonder and pride.

★ ★ ★

"Pat? Will you come up to my office?" It was Norman Rayle, head of the Department of Biological Sciences.

"I want to discuss your future here."

This sounded promising. The lectureship in Evolutionary Biophysics had been Norman's idea, and Patrick was his star player. He studied the door: "Professor Norman Rayle, HOD".

"Come in, Pat."

Patrick sat down purposefully, in the anticipation of some words to his advantage. He looked steadily across the polished, neatly piled desk at an older face, which levelled with his.

"Now, Pat," Norman began. "I've just been nominated as the next dean of Technology."

This didn't seem particularly relevant to Patrick, but he listened attentively.

"This means, of course, that the head of department position will become available."

Now Patrick was interested, intensely so, as Norman added the line "I want you to get it."

He was no fool. As dean of the faculty he would command a lot of power, and in order to wield it, having a head of department in his pocket would be very useful. If Patrick owed him big-time, the payback would be one of unfaltering obedience. In short, he would back him up no matter what was at stake, and at the stake was the Department of Applied Physics, awaiting the final torch.

"There is one snag, however," Norman continued, "and that is your age. You're only thirty-six, which most people would consider too young to be a department head. We need to strengthen your portfolio somewhat, to give you some seniority. If you were to become a professor..."

Patrick stared in disbelief, having been steeped in the traditions of the older universities.

"A professor?!" He looked at Norman to check the authenticity of his words.

"But I've only published one paper." Patrick caught his breath.

"Yes, but it is in *Nature*..." Norman reassured him, "and in any case, that doesn't matter *here*. We have professors on the books with much less than that. We can run the two applications together: you get a professorship because you are going to be a head of department, and the latter on the grounds you are going to become a professor."

"But don't I need three external referees?" Patrick remained unconvinced.

"Well, the rules are open to interpretation," Norman responded. "The exact wording states that '*the opinion of three external referees **may** be sought as to the suitability of a candidate for promotion to a professorship*'. It is not, therefore, a *mandatory* requirement, but the actual procedure adopted rests with the discretion of the committee's chair, which happens to be me!"

As Norman's hearty laughter echoed around the room, and on down the corridor, Patrick knew it was in the bag.

★　★　★

Sandra could hardly believe it. Here was her meal ticket out of the typing pool, and so soon at that. On the recommendation of Professor Patrick Walker, head of the Department of Biological Sciences, as it now read on his door, Sandra was appointed assistant to the departmental administrative manager. This was her first limb on the winding bureaucratic ladder of the polytechnic, and a lucky one too. Twelve months later, Norman Rayle suffered a fatal heart attack, leaving the way open for Patrick Walker to become dean of the Faculty of Technology. And so, when the newly merged

Department of Leisurewear and Applied Physical Sciences (LAPS) emerged, Sandra was appointed as its departmental administrative manager, under the direction of Rod Shine, its head, but working most closely with Thomas O'Grady, the deputy head.

★ ★ ★

"Sandra, can you bring me the department's balance sheets – up to date, please. There seems to be a discrepancy."

Thomas O'Grady, a neat humourless man with an eye for detail, frowned and polished his steel-rimmed spectacles. Having replaced them, he began to work on down the list of accounts one more time. He placed the spectacles on top of his desk, and massaged his forehead thoughtfully. There was no doubt. As far as he could make out, the balance was down by nearly half a million pounds. His figures were correct up to the end of the previous week, so something, someone, must have caused – authorised – some hefty outgoings. But, other than himself, only Rod Shine had that authority of signature, and of course the dean, Patrick Walker, who allocated the money to them in the first place. There must be a simple explanation, he pondered. Perhaps it was just another of their clerical errors ... bloody Financial Services, what a shower they were! You could never trust them. They had probably messed up the computer record. Thomas shook his head in dismay at the thought.

A soft but insistent knock heralded Sandra, who arrived with a neat financial summary, highlighted in yellow toward the bottom of the sheet.

"Here it is, Professor O'Grady. I got Financial Services to check the figures, so they *are* right."

"Please, sit down." Thomas reached over to the print of evidence, which they both scrutinised intently. There was no error, either in Thomas' own figures, or his suspicions that something was amiss. There were several payments made to the Shine Leisurewear Chain, and authorised by Rod Shine's own hand, under the heading of "sundry services", to the sum of four hundred and seventy-three thousand, five hundred and sixty-seven pounds, forty-three pence, as Thomas read from the display, tapping the running total of numbers into his desktop calculator. This was most embarrassing.

A peculiar sense of intimacy drifted over them, brought from the dark matter that only they knew. Then Thomas broke the spell. "I can't believe it. This is embezzlement! How did he think he could get away with it?!"

The picture was clear but not rosy, but what should they do about it? Confronting Rod did not seem to be an appropriate step. He was the head of department, after all.

"I'm only the deputy head," Thomas emphasised the point, but Sandra gave him a foxy look.

"Well, you are *now*," she lifted the edge of her plan. "But they'll have to get rid of Rod after this, won't they? And who would be his obvious successor?"

A glow began to revive in the black embers of Thomas' ambitions. He hadn't thought he would get this far, with his lack of research credibility, but nonetheless, he'd got himself a professorship and the deputy head position. So, why not go for it? Head of department! Sandra's breath fanned softly a small flame. "It's *you*, isn't it?!" she whispered.

The two smiled in a tacit closure of this most private of pacts.

"I'll go to the dean," Thomas declared, "and he can take the matter to the vice-chancellor." He had made the decision, and she motioned in assent of it.

The issue proved unsurprisingly messy. Patrick Walker spoke tersely, "Thank you, Thomas, leave it with me."

★　★　★

"Vice-Chancellor. I need to speak to you on a matter of extreme delicacy."

Stirling George knew that whatever Patrick had to say would be extremely indelicate, but decided to approach it head-on.

"Come in, Pat. Take a seat. Right, what's the problem?"

"It's probably simplest if I show you the figures," and so saying, he placed the sheet which Thomas O'Grady had given him, with its yellow high-lighted columns, between the two of them, moving to a chair next to the vice-chancellor.

"As you can see, this is the current statement of accounts from LAPS. There are several payments made out to the Shine Leisurewear Chain."

"Rod Shine's business, you mean?!" Stirling sounded edgy.

"Yes."

"And presumably it's not above board, then."

"No, it's completely unauthorised, although it was authorised by Rod himself. This is definitely his signature." He pointed accusingly at it.

"We need to keep a lid on the whole business," Stirling spoke firmly. "We don't want even *more* bad publicity!"

Patrick nodded, asking him, "What do you think our best move would be?"

"Have you spoken to Rod at all, yet?" Stirling asked him.

"He's not been in for a few days. I tried to phone him at home, but he's away on business, according to his wife."

"Mmm. Well, we need to talk to him, just as soon as we can. I take it you emphasised that to her?"

"Yes, I asked her to pass on the message to get back to me ASAP, without causing her alarm. She probably knows nothing about it."

"Who knows, then? You, me, O'Grady. Is that it?"

"Yes, only the three of us."

"OK. If we can get Rod to pay back the money, that will balance the books again. But we will have to...um...move him on somehow. A sideways move to somewhere quiet? He can't carry on working here as head of a department. I shall simply get the money back from him and ask for his resignation. We won't press charges. It would be bound to get into the papers and that would be too embarrassing."

Patrick nodded emphatically.

"Yes, what with Rob Robinson and those bloody examination paper fiascos, we don't want more bad press, otherwise nobody will want to come here any more, students or staff!"

Stirling gave him a hard stare, adding, "I vote we leave it till tomorrow. Hopefully we can have a meeting with Rod, or at least speak to him on the phone, and let him know what we propose to do with him. But stressing that we will do it discreetly."

★   ★   ★

"What was that?!"

"Gazette! Gazette! Read all about it! EEU professor embezzles half a million from the university! Extra! Extra!"

They opened the window and both leant out, just to make absolutely sure of what they were hearing.

"Fuck!"

It was all out in the open. They never found out who had done it. Who the mole was remained a mystery all along the whispering corridors of EEU. A loose-tongued secretary, maybe? A disgruntled porter? Someone going through the waste paper bins from Financial Services? That was the worst of it. Some reporter at the Evergreen Gazette had hold of hard evidence, so they couldn't deny it. And to save face, they had to press charges.

★ ★ ★

"Yes, this is Stirling George, the vice-chancellor of Evergreen Epstein University. Could you send over a couple of officers to arrest Professor Rod Shine. We have him in his office waiting for you."

Poor Rod: he had slipped in with a cheque for the full amount. He *was* going to pay it back. It really *was* just a loan that he had in mind. But the beans were well and truly spilled, and there was no putting them back in the tin. Tomato sauce everywhere!

It was indeed messy. Rod got his sideways move: eight years in Evergreen jail – one building in the city, at least, that did not yet have the sign of EEU above its main entrance.

Thus Thomas O'Grady became head of the Department of LAPS, but Sandra had higher aims for him, and more for herself.

16

Tarquin's eyes blistered with expectation. There it was, the envelope stamped: Office of the Assistant-Vice Chancellor. He was sure, this time it would be … *Professor* Tarquin Tupper. His mind exalted. He was as good as all the rest of them. As good as Charles Rae. He'd show him! Bloody upstart. Appointed to a professorship at thirty-two – a bloody kid! Tarquin had just over thirty years on that, so as far as he was concerned it was long overdue. His hands weren't quite as steady as when he was younger, and he was tense with anticipation as he reached out to seize *that* envelope – to take what was finally *his*. He lifted it from the pigeonhole, and nested it in the inside pocket of his sports blazer. He could open it later, alone in his office, savouring the words it contained:

> *Dear Tarquin… Very many congratulations…the university takes great pleasure in your promotion as professor in Industrial Physics…*

But now he had a lecture to give. He was unusually distracted in its delivery, occasionally checking in his pocket that the envelope was still there, which of course it was. He cut the lecture a few minutes short.

"I'll stop there today, as I have something urgent to attend to."

The students didn't mind, and went off for an early break, while Tarquin strode impatiently toward his office. But as he approached it, a group of students were waiting for him.

"Dr Tupper?" one of them began.

"I'm sorry," Tarquin halted him, "but you'll have to come back later. I have some urgent business to attend to."

Tarquin closed his office door. Then he locked it. He took off his blazer, glancing at the golf club insignia on the breast pocket, and, perspiring a little, placed the loop of its collar over the hook behind the door. He reached once again into the inside pocket, withdrawing the envelope, and walked the two paces to his desk, sat down, then inserted the paperknife under the adhesive fold, tearing the paper through with a measured and constant pressure. He extracted the letter, unfolded it, and began to read:

> *Dear Tarquin,*
>
> *Your application for promotion as Professor of Industrial Physics was reviewed by the University Committee for the Conferment of Readerships and Professorships.*

His eyes almost scorched the paper. This was it!

> *I regret to inform you that once again, your application has been unsuccessful. If you wish further feedback regarding this decision, please do not hesitate to contact me.*
>
> *In any event, the university's current regulations do not entitle you to make another such application for another three years.*
>
> *Yours sincerely,*
>
> *Professor Letticia Jolanda*
>
> *(Assistant Vice-Chancellor)*

His pretty bubble had yet again been knocked against the unflattering spines of the external reviewers: burst and deflated, Tarquin stared impotently at "unsuccessful". Then at "once again". Then at "three years". Three years?! He'd be retired by then, and never been made a professor. He was desperate, but his natural opportunism and cunning sustained him. He reached for the phone.

"Letticia?"

"Yeeees ..." came that unique Sloane-tone.

"It's Tarquin ... Tarquin Tupper."

"Ahhh, Tarquin. And what can I do for you, sweetie?"

"Well! Ah'm outraged! Absolutely Outraged, ah say!"

"Calm down, Tarquin. Whatever's the matter?"

"This is twenty-three times ah've been turned down for a professorship, and ah'm just about sick of it!"

"Oh, I see."

"Why, Letticia? Why? It's like some kind of conspiracy! There's bloody Charles Rae. These youngsters, getting Chairs, and me, ah've been 'ere thirty-five years and – nothing!"

"Well, Tarquin, I promised you some feedback, didn't I? So, just give me a minute and I'll get your file…"

By the time Letticia lifted the handset again, Tarquin had recomposed himself.

"I see the problem. All three of the reviewers called attention to your lack of any published work."

"Published work?! It's all very well for people like Charles Rae, with his international reputation, all his *ree*-search grants, *ree*-search assistants, collaborators in world-class *ree*-search groups – 'e's always bloody well off abroad somewhere! – to write papers. It's easy! But me, no one knows who I am! Ah've never had a *ree*-search grant! Not one! Never! Ah've never 'ad any *ree*-search assistants. Never! Ah'm 'ere doing all t' teaching, so 'ow am ah supposed to produce any publications? Tell me that, eh!"

"Oh, Tarquin, there must be something? Some little thing, surely?"

"Well, there are my course notes for the Remote Learning University. And ah 'ave *edited* a couple of textbooks."

"Tarquin, don't you see, there may be a solution…

"The university is revising its policies on professorial promotions. As you know, we used to insist on *some* level of research attainment (a *few* journal publications anyway), which is where you have always fallen down, but we now feel that those who are providing *other* roles, more in keeping with our core business strategies – teaching methods, academic leadership and entrepreneurship – should also be eligible for a professorship."

"But what could ah be a professor of, Letticia?" Tarquin asked in a sense of real awe, his pretty bubble beginning to reinflate.

"Well, what would you *like* to be a professor of?"

"Ah don't know. What did you say the options were, other than *ree*-search?"

"It's really quite flexible, Tarquin. Academic leadership means being head of department, or some other senior administrative role."

"That rules me out, then."

"Entrepreneurship, perhaps? Income generation of some kind?"

"No, sorry. As ah told you, ah've never 'ad a grant."

"That leaves teaching methods, then."

"Well, ah've done a lot of teaching in the last thirty-five years; then there's my work as a tutor and consultant for the Remote Learning University; and as ah say, ah 'ave edited a couple of textbooks; in Industrial Physics though, not Physics Education."

"Now, Tarquin, don't split hairs. I'm sure, if we choose the right title, we can put a nice little portfolio together, which will impress the committee next time around.

"Between you and me, the committee is in quite a shambles at the moment," she giggled coquettishly. "I know. Why don't we make you professor of Physical Education? Then we can also mention your rescue of that poor poodle from the golf club pavilion when it caught fire, and of course, those dramatic improvements to your golf handicap, mentioned in the Evergreen Gazette last week, no less. Everybody's talking about it! My! How you must practise!

"The new regulations also mean that there is no need to wait three years to make your next application – now you can apply as often as you like. And we've also decided to dispense with that anachronistic and time-wasting practice of sending professorial applications to external reviewers. We feel we can make up our own minds on issues of academic quality."

Actually, Letticia was only too glad to give him his professorship and not have to listen to any more of the weeks of whining, every time they turned him down.

"Thank God!" she thought. "He'll retire in two years, and then we'll finally be shot of the old whinger!"

★ ★ ★

"Phone this number – URGENT!"

As he read the message, a seed of disquiet began to sow in Charles Rae's mind. That was all there was. He turned the paper over, but the counter-side was blank. It wasn't clear even who had placed the note in his pigeonhole. He recognised the city dialing code, but couldn't think of anyone there who might want to contact him – and URGENT(ly) at that.

"Hello. Yes, I've just received a message to phone this number."

"Ah, yes, *sir*. Can I just confirm a few details?" The way he said *sir*, did not imply a sense of respect: rather the intonations of a nightclub doorman emerging from a customer care refresher seminar. Unsettlingly, there was still no clue as to who it was on the other end of the phone.

"Your name, *sir*?"

"Charles Rae."

"And your address?"

"89 Atlantic Quay, Evergreen."

"And your occupation?"

"Hang on, look. Who am I speaking to, exactly?" Charles was finding this one-way flow of information irritating, and suspicious too. Something was amiss.

"We are the Arkthwaite Debt Recovery Service."

"What?! I don't owe anybody any money!"

"Yes, *sir*. That's what you all say."

"But I don't! Who says I owe them anything?!"

"I'll just check your file, *sir*."

He was in that twilight zone again, but in the brief silence that followed, the dawn of an answer insinuated itself in Charles' brain. "Oh, God. There is only one place it could be!" he murmured involuntarily to himself. "But surely not. No. Not even they..."

"Yes, *sir*. According to our records, you owe one hundred and forty-two pounds and thirty-two pence to Evergreen Epstein University. They've put your case into our hands, and we've started recovery proceedings against you."

"What?! But I'm a fucking professor at Evergreen Epstein University! Anyway, I don't owe them any money!" Charles was incredulous.

"It says here that the person who has named you is Millicent Mellon," the bailiff offered helpfully, beginning to feel in his water that this was not a normal case.

"Milly Mellon? She runs the library. I'll bet this is over a couple of library books I had stolen from my office recently. I'll phone her to get this mess sorted out!"

According to her voice mail, Milly was out of the office; out of the university, in fact. The cuts to the library budget had provided a testing time for her, and tested her to destruction. As cost centre manager, Milly had been dealt a 50 per cent cut in her budget. The university had to recover millions from the failed Business School venture, in which an eminent US academic, Sharleen La'Coy, had run up a bill of purchase that would never be recovered. Her extravagant promises had failed the test of time, and she went back West again, leaving an aftermath of financial calamity. A burden which could only be borne by cutting all "support provisions" of the university, its academic departments having been cut to the bone already.

There was truly no slack left in the system, which, moreover, was absurdly overdrawn, and more frequently beyond the limit of mechanical failure. The vice-chancellor had warned, "Take my word for it. There are probably three or four universities that will go out of business. We just have to make sure that EEU isn't one of them! What we need is to recruit more customers from the Evergreen inner-city area. We need to attract more mature customers. We should target those who have never considered going to university before. This is our corporate mission. We are the people's university; a noble cause, going back to our true roots as the Evergreen Mechanics Institute of 1823!"

An evangelical light shone from his eyes. Those eyes, it was often said, that "shone with insincerity".

But in that pertinent context of "resource management", Stirling George was spot on the ball, and fully accurate in his telling of the game, and how its play would be contrived. Consequently, Milly Mellon had been forced to take a large pair of pink paper scissors, with rounded ends, to her department. Most of the journals were cut, and a blockade was emplaced on the purchase of any new library books "for the foreseeable future". Despite these draconian steps, she realised that staff cuts would be necessary, and it was making these that had sent her over the edge. Whole families living on a single wage, with mortgages to honour; repossessions and misery all around. She felt she had blood on her hands and, being highly-strung at best, her nerves had finally fractured. In a negligent moment of delusion, Milly sent forward the name "Charles Rae" to the Arkthwaite Debt Recovery Service, momentarily unaware that he was actually the professor of General Physics, and not a miscreant student who had scampered off with his library books, hoping to wriggle out of a hefty fine for not returning them on time.

In the event of Milly's indisposition it was her assistant, Dora Flagg, who bore the brunt of responsibility for the Learning Resources Centre, and when Charles, having eventually discovered by a circuitous chain of phone calls that Milly was no longer in charge, tried to phone Dora instead, he literally shook with anger. Fortunately for both of them, Dora was on leave that afternoon, so Charles' message was more measured than it might otherwise have been *viva voce* and remained as a clipped communication of the relevant facts and events, recorded in her voice mail box, though the anger in his voice passed undisguised.

"This is Professor Rae. Apparently Millicent Mellon has put a firm of debt collectors onto me over two library books I had stolen. This is absolutely outrageous! Sort this out immediately, and get back to me!"

When he returned to his flat that evening, another surprise lay waiting for him. It was a letter from the Arkthwaite Debt Recovery Service. Posted second class, the letter had taken five days to arrive, which was particularly alarming given its contents, and the caveat that "If we do not receive pay-ment in full within five days of the above date, our operatives will make a personal visit to your address, to recover either the full monies owed, directly, or to claim goods to their equivalent value".

Put simply, if Charles didn't cough up the £142.32, the Arkthwaite Debt Recovery Service would send the boys round to sort him out. And it was all down to that mad cow Milly Mellon, over two bloody library books at that! He'd sent her an email too, telling her that the books had been stolen, and she replied that it was a shame...hoped that nothing else had been stolen..." and that "he needn't worry further about the matter..." which seemed fine. Now this. Presumably she hadn't remembered to deactivate the debt recov-ery mechanism before the yellow van had come for her.

"Five days of the above date" was in fact today, Charles observed, so the matter really did need to be resolved tomorrow at the latest. He didn't par-ticularly want the hassle of dealing with debt collectors. Nasty buggers, some of them, so he had heard. Especially the ones in Evergreen. Not adverse to dealing some violence. Your word against theirs. In any case, the whole thing was a preposterous misunderstanding. It was always possible, he mused, that they might try him tonight, if they were very keen, and he looked furtively, sidelong through the third floor window, shoulder to the wall, up and down the street, but could see nothing. It was just another quiet, solitary night in Evergreen.

His dreams had become peculiar, and increasingly recurrent, he noted. In one of them was a small ginger cat, a tom presumably, as ginger females are rare, being chased by a large and fierce dog. The cat would run for all it was worth, leaping up and over fences, in and out of different gardens, but the dog – the breed of which he couldn't make out, just its massive build – was always there. The cat could never quite escape its unrelenting pur-suit, as the dog closed in, like some paranormally impelled hound of the Baskervilles. But before the cat could come to harm, Charles would always awaken. Suddenly, and trembling beneath a clammy dew of perspiration, he would be awake, finding his heart sucked into a mouth drained of fluid. This happened any number of times throughout the night. Then he would drift off again, only to be confronted by the same scene playing out like some horrific loop-video, and then he would be awake once more.

When the dawn began to rise upon the curtainless window, Charles would feel relieved. He could resist the advances of the rerunning *Alptraum*, and try to get on with the day. As he lay among the luminescent streamers of the early morning, Charles pondered over the origins of his dreams. His ambition had been consuming. That was one dream. He *would* be a professor in his early thirties; thirty-three at the latest, and he had made it at thirty-two. Sadly, it had happened at EEU, and the rest truly was history: in achieving it he had destroyed his career. He was finished as a research scientist; now just a glorified technical college teacher, he inferred ruefully. His blood had burned for an acceptance denied him in his youth. Ambitions always have a root cause toward which the ambitious soul looks hopefully to grant an approval. He wasn't *really* a professor, any more than Tarquin Tupper was; it had all become a sham, and the unhealed vacuum which haunted him since his teenage years was opened again, as a hollow ulcer within him. His career had been a displacement from that sense. He *was* worth something. He *was* good at something, and they had no right to treat him like a leper. This was the anger that drove his will to succeed.

Then there was his "dog–cat" dream. What was that all about? Charles concluded that the frightened ginger cat probably represented himself; although it was small and perhaps not fully developed. Was this a metaphor? If it was, he didn't like it much, whether it referred to either his past or present circumstances. But if he was the cat, who was the dog? Who was the oppressor he was unable to flee? The dream had manifested itself only recently, and so it must pertain to present events, he surmised, not his past. He was feeling rather dogged down by his predicament, and hounded, seemingly by everyone he knew, and even more disconcertingly, by some he didn't: the Arkthwaite Debt Recovery Service. He was also dog-tired, and the steaming pile of dog shit that was his life, grew deeper by the day.

★ ★ ★

By a quarter to eight, his usual time, Charles was seated at his desk, contemplating the day's events. He had to supervise a laboratory class, which started at 9.00 and went on until 1.00. However, he was also timetabled to give a lecture at 10.00 and another one at 12.00.

"Mmm. Tricky," he mumbled thoughtfully.

It was always like this, these days. Perhaps he could get Tommy Wakefield to cover the lab for those hours? Then again, Tommy's teaching load was even worse than his! It was like a bloody school, not a university! Charles mused over what had become a typical day for Tommy, what he called "a six-lecture day". Tommy would arrive early, and then spend the next hour working at his computer, writing out lecture notes, while chain-smoking Marlboros, and getting through half a gallon of coffee. By the time he had finished, it would be 9.00: time for the first lecture, followed immediately by one at 10.00, which finished at 10.50, allowing him to stumble back to his office, put the coffee on again, and light up, collapsing in the chair, eyes closed, seeming to draw in half the cigarette in one grateful inspiration. More coffee. Another fag. Same again. 11.10 lecture. 12.00 lecture. Finish at 12.50. Repeat coffee and fags. 1.00 practical class; which finishes at 5.00, but which he has to leave at 2.00 and then again at 4.00 to give two more lectures. "What was the name of the carthorse in *Animal Farm*?" thought Charles. "Boxer, wasn't it?" Worked to death, then off to the knacker's yard.

"You know, my next-door-neighbour's just taken early retirement. Yes, he delivers bread now: out at 6.30, then back by 9.00," Tommy muttered wistfully, staring blankly into space, then adding, "I've been reading *The Wind in the Willows*. It's my favourite book. I've read it lots of times. I don't understand this obsession with reality TV. I've got a pretty good idea what real life is like, and I don't need reminding of it."

Tommy and Charles had become firm friends, in the way victims of oppression often do. This is so, unless the means of oppression becomes so severe that they begin to fight one another like rats in a sack, unable to reach the oppressor and bite him instead.

In that particular field of sniper fire, Tommy was Charles' ally, and who watched his back, as there were any number lying in wait for a clear shot. It was the culture of envy; in the traditions of EEU, as far back as Tommy could remember from the days of the polytechnic, which he had joined twenty-five years earlier.

"Yes, it was just a bit of nostalgia," Tommy remarked wryly. "It's always been bad here. There's never been any real research policy. Most of them are 'anti' research. You just give them an inferiority complex. That's the trouble."

Charles and Tommy would brew up coffee first thing in the morning, as they both arrived before eight.

"Then why the hell was I ever appointed if I'm not wanted here?" was the question Charles kept coming back to, certainly in his own head, if he didn't ask it in Tommy's presence, knowing the idea was down to him and Hamish Humble, and not wanting to hurt a friend's feelings.

"I never thought it were going to turn out like this. It were a mistake." Tommy answered that tacit question, flatly, staring at his computer, and shaking his head reproachfully. "A bloody mistake."

These morning meetings were in part group therapy sessions, in that they reinforced in Charles' mind his belief that he was not mad. That, surely, it couldn't only be he who thought that the Department of Leisurewear and Applied Physical Sciences was a university science department in the twilight zone, if it was indeed a university science department at all. It was like no department Charles had worked in before or even heard of anywhere in the western world. But EEU had unfailingly surprised him in all her winsome ways. She was a capricious mistress, and unique. Not that Tommy's reassurance he was sane raised his morale much; less still the daily caveats that he should "watch X, Y or Z", or that "A, B or C" had been looking for him. Usually they were the same people: "T, B, O'G".

"Have you seen this?!"

Tommy turned ashen, then white.

"Look!"

Charles looked at the screen, clearly an email message:

To: ALL STAFF
From: Professor Thomas O'Grady.

It gives me great pleasure to announce that the University Committee for the Conferment of Readerships and Professorships has inaugurated Tarquin Tupper, reader in Industrial Physics, as professor of Physical Education. I'm sure we would all like to congratulate him on this outstanding achievement.

WELL DONE, TARQUIN. RICHLY DESERVED!

17

Dear Professor Rae,

Thank you so much for your message. Yes, we could certainly consider an application from you for our vacant Chair in Biological Physics. We are interpreting the remit of this post liberally, and so your experience could definitely meet our requirements. You have a most impressive number of publications – all in international journals at that! These are exactly the kind of credentials we are looking for in our efforts to improve our rating in the next RAE. We are currently at 3a, and wish to elevate that to a grade 4. Your publication and career profile, along with your successful record of winning research funding, might well swing the higher grade for us. Please telephone me to discuss further details.

I look forward to receiving a formal application from you shortly.

Yours sincerely,
Professor Angela Leyton-Borden
(Head. Department of Biological Sciences, University of Effington)

It felt as though a dark sky had suddenly separated on a stormy summer's day, and the sun, forgotten above the glum shadows, had pierced the world again, pouring living fuel into its heart.

"This is it!" thought Charles. "I'm finally out of the nightmare!"

He was glad that he'd emailed his CV to Professor Leyton-Borden. The position did seem a little remote from his field of experience, but a desperation had started to seize him. If she was happy to appoint him, he was sure he could do a good job for her. And anyway, *anything*, almost anything at all would do, just to get himself out of EEU. To escape its oppressiveness and dispiriting quality that seemed to emanate from the walls of the place –

a living, seething fog through which the light of lucid vision could not pass. So, Charles applied, the result of which was revealed duly by one fateful click of a mouse:

> *Dear Professor Rae,*
>
> *I am delighted to inform you that your name has been included among those candidates shortlisted for our currently vacant Chair in Biological Physics. There are three candidates: yourself, one internal, and one external...*

Mmmm. The infamous "internal candidate"! Charles cast his mind back, or rather its memories still haunted him. He remembered only too well when he was younger – looking for that first lectureship – there would always be "the internal candidate". Either internal to the institution or internal to the Establishment. This was what he had always found mounted against him: the snow-capped edifice of the Establishment, whose apex withdrew the further he climbed. Not being its spawn, he could never swim naturally along its flows – no salmon-ladder of connections to help him – and was swept away by it. Ever an outsider. And he had offended against the great and the good. How could they uphold their sense of divine right, if one whom they had not chosen had published more than them?

The knives were out for him, and some of them stuck out of the body of his grant applications, job applications and some putative publications of research results, like lethal weapons from the back of a murdered corpse. Often, the internal candidate would have a tenth the number of publications Charles did but, "Well, we know him" (usually male, in fact); "He's one of us,"; "He's working in the right field"; which meant they, or their friends, could manipulate the grant-awarding bodies through either the cooperation or fear of their peers, in that all-essential process of "peer review". And so, the internal candidate was guaranteed research funding, while Charles would be denied it. He would have to seek another trough. Such is the impartial search for truth which is modern science. This maintains a *status quo* by snuffing out any truly original talent which the Establishment has not first endorsed. It is an environmentally pristine process – the ultimate in recycling. No fuss, no mess; just put the dog to sleep.

But perhaps his fortunes were about to jackpot. Biological Physics. He had moved away from the areas of "pure science" where the salad days of his research career had grown. He could definitely describe himself as an "applied scientist" now: he had migrated into such fields as could be pre-fixed by the terms "biological", "medical", "environmental", even, as would secure him the considerable research income he had earned since then. He'd learned to play the game that outsiders have to. And this, along with his lengthy list of publications, gave him an appearance of paper appeal. They could do none other but to shortlist him, or Human Resources would ask them "Why not?"

★ ★ ★

He emailed his wife. She was delighted.

"We can finally be together again" and Charles was happy at the thought.

She clicked onto the computer: "house prices effington". Up they came.

"Not bad at all. We can get a four-bedroom detached house in Effington for the price of our terraced house here," she returned his mail.

In a moment, all the tension had gone. It was only a matter of perhaps a few months and they would be settled once more; and together. Not this weekly haul back and forth to Evergreen. They could get their life back on course; and a better life too! These were the thoughts both shared, despite their physical separateness. And they shared them warmly that weekend, in the terraced house whose space they used to share together, before Charles' ambition had got the better of him, to become *Professor* Rae.

Then Charles' mind began to focus on the interview. It was only a week away. "What kind of questions will they ask me?" he wondered aloud. He remembered the interview he'd had at EEU. Actually, the questions he'd been asked then were very sensible, but that was just the start of their false pretences. Funny, no one, especially its head, Hamish Humble, had men-tioned the Department of Applied Physics was actually bankrupt when they were offering him a professorship in it. Or indeed, that EEU professorships are worthless, by the example of the likes of "Professor Tarquin Tupper", with no published work in the subject they are supposed to be professor of! Yes, he'd been had, but the questions? They were about research funding, what grants he had or could bring with him, and what equipment he needed or could provide, what research he wanted to do and how that would fit in with the research already going on in the department; then finally the agreement that in order to build up research and improve the RAE rating, which was grade 1 at the time, the lowest possible, he would do "not more than a hundred hours teaching a year".

Tommy Wakefield was in full agreement. "It is a research professorship, after all," he stressed.

Reluctantly, Tarquin Tupper had nodded an assent, and Hamish Humble seemed surprised but accordant.

"Och, I suppose so!"

Nonetheless, in the past year, Charles had done nearer three hundred hours, while the total looked set to grow.

"Anyway, it will soon all be over," he sighed aloud, feeling triumphant and vindicated. He expected a similar rota of questions about research, research funding and other matters at Effington, so he prepared himself mentally to answer them as convincingly as possible, that he was their man.

★　★　★

The hotel was very pleasant. Originally a large family home, it had been converted for its present purpose, with four guest rooms on the first floor. As only Charles was staying there on that particular night, the landlady put him in the main room, with its four-poster bed, mirrors, sherry decanter and rain-diffracted view over the formerly industrial town of Effington, the wealth of whose industrialists had emplaced the foundations of its university. As he surveyed the now and contemplated the morrow, Charles thought, "We can stay here when we are looking to buy a house. She'd like that."

Effington University was only ten minutes away on foot, and the day was dry, which Charles felt was a good omen; a sense he found further warmed by the September sunshine, as he stepped into its beam. He was aware of another sense too – women! There were so many of them, and seemed to outnumber the men in a ratio of about three to one. If that were the case in the general population of Effington, once he reached the university campus, the feminine advantage soared – he guessed at close to six to one. Charles searched around quizzically for a campus map, or at any rate, a signpost.

"Ah yes. There it is: Department of Biological Sciences, pointing left." He noticed an increasing tendency to talk to himself of late. A few minutes later, Charles entered what he hoped would be his new working home. Had it not been for the presence of himself and an unrecently washed man clad in beard, voluminous sweater and sandals, the female to male ratio would have been infinity, requiring a division by zero. And all of them were comely young women at that, he observed. When he met her, Charles thought even Professor Angela Leyton-Borden looked pretty good: tall, elegant, about fifty, with short, coiffured blonde hair, and a palpable quality of poise. No wedding ring, although she seemed to like men. Probably divorced, Charles surmised.

The internal candidate had, it transpired, dropped out of the contest. However, the other, external, candidate was deeply internal to the Establishment, and hence a great friend, it appeared, of the external assessor, who, having arrived from his own university a few hours later, would be present at the interview to adjudicate on who was appointed to the Chair. In manner, he reminded Charles rather of Alistair Blakeley: the kind of man who engenders a near compulsion to wipe the hand that has been used to shake hands with him, immediately down the nearest trouser leg. Moreover, when Charles arrived at Angela Leyton-Borden's office, the other candidate had already arrived, and was in deep discussion with her about his requirements when he accepted the post. Angela appeared intent in her persuasion that Effington University was keen to develop the area of biological physics, and really he would sit comfortably with that. It was a *fix*. Charles Rae was there as cannon fodder. He recognised all the signs. Just as when he was first looking for a lectureship, it seemed getting a Chair within the Establishment was no different. But, he thought cynically, why should it be?

Charles knew that he was the better qualified of the two of them, and so expected a systematic and underhand undermining of his credentials. It would be a case of who was "working in the right field" again, otherwise he, Charles, would get it – hands down. Charles began to feel like a shadow on the wall; a wallflower no one wanted to dance with. And Angela would probably make quite a nice partner – the tango, maybe, in shimmering sequins – but the bitch had obviously wasted his time, and rendered futile his heart-raised hopes of redemption. So, after all, it was back to bloody EEU. But he would see it through, do his bit on the day, and give a good account of himself. He wouldn't make it easy for these bastards; but nor would they for him!

Charles' trump card was the talk he had to give – he was, in fact, a very good lecturer – and he had rehearsed his material well. His opponent (in the red corner) shuffled into the ring, then paced a weak delivery, aimed, monotone, and smacking the floor in its effect. He was *not* a good lecturer. Charles punched with more vigour: he was younger and, it had to be said, more desperate. Both Angela and the external assessor, who meanwhile had occupied the ringside seats, could smell his blood. It went well nonetheless: he amused them with his assertion that "the problem with making physical measurements on biological systems is that they are *wet*". How true, of course: the human body, for example, is 90 per cent water. And then he explained his methods for circumventing this difficulty, and obtaining useful research data from blood and protoplasm using adaptations of his original and more fundamental work.

So, that part of the proceedings was done. He had shown them that he knew his stuff, and he could present it with panache. None of their questions afterwards had tripped him up – his subject knowledge was superior to theirs. The research students smiled at him as they left the room. He had convinced them he was a good chap, which is the ace in the hole of a good lecturer. If that was the ordeal by water, next would come the ordeal by fire. Lunch, served in Angela's oppressively heated office, and heated further by the naked flames of spirit burners that kept open salvers of food – *curry* at that! – in a menacing ebullition. As the drops of sweat dripped on down into the curry, Charles gratefully accepted a cold lager. But it seemed like a trap.

"Are you sure? You know you have your interview next, don't you? You don't want to drink too much," Angela patronised him. "Do you usually drink at lunchtime?"

"I'll have an orange juice, please; I want to keep a clear head," Charles' opponent was quick to clutch at any advantage over him, not that he needed to bother as the whole show was rigged anyway.

"I'll take you both along to meet the vice-chancellor," Angela announced, rising and pushing her chair back from the table. So, lunch was over, and it was time for phase three of the trial: ordeal by intractable questions. In the pecking order of universities, Effington was somewhere near the top, while EEU was within clear sight of rock bottom, and no sign of stopping. But because Effington wasn't at quite the top, there was a good deal of overcompensation engrained in its airs and manners. In short, Charles half expected to find a footprint in him somewhere, and streaks of himself wiped off revulsively on its green and hallowed lawns.

★ ★ ★

The vice-chancellor was curt, and cut to the chase.

"Now how much do you expect me to pay you? More, rather than less, I expect." He smiled, unfurling his dour humour. Charles smiled back. He seemed OK but tough; a hardnosed businessman, like the industrialists who had paid to build the original university: self-made men, putting back some wealth into the mine they had hewn it from, in return for a place in posterity. Malcolm McKenzie had, indeed, come from industry. He had advised the Government well concerning some of the thornier aspects of its foreign trade policies, and who, to express its gratitude, had secured his reward of a knighthood.

"Arise, Sir Malcolm." A proud moment. He was sorry his father, who had worked in the Clyde shipyards and died of a heart attack aged fifty, was not there to see it. His mother too, lost to cancer not long after. He was the ideal choice as Effington's new vice-chancellor. The previous holder of that particular post had not really been up to the job, everyone agreed. A distinguished academic, but not a businessman, and he'd run the university rather into the red. It was time for some prudent rationalisation, and the man for that was Sir Malcolm McKenzie. Sir Malcolm had frozen all budgets other than salaries; there would be no "non-essential" spending for that year, including no more promotions. He had started to renegotiate the university's loan repayments with the bank. But more income was required too. Undergraduate recruitment had to be increased, especially from overseas – international students paying their much higher fees. This was particularly difficult in subjects such as physics, where national and global uptake of its courses had fallen into decline. The Effington physicists held their heads in their hands.

"How?" they asked, shaking those heads.

Staff were expected to apply for more grants, and for bigger grants, even though success in winning them was accordingly less likely; it was a gamble, but there was no other way. Sir Malcolm had to balance the books; that was the job he'd been hired for. He then unsheathed the sword of Damocles. All departments that scored below a grade 4 in the RAE would be closed forthwith, especially those running expensive science subjects, and this included the Department of Biological Sciences with its 3a rating. Angela Leyton-Borden implored him, "Please, Sir Malcolm, can you not offer us a stay of execution? Another two years, that's all I'm asking for."

"So, what *is* your strategic plan, then?"

She began to explain, "I have it from a reliable source – someone who was on the Biological Sciences panel in the last RAE – that we only very narrowly missed a grade 4. The problem is that we've lost a couple of our best researchers during the last few years, so our grant income and publication output have both fallen. If we could recruit a leading figure in the field of biological physics, with a good publication record, their reputation will take us up into the grade 4 category in the next RAE in two years time. We need to resource a professorship in Biological Physics, though, no one of the calibre we need would come here for less than a Chair."

Sir Malcolm's eyes narrowed.

"Ay, very well then, I'll go halves with you." There was the dour smile again. By skimming off her teaching budget and dipping into some of the department's research grant overheads that the university's administration didn't spend on their own activities, and let dribble back into the department, she could just about cover half the cost of a professor over the next two years, so if Sir Malcolm matched that, the appointment was viable. But there would be no start-up funds she could offer them, or even relocation expenses, and they *had* to get a grade 4 next time. Then there would be significant income from the RAE – enough to meet the full costs of her plan. Thus, the choice of appointee was absolutely critical to the survival of the department.

Angela immediately set about trying to identify likely individuals. The ideal candidate would be running a large research group, which they would bring with them, along with equipment, research funds and the prestige of high quality publications. If they were really good – baldly rubber-stamped members of the Establishment – they might even be on the RAE panel for their "unit of assessment" (OUA); and that would do no harm to their rating at all. Or at the very least, they might have sympathetic friends who were on it, and that would be almost as good. But, joining a 3a department is risky. It would have to be either a sideways, or more likely, a downward move. The kind of "star striker" Angela had in mind was unlikely to exist in any department below grade 4, so how could they be attracted there? True, Effington *was* one of the top universities in the country, with most of its departments rated at grade 5, some at 5★, and all the science departments at least at grade 4, apart from hers; a matter that had caused her considerable consternation when the RAE results were published, and all the more so since Sir Malcolm's threat to close it should that situation fail to improve the next time around.

The strength of the other departments and the university's prestige was, therefore, a selling point, and because the proposed Chair was in Biological Physics, there was the potential for lucrative collaborations with the Department of Physics, which at grade 5★ would lead to successful and substantially funded research grant applications. Yes, this was the point to emphasise. One name did materialise: Oliver Marshal. He was older than the ideal, at fifty-five, but very well established. His publication list was reasonable, though not exceptional, running to sixty articles, and probably this would not have got him a Chair had he not been working in a medical school. They would have to, at least, match his salary, which as a medical professor was quite a lot higher than they wanted to pay, but Angela thought she could probably still meet her half of it, if Sir Malcolm was still prepared to match that.

Oliver was well connected though, and he had a large research group which was liberally funded by medical charities and by the pharmaceutical industry. He would *do* perfectly. Now, they couldn't just appoint Marshal, or even interview only him. There had to be a fall guy. Someone with excellent credentials, but with an Achilles heel that could be pierced on the day. But who? Then, via the electronic mechanism of the divine, an answer echoed back to her from the firmament.

Click:

Dear Professor Leyton-Borden,

I note with interest your advertisement for the currently available Chair in Biological Physics. I would value your opinion as to my suitability for this post. My CV is available at: www.eeu/crae/cv.html

Yours sincerely,
Professor Charles Rae

When Charles had phoned Angela Leyton-Borden at her suggestion, her voice was a personification of charm.

"Now, I must be honest," Charles told her, "I am not a biologist, but a physicist. Is that likely to be a problem?"

"Not...at...all..." she soothed him mellifluously. "It is a positive advantage. We have a strong relationship with the Physics Department, and we wish to deepen that, so someone with your background would be ideal."

And so, with heart and step lightened, Charles had put his application into the postbag, next to the pigeonholes. He was on his way. Angela thought he was perfect. Sir Malcolm's scathing views of the "new" universities were well known, and where was Charles Rae from? Evergreen Epstein University (EEU), not only "new" but notorious, its academic malpractices being so well publicised that Sir Malcolm would often cite EEU as both the cause and vindication to disgorge his acidic venom, although he didn't know the half of its rottenness. Even more effectively, by emphasising the "biological" nature of the post, Oliver Marshal, being primarily a biologist, would be seen to sit more comfortably within it than Charles would.

Angela aimed her arrows with poise, seeking out his Achilles' heel.

"But what about the teaching? You're not a biologist. How will you be able to teach biology?"

"But the post is in Biological *Physics*, isn't it? I told you I wasn't a biologist at the outset." Charles tried to protect his heel, but the blood was drawn.

"What is a research professor?" It was someone else's turn in the chain. "Isn't that a tautology? All professors do research. It's the main part of their job!" Everyone nodded.

"Not at EEU," Charles informed them despairingly. "There are professors there without a single piece of published work in the subject they are supposed to be professor of."

This was the proof they needed of his unworthiness. He was tainted and damaged. How could they, in all their glory, possibly hand over one of their esteemed professorships to a creature like this? Who knew what kinds of contamination he might bring with him?! EEU? University? Not in the form any of them was aware of; nor Charles, either for that matter, but he had stepped upon the trapdoor. The noose was already round his neck. All they had to do was pull the lever. "Next, please!"

"I'm sorry, but we don't think you can possibly have adequate professorial level experience, in an…um…*institution*, of that nature."

Oliver Marshal, in pristine condition, was their man. A calm silence said it all, muffling the footfalls of his ambitions, like newly fallen snow.

"Look, I just want to get out of EEU and into a more research-friendly university. I'm drowning there, in teaching and administration. All my spare time goes on trying to keep my research going, to try to do my job as a 'research' professor, as opposed to the other kind, whatever they are supposed to be."

Charles shrugged toward the crescent of blank, unsympathetic faces, and in that moment he knew he definitely wouldn't be moving to Effington; it was back to EEU, with lead in his boots and in his heart.

18

Thomas O'Grady glowed. This was wonderful. He'd made a fine appointment. Perhaps one's loss could truly be another's gain. So, Dr Barney Asif, a piece of driftwood from the latest shipwrecked science department, had been picked up on the rocky beaches of EEU. In Thomas' mind, the interview had been spectacular. There wasn't a box on the form from Human Resources he couldn't tick, and that was good enough for him, even though nobody on the panel other than Thomas actually believed a word Dr Asif had said.

"My research had received unlimited funding from multinational corporations. I had a group of twenty research students."

Though, oddly, although he was "mid-career" in age – early forties – he had only published six papers, ever.

"Ah, yes. But it was all subject to confidentiality agreements, so although I had brought over ten million into the department, and we had to buy a cyclonic wave accelerator, and we had made over one hundred thousand measurements, we couldn't actually publish anything."

"Mmm." Jake Parr, head of physics teaching was not convinced. "But, can you bring any of the equipment with you?" he asked him. "Ten million quid's worth of kit would certainly help improve our RAE rating."

"Ah, no. Sadly, there was a terrible fire, and it was completely destroyed, along with the whole physics building."

Then Barney's heroism raised its standard.

"The door of the lab became jammed. My research students were locked in and screaming. The fire brigade were afraid to go into the building, so what could I do? I seized an axe, covered my nose and mouth with a wet handkerchief, and just ran in with no thought for my own safety. As I approached the door, it was red hot, but I hacked away at the lock, and managed to force it open. I have even been given a medal of valour by the fire brigade!"

Barney shone with pride. Jake wondered if he was the only one who could smell bullshit, but Thomas was captivated, seizing and believing every word of it.

"Wonderful!" he shone. "If we continue to make appointments of this calibre, the future of this department is assured."

★ ★ ★

Celia Marchant was the world's leading voice in diagnostic medical physics, her specialist field being the fabrication of devices for detecting likely genetic diseases in children. She was a handsome woman of fifty-eight, and her tall and sinewy frame betrayed the real tennis accomplishments of her younger days, and she remained a keen spectator of the sport. Celia was a champion in promoting the role of women in science, a point she emphasised in the fact that her own research group – the largest in the university – consisted solely of females.

It was a properly balanced group – in model of the German system: with herself as "the professor" at the top; then a narrow tier of readers; followed by lecturers; then post-docs; and finally the research students, the workhorses of the whole effort. The structure enables both mentoring and feedback to be relayed as necessary within the pyramid body of the group's activities, and ensures that research students are not simply cast adrift, only encountering the professor every year or so – if that often, sometimes – who has by then forgotten what the student's project was exactly, they had set them at the start, when urgently accepting the research grant that supported it.

Among Celia's girls, as they were known, was Marylynne Beddoes. She came to the group a few years older than most of the other research students. Her history, accordingly, was more complex than the average. Her life had started well, as a happy country child. Then her elder sister, seeming to recover from an earlier sickness, had not awoken, on a morning that dealt a cold hand. Since it was Marylynne's discovery that changed everything, and in their grief, the parents could not forgive her, almost resenting the time they had devoted to their younger child.

So, a sad girl had emerged, hollowed with the vacuum of rejection, which she would later seek to fill with the approval of others. She left home young, exchanging green for grey concrete and tarmac, but eventually emerging on the other side of those turbulent but deadened years. She had gone through access course to degree, supporting herself entirely by a series of evening and weekend jobs, and then graduated in medical physics with upper-second class honours.

By now an ambitious and determined young woman, Marylynne was looking to do a PhD, somewhere – but where? Then fate took her hand. Reading in the popular magazine *Boo*, which covered all kinds of celebrities, she chanced upon an article about Celia Marchant, and her work in diagnosing childhood genetic diseases. The piece also mentioned her preference for female research students.

"This is my chance!" Marylynne thought, "but how can I contact her...? Of course – the internet!"

On entering the terms "celia marchant" into the search engine, she wasn't hard to find, with more than two hundred returns. Finding the "Marchant Group Homepage", Marylynne copied down her address, phone number and email address, but of the three options, decided to write her a polite letter:

> *Dear Professor Marchant,*
> *I have been reading with great interest your papers on medical diagnostic devices, and I would love to do a PhD with you and work in your research group. I have a 2:2 degree in Medical Physics, and I am writing to enquire whether you would accept me if you have a grant available.*
> *I would be delighted to come and see you to discuss the possibility.*
> *Respectfully yours,*
> *Marylynne Beddoes*

When her secretary knocked, and on invitation entered, placing the morning's post in her in-tray, Celia Marchant's attention was immediately drawn to the looped girlish handwriting, with circles for full stops, and a flamboyancy of purposeful, fluid characters; one envelope, bright as a beacon, among all the other dull routine-looking stuff, and so she opened this first. In an age of endless email messages and letters word-processed on a PC, a handwritten letter can be almost disarming; and this one from Marylynne had the desired effect.

"Yes, I *am* looking for another research student," Celia mused. "OK, she seems keen, so why not have a look at her?"

When Marylynne arrived for her interview she seemed sincere; an impression she maintained throughout. Celia was convinced she would do. There were the "missing years", however, but Marylynne explained without evasion her troubled schooldays, and the years that had become subsequent. This was the clincher, in that she had nonetheless come through it all, by her own strength of will, and achieved a decent degree at the end. Celia had faced her own battles when she was young too, and believed that such things were all intended to "build"; that the strongest and most resourceful transcended adversity and were improved in both qualities by it.

The contract was signed, and Celia's judgement proved not too bad. When assigned to an existing successful project (Celia felt a helping hand was in order) Marylynne quickly ingratiated herself into that portion of the research group, held on to their coat tails, and rose as one with their ascension. With a firm eye on her future, Marylynne also grasped whatever other useful coat tails might be around in the wide world of their scientific collaborators. At conferences, she would flirt, convincing middle-aged male professors and post-docs and younger lecturers who looked like they were going for the main stage, and would make it too, that she was worth knowing (and they were in with a chance).

"I'll sleep with anybody who'll help me get to the top" was the folklore and the aura she both trailed behind her, and projected as rumour to those like Barney Asif, who she felt would never make it, but who would spread the word, which he did; but since anybody might "make it" she hedged her bets, subtly soliciting those in the know to ascertain as toward whom the swingometer of scientific politics was jigged.

"Oh, yes," nodding with a wink, "he's just received a grant of three million for his research on virus analysis." And, "Oh yes, over there, he's done almost as well. It's not been formally announced yet, but I was on the funding committee...so, it's in the bag."

"Good chap. He was with Conrad Connory, you know, so we thought we ought to give him a leg up."

Then more confidentially, "Quite his blue-eyed boy, in fact, and between you and me, since Connory either chairs or advises most of the funding committees none of us wants to get on the wrong side of him," followed by a nervous laugh.

Marylynne began to learn one rule of the game: that it's *people* who award grants to other people. So, get myself noticed – whatever it takes. But in her naivety, she had failed to grasp the counter-rule of peer review: that it's people who can deny grants to other people, block their efforts to publish their work and ultimately destroy them. And since research is about *people*, science has relatively little to do with any of it. Jealousies, imagined slights, control freakery, personal involvements of one kind or another, occasionally a desire to suppress the rise of any stars from outside the Establishment (to maintain its purity), subjective moral judgements of personal character, along with all other human vagaries. All of this more than anything else, determines a career which is successful, or otherwise.

This is a lesson to the young which is never taught overtly or explicitly, to avoid mitigating its emphasis, or perhaps putting them off the whole idea of embarking upon a research career at the outset. But Marylynne was young, she had the support of an influential and respected mentor in Celia Marchant, and while still attached to her apron strings, felt she could begin to spin her own network from among the great and the good. This is a dicey game, of course, since the network is already very well established, and the Establishment has the ultimate means to eject interlopers into the gutter when it has tired of them, like a rampant doorman.

Celia was watchful as a mother hen. Making introductions, she would then stand back, carefully observing her chick as it bobbed up and down among the other animals in the conference farmyard. She had already primed Marylynne as to who was who and who to get to know, and suggested that she read some of their papers beforehand, knowing they would feel flattered by her attention and remember her on other occasions, such as when reviewing her own applications for research grants, when she finally left the security of the hen house. There was, however, one disadvantage Marylynne had: the fact she was nearly thirty.

If she did the normal post-doc thing, she could add two or three years to that, but in any case she had to finish her PhD first. And thirty-three or thirty-four is getting a little on the long-in-the-tooth side of being appointed to a first lectureship. Celia was well aware of this, but she managed to contrive a strategy. It was only in the "older" universities that having done a post-doc was prerequisite for getting a lectureship. As far as she could judge, in some of the "new" universities, to be "shortly awarded a PhD" was all that was necessary. Therefore, Marylynne would be shortly qualified for such a post, and Celia's enthusiastic recommendation would almost certainly secure it for her.

★ ★ ★

But rumours had begun to circulate. Whispers and nudges in urinals and dark corridors. Mutterings by pigeonholes:

"Have you heard about Celia Marchant and Marylynne Beddoes?"

"They've moved in together."

"No? What? Do you mean...?" said with a mixture of mock shock and lascivious delight, each man imagining "what they get up to together", while some of the women felt more than a pang of envy as to the help Marylynne was getting with her career, whatever she had to do in return. But as far as anyone had known, Marylynne wasn't "like that", although everyone had thought that Celia probably was. However, there were, perhaps, no restrictions to Marylynne's ambition; nothing, even committing murder, she wouldn't do to slide up the greasy pole. She wanted to become the equal of Professor "The Lady" Celia Marchant, and nothing short of that would suffice. But first, she had to get her foot on that bottom rung; get a lectureship somewhere, and somewhere that wouldn't expect too much given her lack of experience, and she had yet to complete her PhD – but where?

Marylynne scanned the job ads, but in vain, as all of them seemed to expect post-doctoral experience, and in many cases publications too. After a fruitless few months, the only option seemed to be to post-doc with Celia, who might then be able to swing an experimental officer post for her. That would, at least, be a permanent job, but it would not have the same status and nor could it provide the route to academic ascension that she sought. Then one bright day, the gods conferred their blessing on her, and her eyes rejoiced as their gaze fell upon that one advert she had been looking out for, which read:

> *Evergreen Epstein University (EEU): Lecturer in Applied Medical, Exercise and Leisurewear Physical Sciences. Applicants should have, or shortly expect to obtain, a post-graduate qualification in a relevant subject area. Ideally we are seeking someone whose expertise could be applied to the furtherance of our teaching and research activities, centred around the advancement of the leisurewear industry.*
>
> *For an informal discussion, please contact: Professor Thomas O'Grady, Head, Department of Leisurewear and Applied Physical Sciences, The Albert Einstein Building, Evergreen Epstein University, Evergreen.*

Marylynne's hands trembled as she activated the "print" icon on their computer.

"Celia! Celia! I've found the perfect job!"

"Let me see," Celia called back, as her footfalls skipped their beat from the bedroom, onto the stairs and down into the living room. "Show me!"

she insisted, settling an urgent palm on the back of the younger woman's neck.

"Yes, that will do perfectly. I'll phone Professor O'Grady first thing tomorrow morning."

It was a permanent position; not that Marylynne planned to stay at EEU for too long, but it was that first academic stepping stone. A lectureship. With Celia's support, she would certainly get some research funding, some publications in decent journals, and then secure a post at a more prestigious university. Then she would be independent of Celia; and then, as it is sometimes said, the sky would be the limit, Marylynne's sky being cloudless and airy. Marylynne tingled with exhilaration at the prospect of her future glories; recognition; acceptance; unknowingly healing that hole in her soul of adolescent rejection. She knew Celia could galvanise the initial process, and in that moment, Marylynne was in love. She felt complete in Celia's volition; letting herself slip into the fluent sensation of her; trusting as a child that knows its parent will always be there: solid, all-knowing, unequivocally loving and constant.

★ ★ ★

The sun beat down on Hollworth College, shining its best on a sunny July day – an "awayday", a "staff development day". The proceedings didn't start until 9.30, and all had arrived there in good time, the whole Department of Leisurewear and Applied Physical Sciences standing, coffee cups in hands, enjoying the tranquil, rural setting of the venue. When Charles Rae arrived, he snatched from the general buzz of conversation the name Marylynne. She was there, of course, and her name was on the list against a slot at 10.15 entitled How to Get Your First Research Grant. Indeed, she did know "how" since she had just been awarded £250,000, much, it must be said, to everyone's surprise.

"But how? She's got no post-doctoral experience – only just finished her PhD, for that matter!"

These were the general sentiments that Charles overheard.

"Yes, but you know she's sleeping with her supervisor. And really it's *she* who has been awarded the grant, but she's simply transferred it to Marylynne."

"*She?*"

"Oh, yes. Celia Marchant. They live together."

The group of men turned their gaze as one, toward Marylynne, regarding her with a new and rising interest, but Marylynne was oblivious to them, sitting alone on the grass, head down, her attention entirely absorbed in reading her talk. Thomas O'Grady appeared, clapping his hands to gain everybody's attention.

"It's now 9.25 precisely, so will you all go in and take your seats."

The absence of enthusiasm was palpable, as the assembled looked around for somewhere to put down their cups and saucers, and began to shuffle into the conference room. Having observed that everyone had found a seat, Thomas addressed the meeting, "Good morning, ladies and gentlemen. Thank you for coming along." Not that there was any choice in the matter as an awayday was a big day for Thomas; that special occasion when his true talents could truly shine, and everyone had to be there to receive their administrations. Not even mortal illness, family bereavements, prior engagements of national imperative, flat tyres or any other just impediment could excuse one's absence from an awayday. The staff needed to be developed, and that was that. But Charles Rae, for one, always found the experience less than improving. Awful though EEU was on his usual days, it was only when he saw, and had to listen to renditions from the whole department *en masse*, particularly the Leisurewear staff, that he realised what an appalling shithouse he had been conned into joining. And, oh yes, how Thomas shone; those polished steel-rimmed spectacles glittering imperiously. "Our Leader".

But his real rallies to arms were his speeches. Sounding like the text of some outmoded and discredited tract on 1970s style industrial management, Thomas could call instantly to mind each and every managerial acronym, quality assurance issue, details of the teaching transparency exercise, examination regulations; he knew everybody's teaching load by heart, and it was his crusade that those most heavily involved in research should get the most teaching. Thomas didn't believe in research; he'd never done any and he was all the better for it. He would stamp it out, if that was his final act. However, Marylynne's research grant was the talk of the university, so he couldn't simply dismiss it. Also, she was considered as part of the Leisurewear staff, not one of the physicists. As he was bent on getting rid of the latter staff, two of whom, at least in the shape of Charles Rae and Tommy Wakefield were *good* at research, he could use Marylynne as a good example of success in leisurewear research to action some counterweight against them and destabilise their position. Along with the low student numbers in Applied Physics, in contrast to the booming Leisurewear market – the flag Thomas often waved – he could bury them with burdensome tasks and play down their strengths in research, never allowing the latter or the money it brought in to influence his policy decisions, which passed uncontested, since the departmental management team consisted solely of Leisurewear staff, the physicists all being excluded from contributing to any of its decisions.

At 10.15 Marylynne took the stage, whereupon she made the proud and strident announcement: "I'm going to show you all what I had to do to get my grant!"

Given the rumours that were now rife, both in the department and the wider world for that matter, the prospect evoked an element of licentious amusement. There were loud whispers: "Cor! What's she going to do? Show us a video?! Ha ha!"

But Marylynne remained unfazed, being still rather naïve, neither appreciating the significance of her manner of expression nor the reaction it elicited. The main cause of their response, of course, was jealousy; the depth of which was hardly mitigated by Marylynne's comment: "Your careers didn't have to be just about teaching and admin, you know. You could have made a name for yourselves, if you'd tried at all!"

No trace of mirth now. The audience sat tight lipped through the rest of it. She was wrong though: most of them didn't have the talent to have made any impact, however hard they'd tried. But amid the smug complacency of their collective mediocrity, her words drew blood. All of them would really have liked to be academic stars; so some, like Thomas O'Grady, held a defensive "anti" research ethic, rejecting it as an irrelevance. "Customer service supply is our core mission, not research".

Marylynne held forth, unfazed. "I showed you! 'Who does she think she is?' you said. 'No post-doctoral experience, no publications, she'll never get that grant!' All you have to do is collaborate," she continued. "Just get someone famous to put their CV and name on your grant. And then you collect the money! It's easy! Why didn't you do the same?" she squealed, sowing salt blithely into the wounds she had just opened.

"Well, thank you, Marylynne," Thomas interrupted, "I'm sure we've all learned something useful here."

The next speaker on the list was Dr Anne Wobble, who had given the title of her talk as University Quality Assurance Initiatives. This looked to be right up Thomas' street. Anne was "Doctor" Anne by virtue of a PhD (by coursework) in Business Administration, which she'd studied for part-time, in the EEU Business School. And now, swept in on the wave of Thomas O'Grady's sparkling introduction, she addressed the collected academic staff of Leisurewear and Applied Physical Sciences:

★ ★ ★

"Good morning. Professor O'Grady has asked me to come along today to explain to you all the university's new corporate structure, and the provisions within it which engage with the assurance of quality in the delivery of its modular programmes. To this end, the Executive Quality Assurance Team, of which I am chair, has implemented several new initiatives. There have been a number of embarrassing reports in the newspapers recently, concerning poor quality and alleged malpractices during the examinations at EEU, and in this department particularly. The vice-chancellor has given me a free hand to make sure that you all pull your socks up!"

The assembled hackles began to rise.

Mutterings: "Who is this stupid bitch, anyway? What the hell does she know about teaching? This is bloody typical of EEU; it was exactly the same when it was the polytechnic."

"Top-heavy management; run by managers, not academics. People who have no idea and no subject knowledge. Anyone could do their job, and do it better too; but none of them could do ours! And yet they treat us like shit!"

All these and other sentiments began to form, as they often do these days, in the minds of the oppressed proletariat that academics have apparently become. It used to be that support staff supported academics; then along came "management", and now the academics do the bidding of the managers, with their endless job-creating bureaucracy, in addition to their own work, which is what actually keeps the university running, and with less and less support to do any of it. But as Anne launched herself upon an inexorable flow of management babble, irritation quickly became boredom and Charles found his roving attention finally caught in the intricacies of the fleur-de-lys that spidered the high ceiling. In fact, this usually happened on awaydays, but not usually so early on. He knew he just had to get out of EEU at all costs.

But there was something else too; another sound had started up. A humming amid the drone. Tommy Wakefield, a truly exploited worker, sitting next to Charles, staring aloft, wide-eyed and humming. Then Charles recognised the tune, and some of the words came to mind, which could have been written for a man longing for early retirement:

> "To Bombay
> A travelling circus came.
> They brought an intelligent elephant
> And Nellie was her name.
> One dark night
> She slipped her iron chain,
> And off she ran
> To Hindustan
> And was never seen again
> Ooooooooooooooooo…
> Nelly the elephant packed her trunk, and
> Said goodbye to the circus.
> Off she went with a trumpety-trump;
> Trump, trump, trump.
> No more tricks for Nellie to perform…
> The head of the herd was calling, far, far away…"

Then, as suddenly as it had started, it stopped, and on glancing idly to his side, Charles saw that Tommy Wakefield had fallen asleep.

19

"Ah, good morning, Vice-Chancellor. I wonder if I might see you, on a matter of some urgency." Tony Naismith sounded edgy, as he often did, the lot of bursar at EEU not being a very rosy one, apart from the salary.

"Yes, thank you. Ten o'clock. Yes, that's fine. Oh, it's about the Government's research infrastructure allocation. There is a problem."

Stirling George knew well enough that they were "in trouble" financially, and consequently, he and Tony had seen a good deal of one another during the past year or so.

"That bloody Business School! That bloody woman, Sharleen La'Coy. Damn her!" he cursed. She had cost him ten million quid, which he was desperately trying to pare from the rest of his service departments – Human Resources, Learning Resources, even Security Services, Financial Services and Accounts – since he could cut nothing further from the academic departments without them and the university collapsing catastrophically around a framework rendered too weak to support their burden. But this was an infrastructure *allocation*. Money *coming in*. That had to be good news, surely? So what was Tony's problem, he wondered.

"Yes, come in, Tony. Please have a seat."

Tony Naismith looked a worried man, and his voice and hand trembled as one. "Thank you, Vice-Chancellor," as he placed his briefcase on the desk and extracted from it the university's balance sheets.

"Tony. I was delighted to hear that we are to receive some funding from this new initiative. Well, cutting to the chase, you and I both know perfectly well the state of our finances. Bloody Sharleen La'Coy and her damned promises for the new Business School. However, as I recall, we are due nearly two million from the government research infrastructure allocation – a bit more wouldn't have hurt, mind – but anyway, that has to be all the more power to our elbow, surely?"

Stirling George looked directly and interrogatively at his bursar, but braced himself for a further blow on his house of cards. Tony pushed the statement of accounts toward the V-C, and began to explain what indeed the problem was.

"Yes, I agree. In principle, of course, two million – well, one million, nine hundred and forty-three thousand, seven hundred and twenty-nine pounds, thirty-eight pence to be precise."

Stirling George grew impatient. "Yes. OK. Go on."

Tony continued, "You are right. In principle, of course, this is *good*, but there is a *snag*. Namely that in order to actually collect the two million, we have to match-fund 25 per cent of it," Tony's fingers moved deftly over his calculator, "which amounts to four hundred and eighty-five thousand, nine hundred and thirty-two pounds, thirty-five pence," he concluded.

"Mmm. Half a million quid," Stirling George rumbled.

"Can't you just do some of your creative accounting? Move the money around a bit? Put it under different headings … what do you financial chaps call it…? *Virement*…perhaps? Borrow it, even?" An edge of desperation leaked out from his voice.

"That still doesn't get us out of the hole. We have to be seen to invest the 25 per cent match in…well…*research infrastructure*, and we simply don't have it!"

The bursar went on. "We owe the bank five million, and they're not happy. I keep fobbing them off, but they certainly won't lend us any more. So that option is out. We've agreed that our savings have to go toward paying off the bank loan, so we can't save up the half million from our various prunings to the service budgets. Redundancies are too expensive, and natural wastage is too slow. If we went for the redundancy option, since some of these staff have been here for thirty-odd years, we'd have to give them a massive payout!"

The V-C considered the situation and observed, "Many of them are due for retirement imminently. We could lay off some of our more recent appointments – that would be cheap – but we will need to rehire to replace the old guard as they retire. It would be a purely short-term measure, and in any case we would look like pretty rotten eggs! We don't want any *more* bad publicity, or some kind of investigation into our affairs. God, we don't!"

The bursar nodded in agreement. "There is one other option, of course. The building budget."

"What do you mean?"

"There is some latitude in what might be construed as *research infrastructure*."

"Well, scientific equipment, surely, that kind of thing?" Stirling volunteered.

"Ah, yes, but of course scientific equipment needs to *go* somewhere. Into laboratories, which are housed in buildings. And how would such equipment be transported to the laboratories? They're not all on the ground floor, are they? So, the lifts need to be refurbished to the appropriate requirements. And research workers have infrastructural demands, too. The toilets, for instance. They all need repainting. The canteen overhaul – well, they all have to eat, don't they, and they can't bring sandwiches into the labs, on health and safety grounds. The window replacement programme – the research personnel have to be able to see outside: it's bad for their mental health, otherwise. Actually, the labs themselves need some attention. Repainting, replacing fume-hoods, removing some of the benches so we can get more students into them. Admittedly, the labs are almost entirely used for undergraduate teaching, but students do undertake a final year *research* project, so the point might be stretched that this is all in the interests of improving overall *research infrastructure*, which is, after all, what the money is for. That's what it says: *research infrastructure allocation*."

The dropping penny had activated the costing mechanism of Stirling George. He beamed. This was why he paid Tony Naismith as much as he did. He had come up trumps yet again.

"So, Tony, let me get this straight. What you are suggesting is that we cost our 25 per cent from the budget we have already allocated for these refurbishment jobs, and that way, we don't have to find the extra half million?"

"Exactly, Vice-Chancellor."

"And, Tony, might I be right in thinking that since these, various ...um ... infrastructural improvements, are indeed bona fide benefits to the *research infrastructure* of the university, we would be quite within our remit of that task in spending some proportion of the additional two million on completing the whole programme of building upgrades?"

"Indeed, Vice-Chancellor, that would be entirely within the criteria of the exercise."

Being able to get his hands on the best part of two million pounds, aided admirably by Tony Naismith's skilful accounting methods, Stirling George was now able to pay off a good chunk of the debt incurred through the failed Business School venture.

★ ★ ★

The news of this was, at best, greeted with derision and disgust in the academic departments, whose efforts of a very few in research had engendered the award of the funds at all, since research infrastructure in the shape of scientific equipment would be provided through only the paltry £200K the vice-chancellor had allowed to trickle back to them. It was a body blow, since much of their existing equipment was obsolescent to the extent that bodges and repairs, overridings of safety mechanisms which would otherwise render them inoperative, occupied more time than it actually ran for. The researchers had banked on the research infrastructure allocation to keep their own research programmes viable, unknowing that Stirling George would simply hijack it to pay for the bankrupt Business School.

It was a hopeless situation. Charles Rae had research students he needed to support. They needed the equipment to run full-time; without it, they couldn't complete their PhDs. Charles had already applied to the Research Council to buy a new cosmic ray transformer (CRT), but this had been rejected on the grounds that surely he could do all his work using the National Centre of Excellence, some few hundred miles from Evergreen. How were they supposed to get there on a daily basis? Ridiculous! Ironically, it was he who had stood behind Michael Moynihan and Dai Davis, backing up their application to fund the Centre in the first place. Too late, he discovered that selflessness, in this game, was tantamount to cutting your own throat. Not that anyone was using the bloody Centre anyway, apart from Michael Moynihan and Dai Davis themselves. Charles knew his only chance of getting a new CRT machine was if it was funded from the research infrastructure allocation, but he would have to construct a good case for it.

It was agreed that the Faculty of Technology, which embraced the Department of Leisurewear and Applied Physical Sciences, would receive the lion's share of the £200K available, as its needs were greater than any of the non-science faculties. Nonetheless, there was not much to go round. An "invitation" was next emailed to all staff to compile a "wish list" of their needs by a very short deadline, but even so, it resulted in a rather long list, the sum of whose quotations exceeded £2 million − ten times the amount available. Even in a fair fight, the competition would be fierce, and Charles suspected the contest would not be fought on open ground. It was still worth a try, though, especially with no other option in sight.

Apart from Tommy Wakefield, there was no one in LAPS whom Charles could enlist for support. Bob Bates would do him down out of envy and bloody-mindedness, and Tarquin Tupper would be Bob's ally for these self-same reasons, doubtless in some underhand political coup made at an extraordinary meeting to discuss the research infrastructure bids, which both would attend: Bob as departmental research officer, primarily representing the interests of Leisurewear, and Tarquin as his deputy, ostensibly to embody the interests of Physics. Indeed, among his list of collected titles, Tarquin described himself as "Physics Research Leader", and "Head of Physics", even though both positions were virtual, neither existing beyond his own bombastically inflated opinion of himself.

Charles did, however, secure the support of the head of Biological Sciences, and of the professor of Exercise Technology. This was good. It meant Charles could present a strong case: that the machine was not sought purely for his own ends (although his major immediate concern was to support his research students), but to provide a central facility within the Faculty of Technology, and one which would aid in winning further research grants for the university. Exercise Technology was the strongest department in the faculty, an up-and-coming subject that could attract almost as many undergraduates as Leisurewear did. It also enrolled the largest number of research students in the faculty, with more PhD candidates registered for exercise-related studies than any other subject in the university. The Department of Biological Sciences had faced a downturn in their customer recruitment but more than restored its previously strong position through the launch of a degree in Forensic Materials, which proved highly popular.

Charles convinced them that his CRT machine would benefit their research in both Exercise Technology and Biological Sciences, and should help maintain the grade 5 and grade 4 ratings scored by each subject's unit of assessment, respectively. In common with their peers in many universities, Charles Rae and Tommy Wakefield had recognised the futility of submitting their research for review by the Physical Sciences Assessment Panel, who had dismissed them with a grade1 in the previous RAE, and instead joined up with Biological Sciences. The strategy paid off, in that by including Charles and Tommy its rating rose from a grade 3a to a grade 4, and this brought the only income into the Department of LAPS from the whole exercise.

Leisurewear attempted a similar mission and made two submissions of their own, since they too had been summarily dismissed as grade 1 ("no or virtually no work of national standing") by the Leisurewear Assessment Panel.

171

Bob Bates spearheaded a new "Units of assessment" (UOA) in "Dynamic Fabric Materials", but this proved disastrous, scoring only a grade 2, the lowest rating awarded to any university in the country for its research in that subject. Bob was rather downcast at the outcome, but considering the absence of publications and research grants by himself and the other two "leisurewearers" in his UOA, it did seem an apt judgement. At least he could seek some consolation in the parallel garnering of a nationally minimal grade by a miscellaneous ensemble of leftovers who attempted to cover themselves up with a canvass sheet labelled "Sustainable Subjects", when really they should have stayed out in the rain.

The group leader, and professor of Sustainable Subjects, Austin Oldfield, was a firm chum of Bob Bates and both were members of the same congregation at the Evergreen Christian Reform Church, where they would, when the occasion so required, share a hymn-book between them. In a tune of religious ecstasy, Bob's buttocks would resonate in a miasmic rhythm with the rumble of the organ. At Bob's prompting of the University Research Steering Committee, Austin was promoted to the newly created post of university research manager, and made a member of the EEU Executive Strategy Team. There was an apparent duplication in fashioning this role, since a pro-vice-chancellor for research already existed in the form of Mervyn Omen, the professor of Astrology. Odd too, to fill it with the form of Austin Oldfield, whose UOA's RAE score was the most lamentable in its field. What the hell did he know about "research management"? one might wonder, but the question had not been asked.

As university research manager, Austin automatically became chair of the University Research Steering Committee, and now Bob had his man in place. When the committee met, extraordinarily, to review the research infrastructure bids, Bob had already primed both Austin and Tarquin, whom he set a place for next to him. Officially, there should be no discussion of its agendas outside of formal meetings, but these were a charade, the committee existing merely to stamp a sequence of cards effectively filled out in advance by private arrangement. Yes. No. Who to award. Who to deny? The roll of names was called and each well-rehearsed move played out, turn by turn. When they opened the folder placed in front of them by the committee secretary, Charles' bid found itself at the top of a pile pared down to only eight serious contenders, and was accordingly the first to be dealt with. Austin struck the first blow, opening a contest where the opponent was already down. It was like flogging a corpse round the fleet: seven hundred lashes. The sentence would be fulfilled, although the man was dead by six dozen or so.

Bob, Tarquin and Austin had already agreed to trash Charles' bid, as part of their campaign, and approved avidly by Thomas O'Grady, to destroy his career. By wrecking his research, the magic "not more than a hundred hours teaching" that Hamish Humble had promised among many other inducements to get Charles Rae to EEU in the first place, was no more than a distant echo, which ultimately proved to be a lie, and Charles found himself swamped with nearer six hundred hours of low-level teaching, supervising laboratory classes, doubling up as a technician, marking scripts, and attendant administration. He didn't have time any more to write grant applications or publish anything. He was also trying to write a book, but that now fell heavily by the wayside. His morale had taken a deep dent.

He felt like a fool. Not only for allowing himself to be conned into joining EEU at all – though, in fairness to himself, how could he have guessed anywhere could be as bad as this? How could anybody? But there he was, still struggling through his evenings and weekends trying to get grants, write papers … ah, yes, and the book. And yet, there was Tarquin Tupper, with no published work, who consequently had never been included in any RAE, had never had a research grant, and yet, somehow, he'd been promoted to a professorship, just the same as Charles. It was a smack in the face – the confirmation of how little he was thought of at EEU.

"Why have I wasted so much of my life?" Charles asked himself, aloud.

Working all those evenings and weekends, for years. Why? To get a professorship, which turned out worthless. And yet, there is Tarquin … on the golf course every other afternoon … who takes all his bloody holidays during term time. What does he do during the university vacations that benefits the university? Nothing. He works as a tutor for the Remote Learning University – for extra money, at that. And, somehow, he is accredited "teaching hours" for it, so he does less teaching at EEU to compensate for his extra earnings. Bizarre! Oh, yes, and then there is his "research allowance", so even though he doesn't actually *do* any research, he gets the same allowance for it as I do. Even though only my research is bringing any money into the department from the RAE, since Bates and Oldfield made such a mess of their attempts.

How are all these things possible? Is there some "secret society" operating at EEU?! Curious how Thomas O'Grady endorses it all. Does Tarquin have something on him, or have they made a deal? When he asked such questions, of Bob Bates for instance, they were never answered. Just an awkward silence, or a swift switch of subject to something else. This seemed to confirm that there *was* some kind of conspiracy. Or was he just being paranoid. The two thoughts seesawed in and out of his consciousness. For Charles, though, it was his falling research output, which Bob Bates, as departmental research officer, was gleefully keeping tabs on. Not very good for a "research professor". Both drivers turned the same screw: if they upped his teaching and admin, his research output fell. If his research output fell, there was a more emphatic case to up his teaching and admin.

Charles could see that soon that was all he would be doing. He would be a glorified teacher, with his research achievements mocking him from the dim distance, and the likes of Tupper, Bates, O'Grady and Oldfield sniping at a marginalised form of him, a target on the sidelines; preparing for an all-out artillery assault on him when his RAE rating fell below grade 4 next time around, as it inevitably would. Like his title "Professor", normally ignored as a matter of strategy, his RAE success would be used as a weapon against him, once his position was found sufficiently weakened. They had engineered his vanquishment, and Charles alone would shoulder the blame for being vanquished. It would be entirely his fault for not publishing enough papers or winning research grants – rather like the rest of them, actually, but Charles was an outsider to their closed ranks, which lent them a mutual immunity, while he stood alone in their firing line.

★   ★   ★

"Yes, I have some grave concerns over this bid," Austin signalled the attack. "As we all know, Charles Rae is an internationally respected scientist." He positioned the target on a pedestal to make it fall harder. "But if he has all these publications," he smiled, "and all the research support for his European project, why can't he get research council funding for his machine? If he's *really* so good, that is. There's something not right, here."

Bob moved in to flank him. "I don't mean to be critical. None of all his millions…" Bob smirked too, "actually go through the books, you know." His voice ended in that curious whine, part Evergreen accent, part Bob's usual way of emphasising some point of criticism. He shook his head slowly to reinforce the point, and show mock regret for it.

"It's also worth pointing out…" now it was Tarquin's turn. "Austin. You mentioned Charles' research publications. Well, he hasn't published much lately."

Bob nodded a countersignature to the fact. "I've got a list here, actually. I'm putting the university's research portfolio together, and I seem to have brought the printout of Charles' publications with me, for some reason. Must have got mixed up with the papers for this meeting," Bob sighed. "It's all just so hectic at the moment. So much to do." His expression appealed in a supplication for sympathy and camaraderie. Poor Bob. That workhorse. Good old Bob. Where would we be without him?

"Well, it's probably useful to see exactly what the figures are," Bob continued. "Yes. Now look. Oh! I seem to have his entire list of publications since he came here, not just the last two years that I need for the portfolio. Well, anyway, in his first year with us he published eighteen papers…" (actually more than Bob, Tarquin, Austin and Thomas O'Grady had in all their careers put together, but they were unlikely to be aware of the fact) "then a slight fall in the following year … to only fifteen."

The pads of his fleshy fingers walked on down the list, counting. Perspiration condensed on his forehead. Dabbed away with a fresh handkerchief. On his neck. Soaking into the damp collar.

"Only ten in the next one." He moved on down.

"Twelve. Ten. Fourteen. Eight." He paused.

"Look now: *three!*" Bob whined out the last syllable at a theatrical pitch. "One," more subdued. "And this year, nothing at *all!*" The word *all* was pitched out like *three*.

It was a small committee of eight. One representative from each department in the Faculty of Technology, in most cases the departmental research coordinator, with Tarquin as an *extra*, Mervyn Omen as pro-vice-chancellor for research, Austin Oldfield as Chair, and Letticia Jolanda, as assistant vice-chancellor, representing the University Executive Strategy Team. The three stooges had dealt their stroke and Letticia was fully converted.

"I'm sorry to hear that Charles has stopped delivering." Her tone was reproachful. "I had such hopes of him when he first came. We made every effort to support him after the Applied Physics and Astrology Department was closed. The vice-chancellor instructed Rod Shine to make him welcome in the new Department of LAPS, and to give him whatever he needed for his research. It was all rather awkward as he'd only been here six months. He was going to go back to his old university, so we had to make some promises to keep him. Then, of course, Rod ended up in … yes, well. We don't need to go into all that again. Then that business with the Business School. Oh dear! Hark at me. *Business* with the Business School. And what a business it all was!" Letticia tittered coquettishly.

"The university just couldn't afford to buy him a new particle accelerator. Still, he did get a grade 4 in the last RAE," Letticia began to warm to Charles again. Unpredictable. A bit of a maverick. She liked that aspect in a man.

"Yes. But he won't get that again, will he. Not the way he's going," Tarquin dealt the death blow.

Bob and Austin nodded wisely, and Letticia felt compelled to give her reluctant agreement, continuing, "No. We can't throw more money at him..." (not that they'd given him any, just a sackcloth bag of worthless promises). "I think, on this occasion, we have to pass Charles over for a more deserving case. Bob. You will break it to him gently, won't you? I don't want him upset."

Bob and Tarquin practically squeezed each other's knees under the table in their shared passion: their envious hatred of Charles Rae. And now they'd got him! They'd teach the bastard! Swanning around! All that time in Europe. All those conferences. Invitations to give lectures abroad. All his publications and research grants. They'd stamp that out. He ought to be teaching at the poly and doing lots of admin, serving his time just like them! Research professor! Thomas O'Grady made it clear that position no longer exists! Never should have done in the first place! What the hell was Hamish Humble playing at!

Charles was stuck. He couldn't get away from the place any more, even for a day – his new teaching commitments prevented that – so the European project, and all its millions, went to the wall. His existing machine was knackered, so he didn't dare take on any more PhD students at EEU. He couldn't get a grant from the research council, who would tell him to just use the National Centre to do his work, and the three stooges had just demolished his last-chance saloon. He was finished.

Bob's chins framed a smug smile of self-satisfaction. "Of course, Letticia. I'll be gentle with him. Just leave it to me."

And ever the committee man, Bob bulked the momentum of the moment to his own advantage. "I think we need to adopt a strategy of funding for the greatest good. Charles Rae's grade 4 was a *reasonable* success, although he didn't do it on his *own*, of course. He merely (that whine, again) joined a grouping in Biological Sciences, that was already fairly strong, with a 3a rating. Now, with his failure to produce papers over the last few years – and the problem seems to be getting worse, not better – expecting a grade 4 next time is just not realistic."

Seven, united heads nodded in unison. Their lips grim in disappointed resignation of the fact, which sucked in their teeth. How Rae had let them all down!

Bob continued, "I think we should be focussing more on up-and-coming areas. Subjects that may not have done so well in the last RAE, but which show considerable potential to excel in the future, and could really put the university on the map! Austin and I were talking the other night – now I know we're not supposed to – smacked wrists…" he smiled simperingly, "over a pint, after our church union meeting. Now, there were two new subjects entered as UOA in the last RAE: 'sustainable subjects' and 'dynamic fabric materials'."

With a flourish, Bob donned the veil of self-effacement. "I know we only scored a grade 2…" he switched on his winsome smile "but we take that as a success! It's a platform we can build on. Sustainable Studies contains the largest number of staff in any UOA of the university. It includes staff from all five departments of the Faculty of Technology. Dynamic Fabric Materials is a rapidly expanding area. If we combine the two, we could even make a submission as a UOA to be considered by the prestigious Leisurewear panel. We might even get a grade 4 from them. And then, who knows!"

By now, mists had formed in Bob's eyes, so seduced was he in his own rhetoric abandon. It was the lay preacher, espousing parables and other brands of nonsense, until the unconvinced are pummelled into an apathetic, punch-drunken acceptance of his veracity.

"If the committee is in agreement, Mr Chair…" Bob and Austin exchanged a knowing smirk, "the piece of equipment that we really do need, in order to get this all off the ground, is a 'leisurewear dynamics tester'."

Other than the three stooges, no one agreed, but in their flat mood, they did not dissent either, so Bob had his way. In addition to the purchase of Bob's leisurewear tester, it was agreed they should support a bid for an electromagnetic force spectrometer (EFS) as not quite *all* the money could go to Leisurewear … and so the £200K available was spent.

20

Although Charles Rae's grade 4 was the only one to bring in any money to LAPS from the RAE, Bob Bates was damned if Charles would see any of it. It was an opportune circumstance that Rod Shine had gone to jail, leaving the naïve and ever manipulable Thomas O'Grady as head of department, and therefore responsible for its finances. Rod would simply have given the money over to Charles to use as he saw fit, but Thomas could be otherwise persuaded.

"Speaking as a Christian, I believe it is our duty to support the young."

Thomas listened attentively, as he always did to Bob, accepting with implicit gratitude anything Bob assured him of regarding matters related to research, having no clue about them himself. He was a professor of Educational Quality Assurance, after all, and that was quite separate. A professor of form filling and box ticking; a vagary of EEU, and a residue of the notorious city council that owned the former polytechnic.

"What have you in mind, Bob?" Thomas asked with a thoughtful air of polished impassiveness.

"The RAE income. What I don't want is for it to go directly to Charles Rae. He ought to be able to go out and get his own money. No, instead, it should go to the new, or younger staff." Bob had planned his moves well in advance, adding, "If you can persuade the dean to allocate the money to the department, not directly to the individuals whose research was assessed in the RAE, then we'll be able to set up our own internal research committee to distribute the money as *we* see fit."

"Who do you think should be on this committee?" was the question Thomas was prompted to ask, and Bob was ready with the reply.

"Well, myself, as departmental research officer. Tarquin Tupper, being chair of the normal Departmental Research Committee, is the obvious choice to chair this one. Yourself, as head of department and its financial director. And I think we should have someone from outside the department, just to show that everything is done fairly and above board…but who?"

The question lingered momentarily, then Bob had the answer. "Of course. Austin Oldfield. Who better than the university research manager! Four professors in all. No one could argue at that now, could they?!"

★ ★ ★

Charles felt rather peeved that his name did not appear among the membership of the committee when it was announced. They were going to decide on the distribution of *his* money, all said and done, but it had now become *our* money, and he was once again and thanklessly back in the margins.

"*We* got a grade 4!" he would often hear, usually from some member of the Leisurewear staff, who, typically for them, did no research at all, and couldn't even be included in the exercise. Tarquin was also remarkably proud of *his* success, and Bob was too. The grade and the money were entirely down to Charles and Tommy Wakefield – no one else – but neither was included in deciding the issues of it.

Loyal to his moral duty, Bob pushed on with his plan to cut Charles completely out of the game. He knew Thomas would simply haul along with the main drag, so all Bob had to do was pre-empt Tarquin and Austin as to what the plan was.

"Tarquin. It's Bob. I need to have a word. Can you meet me in Austin Oldfield's office in half an hour? Yes, that's right, it is about the RAE. About the *money*, actually."

When Tarquin arrived, Bob was already there, the door ajar.

"Ah, Tarquin. Right. Yes. I've been filling Austin in with a few details. As you know, the dean has agreed with Thomas to give the money to the department, and not directly to Rae or Wakefield. And in turn, Thomas agreed with my recommendation that we set up this committee. So, it's up to the three of us…and Thomas, of course," he added, "how it gets spent."

Bob resounded triumphantly, "What we should do is allocate half the money to support two PhD studentships," while Tarquin and Austin listened attentively. "Then we invite proposals from our younger staff – or let's say *newer appointees*. We can fix a ceiling on the rank, so that no readers or professors are eligible to apply. Now, of course, being fairly new lecturers, they won't have enough experience to supervise a PhD student on their own. So, a second supervisor needs to be found, to act as a mentor. According to the university's higher-degree committee regulations – I believe I'm right, Austin – until they have supervised five PhDs, under such a mentor arrangement, they are not regarded as free-standing supervisors. So, in order that the mentor can provide, um ... appropriate *support*, shall we say, the topic of the PhD project would have to be in the mentor's subject field. Now, the two newest lecturers were appointed in the areas of General Studies and Leisurewear Dynamics, so that would seem to suggest you and me, Austin. Because of the appalling fall in Applied Physics recruitment, obviously there have been no new Physics lecturers appointed for several years, so that eliminates Rae, for instance, as a possible mentor for these PhD studentships...and Wakefield for that matter," he laughed. "Tarquin. You have all your Physical Education and Professional Development activities, and all your committees and work for the Remote Learning University, so you would probably be too occupied in any case, to be a mentor."

Tarquin gave an affirmative smile, tinted with relief. Yes, chairing the departmental research committee was enough for him. Anyway, now he'd got his professorship, what was the incentive to get involved with research. He'd managed without it all these years, albeit bitterly resenting those who had been promoted on the strengths of their research output. They had to have published something, at least, like the dean of the Faculty of Technology, Patrick Walker, who had notched up the number fifteen on his list of publications, and was therefore one of the higher scoring professors at EEU.

"Bloody Rae! He's just unnatural!" Tarquin would tell everybody. "Two 'undred publications! And at 'is age. It's absolutely bloody ridiculous! Ah don't know why the 'ell we ever appointed 'im!"

Bob continued with the chase. "The other thing we need is a research technician. I think we should also fund this new position from the RAE income. Ideally, we need someone who can run various instruments, but seeing as we are buying a new one, the leisurewear tester," he simpered, "it's imperative that we make maximum use of this in order to build on our grade 2 rating in Dynamic Fabric Materials, so I would argue a strong case for appointing someone with experience in the field of leisurewear dynamics, and ideally also with a background in EFS. EFS could be very useful to some of your General Studies people, too, Austin." Bob looked piously intense, placing his palms in thoughtful deliverance. "So this appointment would be key in fulfilling the university research strategy team's commitment to develop both areas, which, as I recall from the last meeting, were considered to be up and coming."

Austin was not entirely convinced by Bob's sales pitch about the EFS, but since his "people" were such a motley crew, there was always the chance that some good might come from it, possibly in hand with the appointment of a new PhD student, who would become part of that submission in the next RAE.

"OK, Bob. You've obviously thought it all through quite thoroughly, and your case seems convincing to me. What do you think, Tarquin?"

Tarquin looked at him thoughtfully. "Ay. Ah've no problems with any of it, but…" ever the committee man, he went on, "as ah see it, even allowing for *overheads*, paid back to the university on the PhD studentships, we haven't spent quite all of it yet, have we? Ah mean, ah don't know exactly what all the figures *are*, these days, but there must be a few bob left? Am ah right there, Bob?"

Involuntarily, this time, but Tarquin had primed the last act on the bill.

"Yes, Tarquin. I was just coming to that…" Bob tripped on crisply, "According to my sums, this leaves us with about fifteen thousand, give or take. Now that would cover the cost of a maintenance grant to a PhD student, plus the registration fee to the university, but there would be nothing left for consumables, to cover the cost of the project itself."

"Couldn't Thomas simply stump up some departmental cash for that?" suggested Austin.

"Mmmm, well. You know what his attitude towards research is," replied Bob. "He wouldn't wear it. I have another idea, though." Both Austin and Tarquin looked intrigued.

"What other option is there?" Tarquin asked. "Could the University Research Strategy Committee or the University Executive Strategy Team step in?"

"No." Austin answered. "Both bodies merely devise policy. They have no direct financial input. All monies for salaries, research, customer supply, administration and so forth are devolved down to the individual faculties. It is the faculties themselves that have to fund their objectives from their own various allocations. The only exception is the salary bill for the executive strategy team itself, which is top-sliced and includes the vice-chancellor, and he decides what each of them is paid, including me, now I'm on it," Austin chortled. "In our own Faculty of Technology, the dean devolves funding on down to the various departments, so if you want anything, you *do* need to go to Thomas … and as Bob says, he wouldn't wear it."

Bob picked up the lead. "Now exactly, that's what I meant. Which is why I've come up with an alternative idea. We should offer up the remaining fifteen thousand for general bids of up to about five thousand each, for seed corn, pump-priming actions, for instance: consumables, small items of equipment, possibly some travel funds to initiate collaborations with leading research groups in other universities. That way, we benefit the greatest number of researchers. I think it's the fairest and most effective use of the money."

This was a pronouncement, but the lot sounded entirely reasonable, if you weren't in the know, included within a scheme which provided research students to two promising young lecturers. As a superficial strategy, no one could find fault with any of it, and when the email was circulated it read quite plausibly:

> *To: ALL STAFF*
> *Subject: RAE Income*
> *c.c: Dean, V-C; Pro-V-C for Research; Jolanda, Letticia; O'Grady, Thomas.*
> *From: Bates, Bob; Tupper, Tarquin; Oldfield, Austin.*
>
> *An extraordinary meeting was called yesterday, to discuss possible actions on the spending of our RAE income. After much deliberation, the following agenda was drawn up:*
>
> *(1)   It was agreed to provide funding for two PhD studentships. Project proposals are invited from any staff below the rank of reader. They should be submitted to me directly, as chair of the "RAE Income Strategy Committee", which will consider their relative merits in context of the department's overall research aims.*
>
> *(2)   In light of the forthcoming purchase of an Electromagnetic Force Spectrometer (EFS) and a Dynamic Leisurewear Tester from the government research infrastructure allocation, as agreed by the University Research Strategy Committee, it was decided that a research technician/experimental officer should be appointed, and that the funding for this post should be provided additionally from the RAE income.*
>
> *(3)   New initiatives. In order to pump-prime new research identifiers, it is proposed to invite bids for e.g. equipment, consumables, travel to other laboratories to set up research collaborations etc to the tune of up to ca £5K.*

For all bids referred to above, the overriding criterion is that an improvement in the RAE grade is likely to be achieved from them, on the strength of additional e.g. research council funding and publications.

Professor Tarquin Tupper
Chair of RAE Income Strategy Committee
Professor of Physical Education
Head of Physics
Physics Modular Programmes Leader
Physics Research Leader
Fellow of the European Industrial Physics Society
Chair of the Departmental Research Strategy Committee

When the message arrived, Charles read it in a contest of emotions. On the annoyed/rankled side were lined up the standard players: that worthless, bloody professorship, done behind his back at that! If they'd asked his opinion as to Tarquin's professorial worth, as other, better universities did of him about their candidates, he would have dealt him the contempt he deserved! That collection of titles, underliners to his self-importance, though none of them actually meant anything! The lording arrogance, pontificating upon goods he had nothing to do with getting, as though they were a handout, available only through his glory and beneficence.

On the succouring side, stood the single glimmer of salvation, from the lot, but heavily outgunned, and out in the open: the bit about "New initiatives...travel to other laboratories to initiate research collaborations..." And no restrictions on rank, here. Charles was in full agreement that the research students should go to the younger staff. He felt sorry for them. Even though they were all appointed before their own PhD was completed, and none of them had any post-doctoral experience, they had been sold a lie. It was another roll of the EEU savings vehicle. A gravy train in reverse; collecting but never supplying over the length of its piecemeal voyage. Get 'em young and get 'em cheap! But most importantly, *cheap*!

There were a couple of cases – sad souls, scrapped at forty from industry – only too grateful to EEU for a job. Any job. They asked no questions. But those actually young, with undulled shiny faces, were star-laden: "Wow! Just imagine, getting a *university lectureship* straight from my PhD. Before I've finished it, even!"

Such rang out their phone calls to proud parents. They could laugh at those poor suckers doing post-docs, and they did too, especially the ones caught in the "post-doc trap", on their second or third temporary contract, or worse, vainly sniffing after permanent jobs for which they were by now too old. But beyond the glitter lay a deeper truth. When they asked about "research opportunities" at their interview, all were uniformly reassured, "Of course, the department will do all it can to encourage your independent research careers". Thomas O'Grady and Bob Bates voiced the promise in a harmonious accord to all of them, beaming like kindly uncles. That did the trick, allowing them to hire the grateful if not the great, and reject potential troublemakers who might later try to hold them against welshing on their words. And those words pronged upon the trident, *all it can*, which in truth amounted to precious little. Bob Bates interpreted his role as departmental research officer as being partly pastoral, and consequently he adopted each of the new recruits as their personal advisor and research mentor. This was not altogether an act of altruism, since it meant that Bob's name was entered as principal research supervisor of any research students they might end up supervising. It had been a lucrative ploy, at least while the Vice-Chancellor's Research Student Support Fund for Newly Appointed Lecturers (VCRSSFNAL) was in full flood, and Bob was able to claim that he had supervised almost ten PhDs, a keynote in his application for a professorship, which drew away the sting from the empty boxes referring to publications or research grants of his own.

The vice-chancellor's "fund" had since been axed, however, and there were one or two askance remarks thrown around which managed to filter through to Bob's attention, along the lines of "How can a departmental research officer not have any research students of their own?" Such were fair but rather critical questions which Bob deflected by referring to an apparently vast army of part-time PhDs registered with various universities – albeit not necessarily EEU – but working in local industry, whom he claimed he *did* somehow have a hand in supervising.

To shore up his credibility, though, Bob needed at least one PhD student nominally registered under his name, in-house at EEU, for all doubts to be dispelled by the evidence of them. But the V-C had drawn the draw-strings on his fund tight, the sack emptied into other barren coffers, so another source was required. In earlier days, he had co-supervised several PhDs with Rod Shine, but the relatively small amount of money released by the local leisurewear industry to support research at EEU had dried up following the announcement of Rod's jail term in the Evergreen Gazette, and none of the research councils would touch leisurewear research with a bargepole. In short, it needed to be internal money of some kind, which when available had always been targeted toward newer staff, as was stressed in the name of the original Vice-Chancellor's Research Student Support Fund for Newly Appointed Lecturers (VCRSSFNAL).

Then – a gift from God! In the midst of the wilderness, there *was* internal money available. Charles Rae's RAE funding, unprecedented in the department. It was entirely up for grabs, but of course, naturally it would go straight to Rae, and that would not oil Bob's political locomotions one drop.

★ ★ ★

Amid the calm reassurances of religious pop melodies, drawn from live recordings at the Evergreen Christian Reform Church, Bob plotted and pondered, until the light began to glimmer. Of course! He needed simply to invoke the traditions of the VCRSSFNAL. As an embryonic university, hatching into the world of flight, or so it thought, EEU clutched fast to the shell of the polytechnic and invoked its traditions as a mantra against all insecurities of change.

"The RAE money will simply replace some of what has been lost through the dissolution of the VCRSSFNAL."

"Yes! Well done, Bob. That's what we'll do with it!" Thomas was delighted. "Thank God!" he thought. "That saves any decision making on my part." Or rather, he applauded himself for his nifty delegation skills.

"OK, Bob," Thomas beamed. "Yes, as you say, let's create a couple of research studentships – ah, yes, and a leisurewear technician. I hadn't forgotten."

Then, by manipulating and even creating a committee or so, suddenly they were Bob and Austin's research students, registered at EEU and warding off imminent humiliation for both of them.

Charles had been unaware of the politicking. The new staff. Yes. Giving them a research student each was the least that could be done for the poor sods! Otherwise, all they would get is "a research allowance" – not money, as there was none, but of "one hundred hours reduced teaching", just the same as Tarquin Tupper, but as a one-off special dispensation in their first year, while Tarquin had his every year, although he did no research.

"That means you only have to do four hundred hours teaching, to start off with, leaving you *plenty* of time to get your research going!"

While the former statement about a research allowance was stressed as a sweetener and a clause of commitment to research in the department, on the day of the interview, the second one, both qualifier and rider, was handed out along with a box of tissues by Bob a month or so into the realities of actually stepping into the job.

"You wouldn't have got a better deal anywhere else, you know. Who else do you think would have given you a lectureship with no post-doctoral experience? Before you'd finished your PhD, even? We've bent over backwards to give you a good start, and..." Bob's tone hardened, "a little gratitude wouldn't go amiss!

"We're on your side, can't you see? You're lucky to be in 'Leisurewear' too. Confidentially..." Bob adopted a confidential pose, "if you were one of the Physics staff, your job would be on the line. At least you have job *security* with us."

This was their only grace, because after a first year's worth of "reduced" teaching and admin, they would then go up to the full five hundred hours contact teaching. With the associated admin, marking, examinations etc, this made a good 35-plus-hour week, and in their first year the hundred hours "allowance" would not cover the preparation time for lectures, whose delivery was new to them, along with the "EEU Teaching Certificate" they were required to study for; thus ensuring they never did any research, and EEU had them forever. They were indeed "lecturers": leather-patched teachers and paper shufflers for all eternity, or so it might seem, as after a few years without any ongoing research credibility – papers and grants – they would be unemployable in any other university. Thus the generations of EEU staff, especially in Leisurewear, reproduced themselves wholly.

While Charles commiserated with them absolutely, he was in no position to offer much practical consolation. This they knew, and although "Professor Rae" was to some extent a figure of pity e.g. "What the hell is Charles Rae doing here?" Marylynne Beddoes asked Tommy Wakefield, to which Tommy responded laconically, "I think he often asks himself the same question". Charles was also the focus of their respect, since only he, though his glories were mostly past laurels, provided a spectral window on a celestial world that shimmered phantom to EEU. At least, now, two of them had a chance to kickstart some research. In was a shame that the RAE money wasn't available during their first "light load" year, but they could at last put some of the plans dreamed during that time into practice, in the hands of a PhD student.

21

Charles opened the new file in his word processing package, and entered the title in capitals: "RESEARCH INITIATIVES". He felt confident. After all, the RAE money only existed because of him – and he was asking for just fifteen hundred quid of it. The committee could hardly refuse him! That would be more than a little churlish! Moreover, he had a strong case, in the shape of a grant application that was highly rated by the reviewers, but who thought some preliminary results should be got, to show the idea of it would work in practice. If he could get back to the German lab, and spend a month there during the summer – what there was left of it after the resit exams that most of the first and second year students were obliged to take (once again, he would have to tell his wife there was "no holiday this year"), that should be sufficient time to get the results he needed , and then the Big Grant! He had a watertight case, and he would be back on track with his research career, for a paltry fifteen hundred quid, that was his by rights anyway.

The reconvening of the RAE Income Strategy Committee was a perfunctory and virtual affair. Salt and pepper on a set menu.

"Bob. It's Tarquin. I've just been through the Research Initiatives applications. Well, there are only three of them, but ah see that Charles Rae is asking for fifteen 'undred quid to go swanning off to Germany. Ah don't think that's an appropriate use of our resources. Ah'll tell you what. He's asked for two 'undred quid to buy some special sample tubes 'e reckons 'e needs – bloody expensive if you ask me – but anyway, ah suggest we give 'im that, then 'e can't complain we 'aven't given 'im anything, can 'e? Now ah know 'e won't be able to actually go there, but that's 'is problem, not ours! Ah'll email the committee's decision to all staff," and so the message arrived:

To: ALL STAFF.

Subject: RAE Income.

c.c: Dean, V-C; Pro-V-C for Research; Jolanda, Letticia; O'Grady, Thomas.

From: Bates, Bob; Tupper, Tarquin; Oldfield, Austin.

The committee has made its final decision regarding the expenditure of the department's RAE income. It has been decided to support the following:

(1)   Research Student (PhD). Principal Supervisor: Professor Bob Bates.

(2)   Research Student (PhD). Principal Supervisor: Professor Austin Oldfield.

(3)   Research Technician to run Leisurewear Tester. To report to: Professor Bob Bates.

(4)   Research Initiatives (taking account of Faculty of Technology Research Strategy):
(i) Support for Leisurewear Tester: £6K (Professor Bob Bates).
(ii) Support for EFS: £6K (Professor Bob Bates).
(iii) Attendance for important research initiative in Physical Education at the Remote Learning University, office of Western Africa: £6K (Professor Tarquin Tupper).
(iv) Sample Tubes: £200.00 (C Rae).

Professor Tarquin Tupper
Chair of RAE Income Strategy Committee
Professor of Physical Education
Head of Physics
Physics Modular Programmes Leader
Physics Research Leader
Fellow of the European Industrial Physics Society
Chair of the Departmental Research Strategy Committee

★ ★ ★

The electromagnetic force spectrometer was to prove a headache for Bob, on two counts. Though he knew these three words, and their initials, he had no clue what they meant. It was also a much larger machine than he realised, and despite the fact that no one in the Department of LAPS had the slightest interest in EFS, it was decided they, being the most "physical" of the faculty's departments, should take charge of the instrument. This meant that, as departmental research officer, Bob had to find somewhere for it to go.

"Mmmm. This might be a stroke of luck," he murmured, alone in his office, musing in the meditative ambiance of religious melodies. Now that Charles Rae's cosmic ray spectrometer (CRS) was no longer operational, a case could be made to throw it out. Especially if there was pressure on space, which there would be, as search as he might, Bob, wringing his hands, would simply not be able to find any alternative. This is what he would tell Thomas O'Grady and the dean. He could even have Charles help dismantle his own machine, and the technicians to load it into a skip! That would really be carrying his cross: crown of thorns and all! His glittering research career finally nailed. That'll teach him to come here and show us all up! The analogy amused him, ever loyal to his Christian virtues.

One problem still remained, that he, Bob, was entirely ignorant of EFS, a condition that might cause considerable embarrassment for him as the whole process of its installation gathered momentum. He was out of his depth, and knew it. He also knew that the one person who could help him was Charles Rae. Charles had no particular interest in EFS, rather CRS, but to Bob it was all the same: "something to do with spectrometer, the S word" though there was in actual fact, no connection between them whatsoever. Bob wanted to palm off the whole business onto Charles. Charles, however, was not best disposed towards Bob, who town-cried the news that the CRS bid had been turned down, with his customary tact and panache, adding that the leisurewear tester was to be bought, as a pinch of extra salt.

"I'm sorry, Charles. These were committee decisions. Now, there's no point you losing your temper. Shout at me if you like, but it was down to a show of hands. I had practically nothing to do with any of it," but his supercilious smirk gave the game away. With typical deviousness, Bob set about unloading his responsibility for the EFS onto Charles. He called a meeting of himself, Charles, Tommy and Tarquin "to discuss the EFS", asking them to meet him in the room where the EFS instrument would go – not that Charles or Tommy knew this yet. Tarquin had been primed as to the purpose of the occasion, but Charles and Tommy wondered what it had to do with either of them, although they suspected skullduggery since they both had equipment in that room, and Charles had seen Bob and Thomas O'Grady wandering around with clipboards, making a detailed inventory of its contents. This just had to be about "space" ("resource implications"), particularly as Bob's tape measure was purposefully stretched, apparently assessing the floor dimensions of each item.

When Charles and Tommy arrived, Bob and Tarquin were already amid their deliberations. They heard the words "well, this can go, for a start..." which rather confirmed their fears. Another bloody conspiracy! But on sight of them, the conversation was truncated abruptly, like walking in on the locals in a pub in North Wales; just before they switch to Welsh, and the stuffed owl above the bar glints an unwelcoming malevolence: "You're not from round here, are you, boyo?"

Bob intercepted the situation with a sly mouth.

"Glad you could make it. Tarquin and I were just talking..."

"I heard. What's the game?" Charles moved forward.

Tarquin countered: the bombastic bulldog, barking louder since the award of his professorship.

"Now see 'ere, Charles. It's not Bob's fault. Ah mean. Ah was talking to Thomas O'Grady the other day, and 'e said 'e 'ad grave concerns. *Grave concerns*, ah say. Grave concerns about the abuse of space in this department. The dean's told 'im 'e's got to cut back."

It was Bill and Ben. Next it was Bob's run with the ball. "Tarquin's quite right. Thomas and I have agreed with the dean to take some pressure off the overhead on our space allocation by accommodating the new EFS instrument, as a faculty facility. The problem is we have to use some of our *existing* space for it. We also have to find somewhere for my, I mean *the faculty's* leisurewear dynamics tester. Did I say the University Research Strategy Committee agreed to support my bid for this? It was a complete surprise. Now, Tarquin and I have looked all round the department, and – Thomas agrees – the only possible room we can use is this one."

"But it's *full* already," Tommy interjected. "We can't, physically I mean, get any more stuff in here!"

Tarquin smiled that smile. The one Charles recalled from their fateful first meeting, on the day of his interview. He should have trusted his instincts, then.

"Well, now. The dean has made an executive decision. It's out of all our hands, ah'm afraid. Your stuff's got to go."

"What?! You're joking?! How the hell are we going to do any research?" Tommy sounded incredulous.

In came Bob, "Now, there's quite some doubt over the future of physics research here. This came up at a University Research Strategy Committee meeting, recently. I know it was on the agenda of the University Executive Strategy Team. I'm sure Austin Oldfield will give an appropriately convincing representation of your case. He *is* the university research manager, after all! The EST will listen to him. We discussed it *all*, after church, last week." Bob laughed.

"So, what about the RAE result?" Charles demanded.

Bob and Tarquin smirked knowingly, in the behind-the-scenes knowledge that Charles was not party to. Both of them had been there for thirty-odd years, and knew its ways better than him. They were both committee men too, well served, and Charles was not, being focussed on his research. Since they did nothing, they had both time and resentful inclination for politics. They couldn't match him fair, but they could do it foul, killing the golden goose in the process, but that never entered their minds. His image made theirs look bad, so they had to shatter it, being incapable of improving themselves to equal him.

"But we're not *Physics* research, any more," Charles railed incredulously. "The grade 4 was for Biological Sciences."

Charles could scarcely believe the message coming across to him. "Any more than you, Bob, are still *Leisurewear*? You're Dynamic Fabric Materials now, aren't you? And what does it have to do with you, Tarquin? You weren't even included in the bloody RAE." Charles was sure he had slipped back into the twilight zone.

"Ah'm chair of the departmental research committee..." Tarquin responded abrasively, "and professor of Physical Education. Bob is departmental research officer. It's our job to see that the dean's wishes are carried out properly."

Bob, again, "Anyway, Charles, your spectrometer doesn't work any more, does it? That was part of your case for the university to buy you a new one ... which they didn't, of course," he simpered.

"Back in my old university, I could have got it fixed by the electronics technicians," Charles remarked in dismay, "but now the vice-chancellor's closed the electronics workshop here, as part of his rationalisation of non-essential services."

"Yes, well, you're not there any more, are you? You took the job here.

You're at EEU, now, and we have our own way of doing things. We don't care 'ow things are done in other universities," Tarquin announced, with an almost indignant pride, continuing, "As part of the space saving measures, all defective equipment is to be scrapped, so even without the need to find room for the EFS and the leisurewear tester, it would have to go." And with a final shove, Tarquin had rolled the seal-stone over the sarcophagus of Charles' career. Tommy's kit was "down" too, damaged beyond his own practical resourcefulness to repair it, by the same mains power surge that had taken out Charles' machine.

With no electronics backup, neither of them had a leg to stand on. It all had to go. Charles remembered a dog his family kept when he was a child. A large German shepherd called Tiger. Tiger was falsely accused of sheep worrying, a serious matter in a farming community, but really he'd been let out of his pen one night by a malicious local with a grudge. The farmer called the police, who would come for the animal and take it away to be destroyed. But his father had anticipated this and phoned the Air Force, who came with dog handlers and took Tiger away for training. The dog had resisted, breaking open the wooden crate with its powerful back, but they took him anyway, off to a good home where he would be appreciated. That's what Charles would do with his machine: give it away, to be renewed and reinvigoured, not dismantled and dissected, its body parts cast out by the idiot technicians at EEU, who couldn't make up chemical solutions correctly to the concentrations written on the bottles that were supposed to contain them, and would probably ask for overtime to do the job. "That's not in my contract!"

"Now there's just one more thing…" Bob rippled out the final delivery, "the room. We need someone to take responsibility for it."

"The room?" Charles echoed suspiciously. "Now what exactly would that entail? I bet there's more to it than just keeping the keys. Otherwise you – or Tarquin for that matter – could do it yourselves."

"Well, yes." Bob let go with a simpering blush. He'd been rumbled. "I admit there's a bit more involved than just the keys. Tarquin and I were discussing it all, earlier. The room needs to be completely refurbished, first. New floor. Externally located gas cylinders. New workbenches. A replacement air-conditioning unit. Brand new seals for the windows. This will all need to be coordinated with the Estates Department. And you know what they're like!" he tittered. "Then, of course, there's the purchase of the EFS instrument and the leisurewear tester. We'll have to go out to tender for these, so someone will have to liaise with the various manufacturers, and get some costings and quotations. And the delivery of the machines will need coordinating," Bob pouted contemplatively. "And then there is the maintenance and operation of the EFS, once it is installed; day-to-day running; filling it up with liquid helium etc. Now I think about it, there is quite a lot that needs doing, but, Charles, you know about EFS, or at least, it's a lot closer to your background than mine..." It was a case of "industrial training" all over again, which Tarquin managed to lumber him with in his first week at EEU.

"Hang on. I can see where this one's going! Tarquin, you're a 'physical' professor. You must know about EFS, surely?"

"Ah'm far too busy! Any road, mah discipline's Physical Education. *Education*, ah say! It's got nowt to do with EFS. EFS is a *ree*-search instrument. It's not mah business. You're supposed to be our *ree*-search professor! It's down to you!"

"Forget it! CRS is my game. Not EFS! Even though I've been driven out of business." Then Charles' anger was suddenly dispelled by the flash of a solution.

"Of course, Barney Asif. He's your man. He tells me he's an expert on EFS. That's the main reason Thomas O'Grady appointed him, *apparently*. Get him to do it!"

Wonderful! Charles had found the solution. Bob could wash his hands of the whole lot of it! He glowed in relief, resonating uncontainedly in joy.

"Oooh, yes! That's it. Barneee! I'll get onto him at once!"

★ ★ ★

Barney tried to conceal his consternation behind a smile which didn't stretch quite wide enough. He was in danger of exposure, a fate that reared itself sinusoidally, then fell, but marked out the matter of time it only was. He had lied, first on his application form, and then confirmed the story at the interview, being forced to tangle the web of deception further, ever since that first step across the threshold of EEU. Now the honeymoon period was a lingering memory, and suspicions rose constructively on the cool swell of events. Charles' door was part open, and Barney bounced into the frame.

"Charles," he began edgily, "we have a problem. The EFS. We need to sort out the room for the new machine."

"We? I don't want anything to do with the bloody thing!" was the response that met him. Charles was irritated, not only by the whole saga of the government research infrastructure allocation and the concomitant derailing of his own bid from it, and that he knew Barney was trying to dump the job on him, but he was about to leave for a conference. He glanced only perfunctorily at Barney, as he continued printing off some sets of acetate sheets for a lecture he had been invited to give there.

"But Thomas O'Grady and Bob Bates ... and the dean, Patrick Walker," he added, "have instructed me to involve you in sorting it all out." This smelt to Charles like more bullshit; yet another card dealt from his pack of lies.

"Look. Sorry, Barney, you're supposed to be the expert on EFS, not me, and anyway, I'm busy. I've got a train to catch in fifteen minutes. I'm off to a conference. I'm trying to get these overheads printed off for a lecture. I don't want to miss it."

Charles' suspicions about Barney were growing. Barney Asif. "As if" he believed a bloody word the man said. Why too, had he wriggled out of giving a couple of lectures on EFS if he was an expert on the subject? It didn't add up. Unless he didn't really know much about it, of course. Tommy Wakefield had denounced Barney privately to Charles as a "con man". Perhaps he was, or at least a pathological liar. Maybe he started out as a con man, and the habit of his tall tales became compulsive.

"There is one other thing, Charles." Barney eyed him with a shifty sidelong glance. "There is a readership going at Effington. I would like to apply for it and I wonder if I might use you for a reference?"

This was tricky, but the adrenaline of Charles' haste made his thoughts sharp.

"OK. I tell you what, Barney. Let me have sight of your CV, and I'll make a decision." Charles smiled kindly, as he got up to reach for his bag, adding, "The fact is, Barney, you have to be very careful what you write in references these days, especially with freedom of information." Charles laughed.

"I have it here." Barney handed it to him.

Charles was surprised at the correct anticipation of his own response, but he accepted the single sheet of paper, slightly puzzled, asking "Is that it?" to which Barney nodded.

"I'll read it on the train and give you my opinion next week," Charles promised him.

★ ★ ★

Charles arrived at the station with some minutes to spare, and bought a polystyrene cup of coffee, along with a baguette in a paper wrapper. He then boarded the train. On finding a seat, he sat down, and opened the shelf in front of him, putting the coffee down, alongside Barney's CV, which he had extracted from his bag. As he began to read it, the visceral sense deepened within him that the words spelt "bad news" throughout:

> Name: Barney Asif
>
> Title: Dr
>
> Degrees Awarded and Previous Positions (to be listed in order):
>
> BSc Physics, 2:2. Year of Award, 1985...

Fair enough, but then ... PhD Physics. Year of Award, 1996.

Eleven years? Why the hell had it taken him eleven years to get his PhD? It would normally be three or four. So what had gone wrong? What had he been doing? Why was the PhD finally awarded by a different university from the one where he had apparently actually started the project? This was most irregular. The post-doctoral details were vague. Had he, in fact, done one? It seemed as if the university which awarded the PhD had also been his post-doctoral *alma mater*, but there were no clear dates to tell the tale by. Charles noticed that Barney had already put down Professor Charles Rae as his lead referee, and Professor Reginald Haswell, who seemed to be at the same university which had certified Barney's PhD. Now that name rang a bell. Charles had been approached by the vice-chancellor of Reg Haswell's university to ask for his opinion on Reg's application for promotion to a personal Chair there, which he had supported.

The case was not overwhelming, Charles recalled: about sixty-five publications, a lot in good journals though, and Reg had done a prodigious amount of teaching and administration. So Charles reversed the process by asking himself the question: would he be offended if the man were awarded a professorship? He felt not, and anyway at fifty-eight, Reg would be unlikely to get another chance if he turned him down now. By EEU standards, apart from Charles own publication record, the man was a giant! Sixty-five published articles by a professor at EEU would be a world record! In contrast, Tarquin Tupper's professorship did offend him. A man with no published work at all: that mocking aggrandizement jarred every bone of his academic sensibilities to the marrow. Charles decided he would phone Reg Haswell to flesh out the empty spaces in Barney's CV.

What about Barney's list of publications? For a readership at Effington, that should be substantive, surely. But, again, the bones stared bare. Charles counted six – all short papers, just a page or two. Two of the journals he had never heard of – did they exist? Not a Rob Robinson case again, he wondered? Then four patents. Mmmm. Harder to check than journal articles, but it could be done. Then mention of Barney's PhD thesis as a publication. God! That really was scraping the barrel. The only other person Charles had ever known do that was Tarquin Tupper, proclaiming it as an "acclaimed book", on the joke EEU website. This was his main claim to fame, along with his work as a tutor and consultant for the Remote Learning University, which had allegedly qualified him for a professorship, in Physical Education.

Curiously, the list ran on with a number of other PhD theses authored by other people – were these supposed to be students whom Barney had supervised? Alas, the facts trundled into muddy streams once more. There was really nothing there, which even Barney realised, as he had included an implicit apology in the lines above his name:

> I know that you will be looking for someone from one of the world's most famous physics research groups, but I am just as good, even though I have not worked in any of them, since I ran my own group of twenty PhD students and post-docs. I am also aware that my list of publications is probably less extensive than you would expect for a reader in a prestigious university such as yours, but all my research has been funded from unlimited sources by private industry, and therefore its results were heavily bound by confidentiality agreements and I am unable to publish anything from it. I do have some patents though.
>
> There was also a terrible fire in my previous department which destroyed much of our measurements and our equipment. This was kept a secret by the university as we did not wish to alarm our sponsors, so you may not have heard anything about it.

> Yours sincerely,
> Barney Asif

Yeah. "As if." Charles shook his head. There was no way he could put his name to this, for fear of soiling his own reputation. Unlimited funding? Well, whatever had been provided must have gone through the university's books, surely. Or was this the kind of funding "in kind" that Bob Bates had mumbled about at the last awayday, when pressed on the point. In other words, "no funding", despite Bob's railing of Charles that most of his "millions" didn't actually go through EEU's books, compared with *all* Bob's industrial funding, which did. It was another pack of lies. Bob and Barney were a pair of fantasists!

How the hell had Thomas O'Grady been even marginally impressed by Barney's CV? Hadn't the short change even begun to jangle, as he stepped over the potholes in it all? It was preposterous.

Charles had wanted a colleague of his, Richard Michaels, currently in the US, to get the job, and had acted as a referee for him. With hindsight, Charles now observed, this had most likely sealed the kiss of death on Richard's application. Richard was in the post-doc trap. He was nearly forty and needed a permanent job. And soon, as his latest contract was about to end. Otherwise it would be teacher training, and the end of a successful research career. Richard was blocks ahead of Barney, too. He had the publications, a lot of proven expertise, and could account respectably for his time, in contrast to Barney's mysterious meanderings.

Charles felt certain Richard could cope with the teaching at EEU, but moreover, he would make a strong contribution to research there, and his research interests complemented those of himself and Tommy Wakefield wonderfully. He would be a real signal to flare when the next RAE sailed into view. Charles had pointed all this out, so Thomas hired Barney instead.

"There aren't any boxes on the personnel form we can't tick" had been Thomas' response when Jake Parr espoused his reservations. Jake knew Barney had already been interviewed by another university, but all four subject groups that spoke to him sussed him out as a bullshitter. Barney was made as a rubber man. Small and bouncy, but when pressed too hard – wheee, off he would go, propelled from one hand and onward into the grip of some equally rivalling fabrication.

"But there isn't a box we can't tick," Thomas stared back blankly at Jake through the lenses of his impassive steel-rimmed spectacles. And that was that. In an instant, Barney was all theirs.

22

Hanns-Peter Krankenpfleger's head rested uneasily against that sultry night. The mosquitoes which buzzed around the neighbouring tributary of the Southern Saxony river precluded opening any windows, and Hanns-Peter had the proverbial sweet blood. Back in Wuperbaden, he had always slept well with his wife, impervious to heat or cold; but alone in Southern Saxony any stimulus, of noise or temperature or thought, no matter how slight, snapped him into waves of alertness, if he could get off at all. His restless movements over the increasingly crumpled sheet on the air-bed brushed his forehead refreshingly against a cool oasis on its rubber surface.

But being a heavy man, his nocturnal agitations had driven sufficient air from the mattress body to offer no resistance against the concrete floor.

"*Scheisse!*" he exclaimed, feeling a sudden sharp pain of concussion between his left eye socket and the floor. He was fully awake now. Tired, but bucked up by adrenaline. Nothing for it but to get up and read, as he had always done in such dark hours that denied him sleep. It was three in the morning. He rose ungainlily to his feet, stubbing his little toe.

"*Scheisse!*"

He let the pyjama bottoms fall to the floor, reaching into the plastic bag of washing, which he took home on the rare occasions he did manage to get back to Wuperbaden these days, for a clean pair of underpants; then stepping and staggering, he buttressed himself, flying against the wall. He surveyed the room in half-illumination: the barren white walls, the mattress and the plastic bag. That was it. He could hardly be further from Wuperbaden and all trappings of home.

He would give up the flat. He had gone to Southern Saxony to work, after all. Sleep was a distraction, which God had denied him in His perfect wisdom of all things. He would go to the department. Yes, that was the calling to him...

"*Guten Nacht, Herr Professor. Was ist das?*"

"*Ich moechte betreten mich Laboratorium,*" Hanns-Peter explained.

"*Jawohl, Herr Professor. Moechten sie…*"

It was clear the man was not German, so Hanns-Peter switched to English.

"Please, would you let me into the building. I need to get to my laboratory and my office."

"Yes. Of course, Herr Professor."

Hanns-Peter wandered purposefully down the safe corridors, guarded and familiar, but now filled by the certainty that his true purpose had been revealed to him.

It was no longer about Lederbauer, but between his soul and the Almighty. Lederbauer had been merely the agent of his true spiritual destiny. The hand of God incarnate; forcing his own hand, holding the suitcase from Wuperbaden; air-bed in the other; train ticket gritted between his teeth.

Yes. All he needed to do was move the air-bed into his modestly spacious office quarters, rise early around five, if he slept at all, wash in the gents toilets – *Herren* – or even *Frauen*, at that time of the morning before the cleaners arrived, officially at six.

A glance at his watch: four o'clock. There was no time like the present, so he retraced his steps to the security office.

"Yes. I need to collect a few things from home. I should be only about half an hour."

"I will wait for you here, Herr Professor."

That was good. Hanns-Peter did not want to have to hang around on the doorstep while the man made some other security rounds, or went for a cigarette before returning to his post.

It was a brief task. Five minutes there, then five back. Since the inflatable mattress was now well worn, he needed only to unplug the two valves and roll it up, what air it still contained hissing away unresistingly as he did so. Knowing that it would be embarrassing to be seen taking it into the Physics Department in the middle of the night, despite the good intentions of this action, Hanns-Peter carefully placed the two available plastic bags over it, one at each end, carefully overlaying them in the middle, so as not to bring attention to the contents of his bundle.

Everything else: spare socks, pants, shirt and trousers, pyjamas, soap, toothpaste, shampoo, comb and electric razor, he could fit easily enough into the suitcase. Dropping the keys through the letter box in the door of the security lodge, Hanns-Peter walked swiftly down the short street, turned the corner and arrived at the department, not looking backward at all. The whole round trip had taken just twenty-seven minutes.

"Can I help you carry your things, Herr Professor?"

"*Nein!*" Hanns-Peter answered him curtly, loath of any interaction with the man. Looking shifty and uneasy, head turned to evade an untrusting gaze, Hanns-Peter stepped smartly away from him, adding, "I can manage," knowing the guard would not press him further.

Hanns-Peter no longer tried to sleep at any particular time. He just worked at his desk until tiredness defocused his brain, and exhaustion enforced a brief torpor upon him. Sometimes he might make it onto the air-bed, which he rarely remembered to inflate; more often he would slump, brain ringing, back in his chair, or forward onto the desk, in a fog of equations, waking minutes or perhaps an hour later, face down on the papers in front of him, a trail of saliva marking their place.

The wearing of him by his new regime was pitiful to see. His secretary would knock gently to ask him if he needed anything – some more coffee perhaps? He looked like he needed it, she thought. He would rarely answer, but she filled the cup by his hand with a kind smile, nonetheless, as though trying to raise life in someone no longer quite alive. He was thinner, she was sure. Well, losing a little weight was perhaps no bad thing, but the pallor – a greenish grey – was just not healthy.

"Like a ghost," she muttered, closing the door quietly.

His nightly wandering of the corridors became a minor legend among those who worked late in the department, and found themselves startled by the apparition of him coming up on them unexpectedly.

"Mind out for the ghost," they warned each other, playfully. "Don't let him get you!"

The nickname stuck: *"Der Geist"*, a sign all was far from well.

As the sturdy structure that was Hanns-Peter began to fail, he became vulnerable to manipulation. In the hands of Bertie Bantam he could be fashioned into an assault weapon: pointed straight at Charles Rae. Even in happier times, Hanns-Peter had been naïve in his human relationships; and even he described himself self-effacingly as a "bad diplomat". But, in truth, he *was* a bad diplomat, in the same sense that a child is. Which was why Herr Dr Professor Helmut Lederbauer, with only a small stone's throw from his retirement castle, had reluctantly forced the exodus of Hanns-Peter Krankenpfleger, believing that he would be unable to manage the

Wuperbaden University politics, which demanded more mature judgement, and so could not allow his overgrown child to succeed him.

The proof of this fact was that Hanns-Peter would not have recognised the truth of it – not in a million years – and consequently left Wuperbaden not only with the suitcase and the air-bed, but a stunned sense of utter bewilderment about it all. And now, thrown off the underpinning bedrock of his life – displaced from his family and from his church, and even from the complacent familiarity of his old university, with its sweeping marble staircases and priceless portraits all around – worrisome cracks were appearing in the once robust pillar that had been Hanns-Peter Krankenpfleger.

★ ★ ★

Bertie began to work on that structure, fashioning it to his own will; working with skilled hands. As they manipulated the keyboard of his computer, he sent constant emails, amending the machine code that drove Hanns-Peter, in a daily bombardment. Chiselling away at the friendship that existed between the Hanns-Peter and Charles, until his tormented mind began to regard Charles Rae as a legitimate target.

Through the mechanisms of "peer review", Bertie and Hanns-Peter started to play a game of ping pong with Charles' career. When Charles wrote a paper for publication in one of the scientific journals, the editor would send it, say, to Bertie for review, who would of course reject it, inventing all kinds of faults and allegations of misdeed, while a second referee accepted the paper, often being quite flattering about it. So an adjudicator was then required. Then the paper and both sets of comments would be sent to Hanns-Peter, who would naturally side with Bertie, and so it would be rejected. If the journal sent the paper first to Hanns-Peter, instead, he would also invent all kinds of criticisms, in contrast with the second referee's report, and then Bertie would be sent it for adjudication, and "out" it would go: ping pong; ping pong; bounce.

Charles' dismay grew as the pile of rejected manuscripts thickened on top of his desk. They applied the same strategy on his applications for research grants, while mentioning additionally "… and his recent publication record is rather poor". Ping pong; bounce; and so Charles' funding was strangled: a severe blow and the end of his research career. But the *coup de grace* was yet to come. Bertie found a paper already published by Charles in a leading journal, and as he scrutinised it, a plan occurred to him. If he could persuade

Hanns-Peter that Charles had deliberately published one of Hanns-Peter's results as his own, and without acknowledging his work, in an act of academic malpractice, then he might enlist his help in making a joint attack on Charles. It was quite untrue, but Hanns-Peter was persuaded.

After several years of his isolation and manipulation, Hanns-Peter's mind was no longer sound enough to recognise that he'd been had, and Bertie was just using him. In any case, Hanns-Peter was never wrong, and so according to the scourging of logic, Charles must be, and therefore deserving of vilification and destruction, according to these final lines in Bertie's machine code windings:

> Dear Vice-Chancellor,
> It is with great regret that we are writing to inform you of the shocking behaviour of one of your professors, Charles Rae...

Thomas O'Grady printed off his spreadsheet of staff teaching hours and placed it in front of him. Removing his steel-rimmed spectacles, he reached into the breast pocket of his grey suit jacket, and extracted a plain white handkerchief by its corner, which he flicked from its carefully pressed pleats into a fully available cotton surface. He rotated the steel frame to give each lens, in turn, a measured but vigorous polishing, then turned the orientation of the glass between his eye and the light, repolishing it several times if necessary, until the result sparkled to his approval. Replacing the glasses, a thin smile played momentarily on his lips, as his eyes scanned down the hours column, gauging the number of hours against the name of each member of staff, one by one, from which just one name stood out towards him: 250 hours, Charles Rae. Mmmm, he surmised, he would need to do something about that.

★ ★ ★

Charles felt there was just one thing he could do, to stake his position. Get a DSc. His erstwhile mentor Ray Chambers, with whom he had done his own post-doc, had been recommending this to him for several years now, and perhaps he was right. Given that his professorship was now worthless among that of all the other similarly entitled creatures at EEU, at least a DSc would show that he actually deserved a professorship, according to the accepted standards of the world's universities. He would submit his publications to the ordeal by fire and water, in which they were scrutinised by two professors from Establishment universities, and if they survived, he would be awarded a Higher Doctorate, the *Doctor of Sciences*, DSc.

He first prepared the ground in a phone call to his former PhD supervisor, who, though now retired, still had an office in the university where Charles had studied, to avoid the dean there choosing as an examiner his nemesis Archibald Hammond, who had caused him so much trouble for so long, and would almost certainly try to block the award. The work passed muster, and both examiners were very flattering about what they had read, so that the DSc was awarded; not surprisingly the only one ever to a member of staff at EEU. Charles chose his moment, and emailed Thomas O'Grady the good news, thinking, "He can't ignore this. Maybe they'll start taking me seriously now. Presuming that Thomas actually knows what a DSc is, that is?"

He copied the message to the dean, Patrick Walker and the vice-chancellor, Stirling George, both of whom immediately sent back their message of congratulation. The response from Thomas O'Grady was rather more muted, and as he stared at the email message, Charles felt utterly confused. Was Thomas being funny; undermining him?

> *To: ALL STAFF LAPS*
> *From: Professor Thomas O'Grady*
> *Subject: DSc*
> *I am pleased to announce that Dr Charles Rae has been awarded a DSc.*

That was it. But, *Dr* Charles Rae; had he genuinely forgotten that Charles was a professor? Which is why he had come to the accursed bloody place at all! Or was he just so academically uninformed that he truly believed the award of a DSc somehow amended Charles title back to "Dr"? Had he confused it with a PhD, perhaps? "Dr", as he was at his "old" university, where he was appreciated, before being seduced by false charms into this unrelenting nightmare, by the allure of a "professorship". The message stung him. Charles clicked on *reply*:

> *Thank you, Thomas. It is of course 'PROFESSOR' Charles Rae!*
> *Regards,*
> *Charles*

But Charles couldn't help but stare at the message, which made no sense. With the sweep of one hand, Thomas was praising his achievement, while with the other he demeaned it. Charles was confused. He remembered when he was 16, sitting his French O-level. Through a linguistic fog had emerged the conviction that a *canne-a-peche* was a "can of peaches", rather than the "fishing boat" the text intended. Charles recalled his similar anxious confusion; over a text that made no clear sense …[The] "can of peaches" [was] floating in the sea. Why? How had it got there? Had someone thrown it in? But the words gave no frame of reference or clue about the enigmatic can of peaches.

Stare as he might, it was hopeless! He laughed about it now, twenty-five years later; but even now he could recall that "fog" from the archive of his emotional memories; as he could recall so many other memories, in the sudden and instinctive emotional archeology that almost defines the onset of middle-age, which feels, cynically, that it has by now "seen it all". But such cynicism is deceptive – there *is* more to come – and from quite unexpected sources. Was Thomas just fishing for Charles? Playing the line out and back; making continued jolts on his mental equilibrium; making him paranoid? Trying to drive him mad? Charles stared frantically, but it was hopeless.

Now that Thomas was head of department, he could make life very difficult for Charles. He no longer had to stir up anyone, like he used to Rod Shine, to strike out at him. He controlled Charles' duties. Doubled his teaching load, trebled his admin. Gave him all the tedious stuff: running all the lab classes, and all the marking. And when Charles complained, "What about my research?"

"That position no longer exists."

"What about the RAE income. It's worth half a million a year to the faculty overall. How the hell are we going to get a grade 4 next time?"

"You are talking irrelevancies. You are here to teach and that is that! Customer Supply and Quality Assurance are our game. Regarding research, that is well dealt with in the hands of Bob Bates and Tarquin Tupper!"

There was no point in arguing. Clearly the man was an idiot, barely sane, and with a death wish for the department, whether he was aware of the fact or not. A kamikaze pilot at its helm: *"Banzai!"*

Thomas' eyes revelled in his new role of authority. He loved it. It was Dudley Dudd all over again, but with power! If he could control a senior academic, then he was quite a man, wasn't he? A real success. The sentiments of his words glinted tacitly behind his steel-framed spectacles. Polished impassiveness.

"Now get out of my office."

Charles felt dazed by irony. He was now doing four times as much teaching as a professor at EEU as he had as a lecturer in his "old" university. And his research career was over, which was supposed to be the point of Hamish Humble hiring him in the first place.

Charles stumbled past Sandra as he left. He glanced at her. She looked sympathetic: one eyelid drooped. He had never noticed that before. But it now blinked at him with insincerity. Blink blink. Like a metronome, measuring the pulsating waves of his frustration and dismay. Blink blink. Moving off scale. She had nothing against Charles: he was just a pawn in her game; everyone was. If piloting the inept Thomas O'Grady into waters of seniority, beyond his depth, would raise her own mast, it was fair play, whoever else's career would be washed away. And now it was Charles' turn.

"How are you?" she asked. He looked incredulously at her and found that adequate words would not form.

"Oh dear. All that extra teaching." How did she know?

Of course, as departmental administrative manager, she was a member of the departmental management team while he, Charles, was not, and so was denied party to such discussions of changes to his duties, which she, who "in old money" would have been simply the departmental secretary, could even contribute too, endorsing Thomas' assertions that Charles Rae does too little teaching, and that he was simply a resourcing problem.

★ ★ ★

The Physics arm of the Department of LAPS continued to wither in its undergraduate recruitment, while that of Leisurewear developed its muscle mass. And in its hand, Thomas O'Grady would bear aloft a blunt instrument – actually his spreadsheet of teaching hours, salaries and undergraduate fee income for the applied physicists – menacing their survival.

"It's just not good enough! Your customer numbers are down yet again! This has happened every year for the past five years! Why can't you be more like Leisurewear?! We don't have any trouble attracting *our* customers."

The applied physicists had heard it all before. Every year for the last five years, this charge had been levelled at them; and even before that, when student numbers weren't too bad, this unflattering comparison with Leisurewear was made. Suddenly their intake had plummeted. No one knew why exactly, but it was an indisputable fact. Not only at EEU, but virtually everywhere else as far as they could discern. But they had been hit particularly hard. At one time a thriving part-time degree course in Applied Physics flourished at EEU, attended by technicians from local industry. Then there were cutbacks and closures, and more companies seemed inclined to train their staff "in-house" these days, as they were less than impressed with the quality of their EEU graduates. The part-timers were generally the better students, at that. All their "firsts" were usually awarded to them, the best of the full-timers only barely scraping a "two-one".

As numbers fell, they had to accept anybody who applied, following the most rudimentary and dispiriting of interviews, and then deal with the inevitable consequences. They opened an in-house "access course" as a route to the degree in Applied Physical Sciences, as it became, to accommodate those students who had never studied physics before – not even to the equivalent of O-level. But still the numbers fell. They had to dumb down the course by removing as much of its mathematics as possible, to the extent that they prayed silently or even aloud, upon waking shakily, amid those nights before exam board meetings, for fear that the course would be closed by the external examiner; but the full-timers couldn't hold even this watered-down spirit, and still failed. In consequence, the academic value of the degree was depleted until the part-timers were withdrawn by their employers, until finally there were only three students enrolled in the first year. The end of the highway was at hand for Applied Physics, and they waited, cowed, for the unyielding shadow of the blade to be made firm, and their heads to tumble together resignedly into the redundancy basket.

Charles' head reeled. He knew the real decisions were made in the "nineteenth hole" at the Evergreen Golf Club, of which Tarquin Tupper was a staunch member; and a token member of the "leisurewear" circle who met there and plotted, usually swapping dirt about himself, he had no doubt of that. But why had Barney been sitting in his car outside Charles' flat? How did he even know where he lived?

"I was just passing. Would you like a lift, Charles?" It was strange, and unnerving. The car journey was nonplussing, to say the least. Clearly Barney was into gadgets. Perhaps he fancied himself as James Bond. Nice the way he installed the speed trap detector. But what else did he have? His comments about the inside of Charles' flat. Did he have a set of skeleton keys? Charles was sure the pens had been moved on his desk, and the book wasn't on the floor when he left. Was the flat bugged, even, and perhaps his office too? Maybe Barney had installed a hidden camera. Was Barney trying to make him paranoid?

"You walk past the burger bar in the mornings, don't you?"

But Charles came in early, usually a couple of hours before Barney, so how did he know that? Was he following him? Had he deliberately shown him that speed trap detector? Yes, he was trying to unnerve him. But if he *was* following him – searching his flat, his office maybe – why? He must be after something. Some dirt on him? Blackmail? Coercion? If Barney was rumbled – God knows what he was into – he could threaten to expose Charles (for something?) or take him down with him.

"Professor Rae knew. We were in it together. It was his idea. He made me. He threatened me."

Newspaper headlines! What the hell was he reporting back to O'Grady? Maybe he was part of the nineteenth hole club. That was it. He was a stooge – appointed by O'Grady as a stooge, to bring him down. What other reason could there be, given his CV? Charles' brain swirled.

Then there was the awayday. First, Bates' lies about his "funding in kind", then the blatant claim of Charles' RAE income as his own. Nobody batted an eyelid. Thomas even congratulated him on it. It was as though Charles was a ghost, not solid or real. Then the rumours that Thomas had been looking for him. Why? Couldn't he see him.

"Tommy, have you seen Charles?"

"Jake, have you seen Charles?"

Ah, he was just making the point that he had his eye on him. That he should keep looking over his shoulder. He knew they would feed it all back to Charles, knowing they were his friends. They had also told him that Thomas was making a list. There had been complaints about him. That one of his courses was unprofessionally organised. The university had set up a committee to pick him over. There was bound to be a disciplinary outcome. The vice-chancellor had received a letter of complaint about his "unprofessional scientific conduct", signed by two senior professors. Who could they be? What was he supposed to have done? This was why O'Grady had put Tarquin Tupper in charge of his "new" duties, to report back, compiling the dossier for the committee. Charles began to shake; his head spiralled down. Was this just paranoia? But it *all* made sense.

Back to the car journey. Barney pretended to reveal things about himself. About his family. True or false? Funny how it all sounded quite like his own family relationships. Could Barney read his mind? Charles played the good listener. But then the claims became steadily more outrageous, attempting perhaps to provoke a reaction.

"I went to school in the School of King Aziz ... with his own children. 'Brother', they call me. Even now Aziz calls me his own son."

Charles' stomach muscles clenched, holding in an explosion of laughter, detonated by the contradiction between (surely?) such embellished bullshit and common sense. Did he really think Charles believed any of this, and therefore that he was a fool? Or did Barney really believe it himself? A very poor con man or Walter Mitty?! Or playing a game? Then all the flattery about Charles' work, and the comment that "You are resented for your success. Thomas O'Grady told me the other day".

"Bullshit!" thought Charles. He hated being sucked up to. It's one thing when a mate says "well done!" and pats you on the back, but Barney ...

To his credit, Barney had a damned good memory. All good liars do, so they say. He could recall Charles', probably too frank, confession of his feelings toward O'Grady, Bates, and the other members of Leisurewear ... and, yes, of Tupper too. "Professor" Tupper, what a joke!

Charles remembered happier days, when he felt on the same wavelength as other people. When he and they all inhabited the same world and shared three-dimensional space. But now he felt restricted – put on the leash of a geometry reduced by one dimension, while being watched from the third; an exercise in experimental psychology. Dogs and people can be tortured and broken through psychological stress and sleep deprivation. This is said to work more effectively than pain. It reaches deeper recesses of the constitution. Perhaps his waking, shaking at 3am was the subtle outcome of a deliberately imposed mental stress. But why had they appointed him, just to destroy his mind?

The goal to unnerve Charles. Again to make him feel that he had been projected into a twilight world; where his logic, his values, were merely two-dimensional parts of a more threatening three-dimensional structure? Were these people even made of the same flesh and blood as him? He was sure Tommy and Jake were; his friends. But they could be part of the plan. He confessed all to them; could their offices be bugged too? Charles' mind swung between the absurd and the paranoid. Perhaps he would later – when found walking incoherently, with days lost and unaccounted for – fall convinced that he had been abducted by aliens. It did, indeed, all feel very alien. But Charles now felt like the alien; that he *had* been abducted.

That must be it. They *were* an alien race, who were taking over the Earth. But they needed to be sure they could conquer and destroy those such as Charles; he was their experimental animal. The experimental psychologists of this race, whose purpose and values Charles could not comprehend, had chosen him as a perfect example, and were testing out the methods of their psychological weapons, before using them *en masse* in the final subjugation of humankind. True weapons of mass destruction (WMDs), of far greater and more subtle force than atom bombs. And they would leave the world and its population unresisting and malleable to their will. A refurbished genesis, rec-reating us all into their own image.

As he looked into the sea of faces. Slow. Slow. God. A child with a crayon can write faster than this...

Suddenly he had the attention of them all. Even the slowest of them had stopped writing. He heard a strange humming: "Nellie the Elephant..."

Then he realised it was him.

"Ahem. As I was saying... Well, perhaps that is enough for today."

They watched him leave.

★ ★ ★

"Where would it all end?" Charles wondered. He could imagine the final straw: being borne out of the front entrance of EEU by two male nurses, struggling, his arms straightjacketed, shouting, "I'm not mad!"

Into the EEU private ambulance, amid a growing crowd of growingly bewildered students and colleagues. Into the hospital. Tall, gaunt figure by the bed. Soft Scots call, extended hand.

"Aye, well." Hand withdrawn in the realisation that Charles was cur-rently indisposed to accept it.

"Och, it's no'so bad. Don't take it so hard, Charles."

"Aaaaaaaahhhh!"

Cords straining against them. Charles re-emerged from his reverie – surely, it couldn't come to that!? Surely not?!

★ ★ ★

"Tarquin. It's Thomas. I see the Department of Canine Care Technology is rather short-staffed at the moment."

"You don't mean the Poodle Parlour, do you?!"

"Yes. I think Charles is due for some retraining."

"What they need is to get somebody really *good* in from outside."

"Aaaaaaaahhhh!"

EPILOGUE

Ten years on. Where are they all now?

Financial pressures within both institutions force the instigation of a merger between the "old" University of Evergreen and EEU. The "old" university, guarding its professorships jealously, has a large number of staff, all with well over one hundred publications, whom it nonetheless refuses to promote above the rank of reader. On being turned down, yet again, a physicist Roger Aldgate, an extremely fractious and bitter man, spots the name Professor Tarquin Tupper on the EEU website under the Department of Leisurewear and Applied Physical Sciences. He logs on to the web of science site, and types in the name: Tupper, Tarquin into the author field, along with the address: Evergreen Epstein University. On finding no citations at all, no matter what combination of these terms he enters, and only *one* under the name: O'Grady, Thomas, his suspicions are confirmed that an absurd differential would exist under the banner of the putative conglomerate "University of Evergreen City", and immediately complains to the Lecturers' Union, whose lawyers smell a ripe round ahead of them, which they threaten to take on.

When approached officially by the union, Sir Colin Maybridge, vice-chancellor of the University of Evergreen, is aghast in fear of the further financial burden that would be incurred through a wholesale round of promotions, since *all* his staff would qualify for a professorship by comparison with the credentials of the EEU professoriate, and through compensation payments to the likes of Roger Aldgate for loss of earnings over the years during which he had been denied promotion. Sir Colin is also plainly aghast at the laughable academic standards at EEU, and personally insulted that he had very nearly been duped by Stirling George into getting under the duvet on the shagpile with him. He immediately aborts the merger, but further informs the Higher Education Funding Council, which is forced to launch an investigation into the quality of senior academic staff in all the country's universities.

Admittedly, a few wrigglers are winkled out in the "older" sector, mainly in subjects such as leisurewear practice, which all universities now vie with one another to offer courses in, since in order to match the lucrative salaries offered by the leisurewear industry they are compelled to offer professorial appointments even to feebly qualified candidates. However, no equivalent showing is found to compare with the likes of professors Tarquin Tupper and Thomas O'Grady, and indeed virtually all the professors at EEU, including the dean of Technology, Professor Patrick Walker. A scandal ensues, and the Government is compelled to inaugurate an independent committee of academics to evaluate all professorial applications, no matter which university they came from, to a nationally acceptable standard, namely that required to be awarded a DSc. This criterion is further applied retrospectively in a round of reapplications for their own positions, with the result that all but two out of the hundred or so professors at EEU are ignominiously reduced to ranks commensurate with their actual level of academic achievement, namely that of lecturer, including the vice-chancellor, Stirling George, and his senior staff, Tony Naismith the bursar, Letticia Jolanda the assistant vice-chancellor, and all the deans.

Once he realises that this immediately knocks £4 million off the EEU annual salary bill, Stirling George begins to warm to an otherwise extremely embarrassing situation, especially as his own salary is protected, as vice-chancellor, not as a professor. One man who is not best pleased, however, is Tarquin Tupper who, having been now forced to retire on a lecturer's pension, rather than that of a professor, which he was banking on, and with heavy alimony payments still outgoing, accepts an appointment as a tutor and consultant at the Western African office of the Remote Learning University. Here, he achieves a spiritual transcendence, which imbues him with enlightenment and humility. He later patches things up with his wife, remarries her in the church where they were originally married, and is now a self-effacing and well-liked member of the local community, having retired back to his home county.

★ ★ ★

Having risen to the rank of dean in consequence of the scandalous departure of Patrick Walker, engineered by Sandra (you remember, *Sandra*, from the typing pool), and that nobody else wanted to do the job, Thomas O'Grady found himself completely and hopelessly out of his depth in dealing with all matters beyond utter trivia. While his ex-colleagues even now remain quite flattering when they refer to the vibrant and innovative colour management and command of his leadership in directing the repainting of the gents toilet on the tenth floor, they have to concede that his running the Faculty of Technology into bankruptcy and the complicated legal suits made against them all personally by international students under Thomas' tutelage (having made the most outrageous promises and claims in order to get them to part with their fees), *was* fairly dealt with by his rather public and embarrassing dismissal.

But they still wonder how, exactly, Thomas had managed to fall from that tenth floor window of the Gents. Was it a terrible accident, perhaps? That he had gone in to take one final nostalgic vista of the only sensible job he'd ever made of anything, and had slipped on the wet floor (that drain never worked properly), falling headlong, crashing through the splintering glass, then shattering himself on the concrete slabs, a hundred feet below? Or, perhaps the humiliation had been finally all too much for him, and he had jumped through the red mist, either oblivious to his oblivion, or needful of it? They ask themselves these things – and many others – every other Thursday morning, as they queue up in the cash queue of the Evergreen Post Office, giro in hand. Then, shaking their heads thoughtfully, they murmur as one:"Poor old Thomas. I guess we'll never know, really."

★   ★   ★

Stirling George took early retirement from EEU some years previously, but since then he remained a high-profile figure in the public arena of Evergreen. He was, therefore, the clear choice, and duly elected as chair of the Evergreen City Development Committee. The connections he made during his time as vice-chancellor of EEU with key Establishment figures and his detailed and personal knowledge of some senior political figures proved invaluable in his new role, which recently culminated in his award of a knighthood.

★   ★   ★

Rod Shine proved to be a model prisoner and served only five years of his original eight-year sentence for embezzlement of EEU funds. Actually, Rod didn't have too bad a time in jail, being generous and popular, and well able to advise his fellow inmates on any legal, financial and business concerns they might have. In any case, Rod was able to continue running his chain of leisurewear stores from the inside, having placed his wife, who is herself a sound businesswoman, as its overall acting manager. Indeed, even without Rod's presence "on the ground" the two managed to build up the chain massively, so Rod was successful in fulfilling his promise to his grandfather to create the SHINE Leisurewear empire. On his release, Rod formed the chain into a limited company: "Shine Enterprises Ltd", of which he is CEO.

★ ★ ★

Now in his dotage, Jasper's bowling days are finally done, but he still visits the green, even though that has been closed too. On sunny days his youngest granddaughter helps him into his bath chair, wraps the tartan blanket around his knees, and patiently pushes him around its perimeter fence, past the chains and padlocks. He doesn't say much, and when he does, she wipes his mouth with her handkerchief. His memory fails, then he remembers something distant and happy and sheds a tear, which she wipes away too.

★ ★ ★

Bertie Bantam is found murdered. Initially, the Midwestern PD think that his death is the result of a sexual mishap, but having cut down his body, clad only in silk stockings and a green suspender belt soaked in a rush of semen whose provenance only a subsequent DNA analysis would confirm, a later postmortem reveals the aftermath of an unfeasibly large rectal object, expanded violently from its original point of dimension. Reluctantly, however, Captain Luigi Marconi, having interviewed over five thousand suspects, all with a credible grudge against Bertie, but with nothing proven, and amid stringent cuts to his budget, has just stamped the file: *UNSOLVED*.

★ ★ ★

Rather than risk bringing shame on the family in their small, fundamentalist community; though estranged, Regina and Hanns-Peter Krankenpfleger agreed not to divorce, but to remain separated. On hearing of his catastrophic mental collapse, Regina agrees to her husband being brought back to Wuperbaden, to the Nervenklinik (Experimental) Wuperbaden. There he has received regular *Behandlung*, personally administered by the adept hands of its director, Herr Dr Geldgruber, using a modification of the original *Electrikalische Verhoer Apparat*.

The bitter-tasting rubber guard would be thrust between his teeth, forcing the upper and lower sets apart; shoulders, wrists, thighs and ankles rubber-manacled down onto the leather-topped table. Then the electric probe would be applied, according to the body plan drawn on the *Nerven-karte*. His teeth and mind would clench into the subsumation of a martyr's smile, his eyes becoming wild blades of flame: "Ha ha," he reasoned, it was all part of God's test upon him.

Dr Geldgruber placed his polished steel-framed spectacles kindly on his desk, and looked at her sympathetically, speaking in a resigned voice, "I'm sorry, Frau Krankenpfleger, but there is no cure for him. We have tried all we know. Never before have I encountered such a hopelessly resistant case of trauma."

★   ★   ★

Herr Professor (Baron von) Lederbauer has since retired to his ancestral seat – Schloss Lederbauer, an impressive castle, set high upon the side of a mountain, Berg Lederbauer, overlooking the estate's private lake, Lederbauersee. He has long abandoned his study of Physics, but has recently detailed an impressive treatise entitled *Der Psychologie aus Trauma*, the subject for which he has found a considerable inspiration in the sad case of Hanns-Peter Krankenpfleger.

★   ★   ★

Letticia Jolanda formally resigned as assistant vice-chancellor and professor of Retail Therapeutics at EEU. She is now CEO of the Evergreen Epstein Fashion Centre (EEFC): in fact, a spin-off company of EEU. Here, Letticia is in her element, being able to combine her artistic eye with sound business acumen. As a consequence, EEFC yielded sizeable profits, which forced the final closure of the contrastingly bankrupt Faculty of Technology at EEU, and allowed the university to provide a one-off severance payment of £3000 to all its remaining academic Technology staff, irrespective of their length of service.

★ ★ ★

Professor Marylynne Beddoes was recently elected a Fellow of the Royal Society.

★ ★ ★

Professor Sharleen La'Coy was recently elected chair of the Advisory Committee to the Government on Business Development in the Emerging Global Markets.

★ ★ ★

On his elevation to the rank of dean, Thomas O'Grady promoted Sandra (that's *Sandra*, from the typing pool) to the rank of faculty executive administrative manager. The formerly *Professor*, but now *Ms*, Sandra Leyton is now assistant vice-chancellor of EEU.

★ ★ ★

Tommy Wakefield took early retirement, and can often be seen walking his golden labrador, and mulling over a pint or two of mild in his local pub. He's since given up smoking, looks ten years younger, and is a very happy man with a renewed interest in gardening.

★ ★ ★

Bob Bates and Austin Oldfield find their hands touching over a hymn-book one Sunday morning in the Evergreen Christian Reform Church, and are finally forced to confront their true feelings for one another. They were last seen skipping hand in hand over the hills beyond the city, and there are rumours that they have moved into a cottage in the country together, with honeysuckle round the door. Bless!

★ ★ ★

With the proverbial "strength of ten", Charles Rae was finally captured and restrained; held down on the flagstones outside the Faculty of Technology, by several members of Security Services and the local Evergreen Constabulary. Straightjacketed and staring wildly, he was transferred in the yellow EEU private ambulance, screaming, "I'm not mad!" But, sadly, he was. However, his latest medication is at last yielding promising results…

★ ★ ★

Charles felt happy. Relaxed. Poodle care. This was what he really enjoyed. He still occasionally had the vague and passing feeling that he had done something else before.

"Well, if I did, I can't remember what it was," he smiled to himself. Clip clip. Clip clip.

"It can't have been as good as this, anyway." He was quite sure of that.

He smiled at the smiling face in the mirror, which smiled back. That was what was so nice. Everybody smiled.